I0628408

The Merlin Box

Lawrence Clayton Miller

Acclaim for *The Merlin Box*

Adam Dekker is back and boy do we need him now. "The Magic Box" is Lawrence Miller's fourth installment in the Abaddon series, an ongoing chronology of one of the most unusual battles against terrorism in modern literature.

Miller did not come to the table with any prior literary works before Abaddon arrived on the scene. It was a leap of faith a few years ago to open that first book and begin the journey with Adam Dekker. But now, many of us are gasping for breath and marveling at this new genre in fiction. Is it espionage fiction? Warfare? Magic and witchcraft? And imagine the plight of the booksellers when stocking their shelves and trying to decide where to display the books – what category? The answer of course is that the really good ones defy categories and refuse to be put in boxes. What box is best for Miller's works? And maybe the answer is – THE MAGIC BOX, or perhaps THE MERLIN BOX.

To further explain Miller's path to the title of this fourth Alex Dekker book would be to give away too much. But when Jim Lynch, Deputy Director of the National Counterterrorism Command (NCTC) needs a hero, he turns to his assistant, Marilyn and says the magic words – "Get me Dekker – NOW!" An ocean and a continent away you can almost hear "M" saying "Moneypenny, get me Bond!" Fortunately, Lawrence Miller's work is not derivative and it sparkles with creativity and a sense of other worldly dimensions and threats not being addressed by other authors.

At the risk of creating a spoiler for readers new to Miller's Abaddon world, let's just say that Dekker (everyone calls him Dekker – never Adam) is at emotional loose ends, having said goodbye to the love of his life. But, as Special Projects Director for NCTC, he is the "go to" guy for crisis management and US Air Force Special Operations Command has a doozie on their hands. What to do when an unmanned military drone takes off in flight and gets redirected despite supposedly insurmountable safeguards resulting in significant foreign casualties.

"Marilyn – Get me Dekker – NOW."

And with that, Miller takes us on a round the world adventure and a Cook's Tour of old Egypt and current Egypt. And we meet Dekker's new international partner Hannah Ahmed as they lock on to Majick and the Flows and arch-villains and plot twists worthy of this series of books. Miller is blessed with a fertile imagination and an impressive command of geography, geopolitical affairs, and history.

To say more would give away an excellent effort. I am guessing the lights will be on late tonight at NCTC and Special Ops Command inasmuch as many will be reading and wondering where Miller gets his insights and knowledge. He knows a great deal about the world of the NCTC and modern technology. It is a very enjoyable read. The Abaddon series is alive and well and there should be lots more coming in the future. Holy Hannah!

Paul Kelbaugh, Attorney at Law and best selling author

Miller Delivers Again!

Abaddon is back and is more dangerous than ever with a new host, an Egyptian mystic and master of the darks arts of his ancient ancestors. With a fanatical band of followers and the power to hijack the West's most technically advance weapons, he will pit West against East and stop at nothing to bring Egypt back to its ancient glory.

The pace is fast as Miller keeps tightening the screws by upping the stakes and doubling the jeopardy. Miller walks a tightrope of tension from the opening sentence to the thrilling conclusion. If you liked the Abaddon series, you will love *The Merlin Box* as Miller's skill as a storyteller grows to even loftier heights.

Dr. Scott Carroll

The Merlin Box is yet another great read from Lawrence Miller. It is written with a great pace and is exciting. It works well in that it is a work of fiction, but he makes it believable by throwing in actual "In Use" technology and locations. His use of characters is also well done. He has a real "Merlin" character in Galdur and I felt like Adam Decker and his sidekick Dennis were a modern version of Batman and Robin.

Hannah Ahmed is a great addition and shows she can continue in the next book as the team of scientist, mystics and real life defenders of justice go after the bad guy Kamenwati.

I have read all of Miller's books and look forward to his next one. I have over forty years of experience in communications and electronics so I find myself enjoying his use of technology in most of his solutions. I highly recommend them to anyone who likes an easy and entertaining read.

Pat Orell US Army (Ret)

Continuing to mix bleeding edge technology with the mystique of ancient Egypt, Miller once again immerses the reader in a story of his own unique brew… of mysticism and potential world-domination by an ancient force of evil that continues to plague humanity.

Fast-paced, laced with political intrigue and cinematic with images of the Egyptian desert and Stonehenge as the backdrop – the main characters fight for both their own survival and mankind's – the novel takes us into the laboratory of the military's weapons scientists and engineers…and to places that we never new existed.

Can't wait for the next installment – or, for the screenplay to make it to Hollywood and hit the big screen as the next summer blockbuster!

Steve Appel, Appel Graphics & Web Design

The Merlin Box
By Lawrence Clayton Miller

Cover design by Jason Miller, fluiddesigns@yahoo.com

ISBN 13: 9780997694109
ISBN 10: 0997694106

Printed in the United States

This is a work of fiction. Names, characters, places, and incidents are products of the author's imagination and are not to be construed as real. Any resemblance to actual events, locales, organizations, or persons, living or dead, is entirely coincidental.

As always, for Susan.

ACKNOWLEDGEMENTS

There are many people who contribute to an author's creative process. It is often a casual conversation with friends, or a question regarding a plot point that sends me in an entirely new direction. For example, in this book a comment by a career Army officer regarding the highly classified nature of drone command and control caused a complete change in the method I used for that aspect of the story.

I do have a few people to thank for their contributions to making *The Merlin Box* not only entertaining, but also believable.

Neal Singer, science writer/media communications and Distinguished Member of
     Laboratories Staff of Sandia National Laboratories.
Your analysis of the relative merits/problems with Marx Generators, Railguns, and Pulse Forming Networks put me on the right path for a believable solution to penetrate an electromagnetic field. You answered difficult scientific questions in understandable language, and given the questions I posed, this was no small accomplishment.

Jason Miller, graphic designer, FluidDesigns, Colorado Springs.
Thank you for another great cover.

Michael McIrvine, Founding Writer and Editor, Pro Novel Editing.
     Thank you for being a collaborative editor. It makes all the difference.

The Merlin Box

Lawrence Clayton Miller

CHAPTER ONE

DAWN LIGHT BATHED THE STATUE of Ramses II in a golden glow. This day, February 22, the anniversary of the ancient king's coronation, was special because on this day the light falls directly on the king's face. Kamenwati looked on the great king with mixed emotions. How had his Egypt gone from such great heights and worldwide domination to, he looked around and sighed, to this? Egypt was still relevant but only as a regional leader, not on the world stage. Kamenwati grieved for his people, the true Egyptians who inhabited this land for millennia and built the greatest civilization in the world. The true Egyptians had been overrun by the Islamic Caliphate, their ancestral land invaded by Arab hordes led by Mohammed hundreds of years ago; but in the sweep of time of Egypt's existence, it was only yesterday.

He looked again at the face of Ramses II and then down to the statue's feet where stone carvings represented the nations he conquered: Africa to the left, Asia to the right. "That is the way it should be and how it shall be again."

The Egyptian mystic had wrested a concession from the government long ago. They had ceded him an island in Lake Nasser, the body of water created in the 1960s when construction of the Aswan Dam was completed. The temple of Abu Simbel, where Ramses II and the pantheon of ancient Egypt were depicted in stone, was moved to this location to prevent its submersion in the new lake. Kamenwati was pleased the world community came together to save the magnificent structure, but he was also sad because the site had become an attraction for tourists who understood nothing of the ancient ways. In his youth he studied the ancient arts and became powerful in the practice of Magick, the ancient art of using invisible forces to influence events, of effecting change in material conditions, or presenting the illusion of change, by spiritual means. With his skills he could create many of the miraculous events depicted in the Bible; the ancient priesthood held the secrets of nature and the world, which allowed them to copy each of the plagues brought on by Moses. All except the death of the firstborn, which caused the priesthood to petition Pharaoh to release the Hebrews. Their leader, Moses, had bested and embarrassed the priesthood, and so they wanted him and all his people out Egypt.

In his meditative state Kamenwati felt the powerful presence of the Abaddon spirit, so intense it was nearly overwhelming. Kamenwati remained still, waiting for the spirit to speak.

You long for those days of glory, do you not? While it seems long ago to you, I assure you, it is yesterday to me. You can recapture what was lost. Is that not what you want?

"Yes, Master, it is what I want."

Do you not have followers of the ancient blood? Do they not stand ready to do your bidding?

"Yes, that is true. But it is only a small group, hardly fifty men."

And fifty will do. Together we will remake this ancient land into the world power it once was. We will push the Islamists out and once again a Pharaoh will sit on the throne in Thebes.

Kamenwati, caught up in the vision offered him by the spirit that possessed him after the death of the original host, nodded in agreement. The day he lost Kambrian was a terrible day, but it was wonderful as well because the Abaddon spirit selected him. The spirit gave him foresight and wisdom, allowing him to escape Krugerschloss in Germany and make his way undetected back to Egypt. He felt the spirit's hand on his shoulder, directing him so that he remained invisible, prompting him to turn left, stop, move ahead. His journey ended here at Abu Simbel where he contemplated the greatness that was Egypt.

"Yes, a new Pharaoh and a new era for my Egypt."

I have a warning for you: there is a force of men coming from the Caliphate. They are intent on possessing your Egypt.

"Master, how do I stop them with only fifty?"

You have skills to manipulate men. Use that to turn this new invader away, just as your ancestors once drove off the invading Hyksos. When you have defeated this present enemy you will turn against the powers that truly hold Egypt down.

"Yes, I see, and I think I know how to repel these invaders and how to use their attack to build my following."

You do well, much better than my previous host, Kambrian. He was weak and in the end blinded by his need for revenge. He forgot that I am the giver and taker of life, the avenging spirit.

"Yes, Master." Kamenwati sensed the spirit withdraw and he emerged from his meditative state. He knew controlling this spirit may be difficult, but it was not impossible. He was much stronger than the previous host and believed he could restrain the Abaddon spirit while tapping into its great power.

He stood and walked to a small inlet where a felucca awaited him. Boarding the small sailing ship, he looked once again to the stone temple in the distance and then shifted his attention to the captain of the ancient-styled single lateen craft. "Take me home," said Kamenwati. Halabi, the captain, made no reply to the man he had served for decades; he cast off the single line holding the boat and, with a long pole, shoved the felucca into the Nile's north flowing current.

The quiet and calm transportation suited Kamenwati. It gave him time to consider his latest encounter with the Abaddon spirit and how he was going to accomplish the order to drive the Islamists from his Egypt and then the entire Western world.

IT HAD BEEN less than one year since Kamenwati left his private island home on the Nile, and yet he felt strangely foreign, out of place in his once tranquil retreat. As the felucca approached the small dock Kamenwati recognized his senior followers, men who pledged themselves to his service years ago, men he knew to be deeply devoted to his dream of a new Egyptian age. He was returning to realize the dream, but the method and means would be far different than they or he ever imagined. *Will these followers remain with me*, he wondered as he stepped out of the boat, greeting each by name.

The compound, which was designed in the ancient manner, faced the eastern shore of the island. No walls interrupted the view of the river; any vantage was open to the beauty of the Nile. Colorful columns supported the wide roof and large terrazzo tiles covered the floors. A garden pathway led down to a small cove set apart from the Nile by a sandbank to serve as a private lagoon. A low-columned gazebo peeked from the river foliage, and Kamenwati pictured the comfortable couches and chairs scattered beneath the structure as he took in the scene, enjoying the breeze coming off the river. His followers stood behind him, respecting the thoughtful silence of their master. None would think to interrupt. They simply waited for his orders. After a time, as if reaching some decision, Kamenwati swung around to face his followers.

"You are no doubt curious about my recent absence," he began. "I left this land, our Egypt, to deal with an old threat. I managed that situation but the Brotherhood I told you about is now in disarray. However, something new and unexpected has come to my attention from the turmoil I encountered." His followers looked from one to another wondering what their master found. "I discovered there is a threat to subvert our Egypt." The followers said nothing but their eyes widened with alarm. "It is the old threat, the invasion our people were too weak to turn back centuries ago: Islam, a new wave of invaders who represent a mindless fanaticism that will pull down what is left of our ancient culture." Kamenwati's followers murmured in frightened anger.

"The threat is still small, only a single group now entering northern Sinai in preparation for infiltration. But you needn't fear because I have the power to deal with them." The group settled down, all obviously wondering what new power he possessed.

Rahotep, the senior among them, gave voice to their questions. "Master, how can you find, much less destroy, a group in the desert?"

Kamenwati gave a small smile. "I will harness the technology of the West to crush the Caliphate's incursion, and then I will use that same technology against the imperialistic nations that seek to keep us hobbled and ineffective."

It was an enigmatic answer and Rahotep was concerned about embracing the modern world's technology; it was against the principles of the Old Truths. The others, less concerned with philosophies, were appeased by their master's confidence.

Kamenwati retreated to his private suite.

For seven days he did not eat or drink, and none of his followers saw him. He spent those seven days deep in the Flows under the influence of the Abaddon spirit. In the Flows he saw the Caliphate group making plans for Egypt, the one nation that did not embrace Wahhabism and Sharia law.

Under Abaddon's direction he was shown the Joint Special Operations Command half a world away at Ft. Bragg, and Kamenwati began exercising a newfound power within the Flows: the ability to reach across the world and take control of both the operator and the drone device being piloted. Kamenwati did not know such power was available, but considering the nature of the Flows and his ability to influence men's actions and thoughts, he thought it a reasonable extension of his already deep skills. But this new power was nevertheless intoxicating.

On the seventh day Kamenwati was ready. He reached out to take control of a drone operator with an aircraft already deployed for a target. It was so easy. He reached out to the mind of the operator and created a blank in the man's consciousness, easily taking control of the operator and making him redirect the drone to a new target.

"It is so simple," said Kamenwati.

Under his direction the drone found its new target, fired its missiles, and flew on, eventually dropping into the Great Bitter Lake.

SERGEANT DANIEL BAINES sat comfortably before his console of monitors, coffee cup in hand, ready to begin another day's work fighting a war half a world away. Sergeant Baines, a newly promoted E-5, was attached to the 24th Special Tactics Squadron, a unit of the United States Air Force Special Operations Command. His unit operated unmanned combat aerial vehicles, drones, with deadly effect. The job was exciting; after all, Sergeant Baines got to play the most sophisticated gaming system in the world without leaving the comfort of the Ft. Bragg UAV facility. He prepared for this job all of his twenty-six years by mastering ever more difficult video games, and when he had the opportunity for the AFSOC position, he jumped at it.

Sergeant Baines went through the special Air Force training school for UAV operators and finished with top marks. His assignment to the Special Tactics Squadron six months previously marked the highlight of his military career, one he saw as participating in the future of warfare and peacekeeping. This day began as usual: sign in, attend the morning operations meeting, take his station, and work through his list of targets. The day was exciting but ordinary. Nothing exceptional, nothing to indicate the catastrophe about to befall him.

CAPTAIN TIMOTHY DUNN swiveled the chair on his platform overlooking the drone operators. An expansive array of monitors allowed him to watch the dozen operators' activities. The room was darkened to reduce distractions, the glow of computer monitors creating and eerie science fiction atmosphere. The captain watched his monitors for any sign of mechanical problems or ground-based hostility. The missions were going as planned, his techs operating drone flights from three different bases in the Middle East. It was, he reflected, a normal day at the office, albeit a day of death for some.

Dunn spotted something odd at station three. He stood to look over his low wall of monitors to verify what he was seeing. He spotted Sergeant Baines hunched over his control console, staring at his monitor and moving the joystick controller. An alarm went off on his console and another operator called him.

"Captain, UAV-Three is not on-mission. The drone has been diverted to a new heading."

"Where?"

"It looks like somewhere in the Sinai peninsula."

Captain Dunn watched with growing alarm as the drone's camera showed activation of the targeting system, a certain sign the payload, two Hellfire missiles, was about to deploy. He watched as the image closed in on a remote camp, more of a bivouac really, made up of a few tents and vehicles. The targeting system focused on a tent in the encampment's center. Dunn couldn't move or speak, but could only watch as the drone fired one missile and then another. The small center-frame crosshair showed the tent going up in a large explosion, which he could almost hear. The drone pulled up and continued flying, the camera swiveling to show the aftermath of its strike. The target tent had been destroyed along with a good deal of the rest of the camp. Vehicles were burning and there were bodies scattered over the area.

The captain asked rhetorically, "Who did we just hit?" He sat back in his chair and muttered an oath, "Damn." He continued watching as the drone flew on until it ran out of fuel and dropped into the Great Bitter Lake.

Captain Dunn punched the intercom connection for station three.

"Baines! What's the problem?" The sergeant didn't even look at his captain but simply continued to stare at his monitor. "Baines!" There was still no reaction from the man.

Dunn stood and left his observation room and went to the operators' floor. When he was standing behind Baines he grabbed his shoulder and said, "Baines, what is your problem?"

Baines shook his head as if waking from a dream. "I don't know, Captain. We were operating five-by-five when I...Well, I don't really recall."

"What do you mean, you don't recall? I watched that UAV go off-mission and fire on a site in the Sinai."

"I don't know, sir. One minute all was normal, and the next, well, it was like I blacked out. No, it was more like a dream and I was sleepwalking. That's all I can tell you. I can't recall anything about the drone."

Captain Dunn feared the worst, a major hack on his drones. How could that be? These drones operated on a highly sophisticated transmission system that changed frequencies constantly. He reached for a telephone, punched a preprogrammed button, and was immediately connected with the squadron commander. His rapid report started a cascade of activity and inquisition, an investigation that would go to the very highest levels of the Intelligence hierarchy.

JAMES LYNCH, DEPUTY Director of the National Counterterrorism Center, received the flash message on his computer. He read the transcript of Sergeant Baines' interview as well as that of Captain Dunn. Baines apparently experienced a period of mental confusion and his drone simply went...somewhere else. Reports from scientists and engineers indicated they had found no technical problems or any indication the system had been hacked. What caused this so-called mishap was a mystery up and down the line, but one with significant implications for national security. Lynch understood the security ramifications and knew the NCTC must move quickly. He needed his best man, Adam Dekker, to unravel this mystery.

Lynch punched the intercom button connecting him to Marilyn Stamm, his administrative assistant. "Marilyn, please find Dekker. Tell him leave is over and he is to return as quickly as possible." Marilyn was taken aback by Jim's tone and his order. *This must be serious*, she thought. "Right away sir."

She prayed Dekker's cell phone was on as she dialed. He was known to turn it off while home in New Mexico, or he might be somewhere in the wilderness with no cellular coverage.

THE SKY WAS filled with angry gray clouds that seemed to boil over the deep purple mountains, threatening to unleash a downpour. The surrounding peaks of the Jemez Mountains were covered by rain-heavy clouds, offering no protection for the tiny valley below or for Vallecito Ranch, Adam Dekker's home.

Dekker watched the spectacle from his covered patio, marveling at the majestic spring storm. A rain squall was moving across the valley and he knew it would not be long before it reached his ranch. With a respectful nod to the storm, he retreated into the house, closing the French doors. He took a new observation position on the couch. Rain storms were not unusual in the mountains of northern New Mexico, but they were infrequent enough to be notable. Dekker knew it would all change in a day, and the sky would be restored to its normal robin's-egg blue. He also knew the rain would cause the meadow surrounding his home to erupt with colorful wildflowers, a beautiful benefit in this high desert country.

The solitude of Vallecito Ranch did not bother Dekker. In fact, he was comfortable being alone and was grateful for the break from his "other" life in Washington, DC as the Special Projects Director for the National Counterterrorism Center. The storm's deep gloom put him in a melancholy mood and he found himself reflecting on the highs and lows of his career, especially his encounters with Abaddon, the madman able to control people and events from his massive cave complex deep in Germany's Black Forest. Dekker brushed over the death of his wife when it came to his memory. Kelly's loss at Abaddon's direction was still too sharp and the wound too deep to fully confront. Instead, he chose to remember the final act of the incredible drama: the death of the man Kambrian and expulsion of the Abaddon spirit. He marveled at the mystical world that was now so central to his life, and idly wondered where the Flows and Magick might take him next.

His cell phone rang. He knew it could only be the NCTC, and he was supposed to be on leave, he also knew it would not be good news.

"Hello, this is Dekker."

"Adam? It's Marilyn. I'm glad you didn't turn off your cell phone."

"I'm never really off-duty, Marilyn, even when I'm on an extended leave."

"I'm sorry, Adam, but something's come up and Mr. Lynch asked me to get you back here ASAP."

"That sounds serious, Marilyn. What's the problem?"

"I'm not sure. There has been a lot of activity in and out of the office and I overheard some talk about drones. It sounded like someone may have taken control of one."

Dekker considered the implications. Drones were the favored method of fighting terror groups throughout the Middle East, and their effectiveness was a significant deterrent to the expansion of terrorist groups and limited their conquests. If what Marilyn suggested was true, and he had no reason to doubt her, the loss of this strategic asset could signal a new chapter for radical Islam. It took only a moment for Dekker to respond, his melancholy suddenly vanishing.

"Tell Jim I'll be on the next flight." This was a situation he knew almost nothing about, but he had a peculiar feeling. The very thought of terrorists interfering with drones had a core "weirdness" that unsettled him, and he wondered if this had any connection to his old nemesis, Abaddon.

"I'm just imagining things," Dekker admonished himself.

Despite the positive self-talk, however, he could not shake the feeling there was more than a technical glitch at Ft. Bragg in play here.

CHAPTER TWO

THE FLIGHT TO DULLES INTERNATIONAL Airport was uneventful. Dekker chose Dulles over Reagan National because of its proximity to NCTC headquarters and his McLean condominium. He called Marilyn twice while in flight, first to arrange a meeting with Jim Lynch and then to confirm a meeting with Dennis Allende, chief of the NCTCs forensic information investigation unit, and his counterparts from the NSA, FBI, NCIS, 25AF, and CIA. Each agency had been briefed on the drone loss and was anxious for NCTC to take a leadership role in solving this problem.

Dekker went straight to NCTC, a cluster of modern but unidentifiable buildings diagonally across from Tysons Corner. Dennis was in the lobby waiting for Dekker, his mentor and friend. Dekker followed him to the large conference room on the Director's floor. The heads of the assembled agencies were not in attendance. Instead, a group of the brightest and most capable computer experts in the country were gathered. Jim Lynch stood at the podium as Dekker took a seat in the rear of the room acknowledging his presence with a nod.

"Ladies and gentlemen," began Lynch, "I am James Lynch, Assistant Director of NCTC. Most of you know the purpose of this meeting and the urgency attached to it. Our national security has been compromised or in your parlance, hacked. A military drone was seized mid-mission by an unknown source. This is a very big problem because we don't know who is behind this and that is why you are here. Thank you for attending, and now I'd like to turn the meeting over to our chief of the forensic information unit, Mr. Dennis Allende." Dennis stood, shook Lynch's hand and took the podium.

Lynch left the room, motioning to Dekker that he wanted to meet. Dekker nodded his understanding.

"Hi, everyone," began Dennis. "I want to start by telling you this meeting will not be formal. We're going to be decidedly more relaxed than what you might expect in this setting, but no less serious. We are here to unravel a mystery, to identify the mechanism of a serious breach and figure out who's behind it."

This approach to a meeting suited Dekker and he saw Dennis' style fit nicely with the other computer geeks in the room.

"Let me begin, but be assured each of you will have an opportunity for input." Dennis then launched into an overview of the situation, including videotaped interviews with the drone operator as well as his supervisor, Captain Dunn. The video identified more questions than answers, and there was vigorous discussion all around the room. Except for Dekker. He sat quietly, letting the technology experts battle it out. After two hours of discussion the group arrived at consensus: NCIS would visit Ft. Bragg, the "scene of the crime," and inspect computer and communications systems looking for a lead. FBI and 25AF agreed to begin a nationwide search for people and facilities capable of mounting a hacking operation, while CIA would begin similar searches worldwide, with a particular emphasis on Russia, China, North Korea, and Iran. NSA was assigned to support the overall effort with a massive new signals intercept program, and the results were to flow back through NCTC.

With agreement reached, one of the attendees, a woman, noticed Dekker sitting quietly and nodding his head at the division of work. "And what will your role be, Mr. Dekker?"

Dekker looked questioningly to Dennis, who answered for him. "Dekker will be our man on the ground, a special operator if you will, tracing any leads the rest of you might develop."

"I'm going to Egypt," Dekker said over Dennis.

"Why there?" asked the female questioner.

"Because that's where the drone struck. It means something, but I don't know what yet. These are questions best answered from the site." Dekker's answer seemed to satisfy the group and the meeting came to an end.

"EGYPT? DO YOU think it's a good idea to run halfway around the world before we've developed any real intelligence on this?" The meeting was over but Dennis was having a difficult time accepting Dekker's plan. For his part, Dekker thought going to the site of the drone attack was the obvious next step in this investigation.

"Dekker, you know this hack could only originate in a few countries, and I don't think Egypt is one of them."

"You're right, Dennis, but I need to know who was targeted and why. Meanwhile, your people need to work on plugging whatever leak let these people in." Dennis shrugged in general agreement.

"Okay, but you've got to promise to take a cell phone *and* a Sat phone with you. That way we'll have access to you at all times." Dekker smiled and pulled both phones from his coat pocket, holding them up for inspection.

Dennis punched a button on his telephone and spoke with Marilyn. "Would you please make a reservation for

Dekker on the next flight to Cairo?" He waited a moment for Marilyn's response. "Right, I'll tell him." He replaced the telephone receiver and looked at Dekker.

"She says to remind you to see Mr. Lynch before you go." Dennis walked Dekker across the hall to Lynch's office. "Touch base with me before you go. I've got a couple of new gadgets I want you to have." Dekker thanked the young computer expert and opened the office door.

He stepped into a small outer office occupied by Marilyn Stamm, who greeted Dekker with a hug and a kiss on the cheek. "You look well, Adam." He could only look down, slightly embarrassed.

"I guess the boss wants to see me."

"Go right in. He's expecting you."

Stepping into the inner office he found Lynch seated behind a modestly sized desk backed by a wall of windows. Lynch stood as Dekker entered, gesturing toward a small sitting area along the wall.

"Good to see you, Dekker, even if I had to cut your leave short." Dekker muttered an incoherent reply and took a seat on the couch. "Let's get to it. I realize you just finished Dennis' meeting with his counterparts from the other agencies, and I don't mind telling you their job is unenviable. They have to tackle the *how*; I called you back to work because I want you to tell me *why*."

"I was the odd man out in that meeting, Jim; but watching them divide up the tasks made my choice obvious. I told them I'm going to Egypt."

Lynch waited for a moment before giving a reply. "I agree, Adam. You want to discover who was hit in this drone strike and why." Lynch stood and stepped to his desk where he wrote something on a notepad. "I want you to make a stop in London before going to Cairo, a visit to SIS in Vauxhall Cross. Ask for C, Alex Younger who is the Chief. I'll call to brief him while you're in flight."

"London? Isn't this an American problem?"

"Egypt has ties to England going back generations. I think they can provide you a suitable liaison to cut through the red tape."

Dekker nodded and took the note, folded it neatly and placed it in his shirt pocket. As he reached the door he turned. "You know, Jim, I've got a funny feeling about this. Something's off, but I can't put my finger on it."

"I feel the same, Adam. That's why I wanted you involved. Good luck."

BEFORE LEAVING NCTC Dekker went to the basement where Dennis ruled over an astonishing array of data collection, processing, and computing equipment. His staff had grown steadily over the last few years, and now he had one hundred people working for him, collecting intelligence reports from all government agencies and sifting through the mass of material to identify trends or rumors of new terror strikes aimed at the United States. Dennis' staff was young, and all were very bright.

Dekker found Allende hunched over the shoulder of a staffer, pointing out some arcane principle of coding. He tapped Dennis on the shoulder, who left his worker with a last word of wisdom before standing to face Adam.

"You said to find you before leaving," said Dekker.

"Right, I did. Come with me. As I told you, I've got a couple of things to give you." The pair walked to an enclosed room in the massive basement. Dennis walked to a long table set against the wall and picked up a small box.

"This is the latest in communication technology. It's strictly military, but I think it may come in handy." He opened the box and handed Dekker a tiny object.

"What is it?"

"This is a satellite phone. You put this small bud in your ear and this box in your pocket." Dekker looked skeptical but pushed the earpiece into place. "It's colored to match your skin, so only someone looking very carefully at your ear would notice."

"How in the world do you dial it?"

"Simple. You speak the name of the person you want to call and the device connects you."

"How does it know everyone I might call?"

"We've downloaded your contact list." Dekker nodded his understanding and decided to give it a try.

"Call Dennis Allende," he said loudly.

"You don't have to shout. Speaking *soto voce* is sufficient." The telephone in Dennis' pocket rang and he answered, smiling at Dekker. "See? It's pretty sweet." Dekker shrugged his acceptance. He was always impressed with Dennis and his technology.

"You said there were a couple of things…"

"Yes. You're going to be traveling to countries where you can't carry firearms." Dennis opened a drawer and lifted out a box. "I have a prototype weapon made entirely of composite material that fires hardened plastic bullets. No metal at all."

Dekker opened the box and lifted out a dark gray handgun. It was slimmer than the weapons he normally favored and very light in his hand. "Is this a toy?"

"Not at all, but it is the latest technology. It came from the stealth aircraft technology."

"No kidding," deadpanned Dekker.

"It is quite accurate at distances under one hundred yards, and deadly. The composite nature of the gun and the plastic bullets make it invisible to airport and border security." Dekker hefted the weapon, inserted the magazine, and chambered a round. Again, he was impressed.

"Feels pretty good. It's a little light, but I guess I can adjust." Dekker cleared the chamber and ejected the magazine.

"Here's a holster to put in the small of your back. That's the least obvious place, and the narrow size makes it especially suited for that carry position." Dekker accepted the holster and slid the pistol snuggly into place against his back.

"Thanks Dennis…for everything."

"Just a minute! Don't forget the antenna booster for your Sat phone and the charging station." Dennis handed him the small box for the earpiece and its charger. Dekker took the box, gave Dennis a small salute, and left.

LYNCH WAS TRUE to his word. Dekker stepped out of a taxi in front of SIS headquarters in Vauxhall Cross, walked into the building and up to a reception desk. He asked for C. The perky young woman seemed to know he was expected. "You'd be Mr. Dekker. I'll ring *him* straight away." Dekker noticed the emphasis on "him."

In a few moments another woman escorted him to a private lift with only one button. "I guess we have only one way to go," said Dekker. The woman gave him an annoyed look. She was obviously a professional and wearing a dark suit, white blouse, and sensible shoes with kitten heels; and he saw the slight bulge of a weapon under her coat. She kept her gaze forward and did not look at Dekker.

The Secret Intelligence Service, formerly known as MI6, is Great Britain's answer to the CIA. They are responsible for all non-domestic intelligence operations, and C, Alex Younger, carried the burden of distilling all reports regarding suspicions of pending threats and outright attacks on British interests and leveraging his dwindling assets to counteract these threats. His was a lofty position and precarious, having to report to Parliament, the Queen, and an ever-critical press. Dekker couldn't imagine how C could keep all those balls moving in harmony, and he knew he would not like to trade places.

The lift doors opened on to a spacious well-appointed lobby. The agent escorted Dekker to another reception desk that, Dekker noted, was more of an antique table and handed him off. Without a word the escort returned to the lift and disappeared. Dekker noticed the lift doors facing into the room were painted to match the walls, making them effectively invisible when closed. The woman at the desk was older than his escort, and she was not wearing a weapon under her carefully tailored coat. "Mr. Younger is expecting you, Mr. Dekker. Please go right in."

The interior office was nothing like Jim Lynch's. This office had a rich, ornate tone: all antique furniture, flocked wallpaper, heavy-framed portraits, and delicate tea service stations. This was the environment of a man of power and prestige, and Dekker felt awed and somewhat humbled by it all. C stood and stepped from behind his large Queen Ann desk to greet Dekker.

"Welcome to SIS Mr. Dekker. I've wanted to meet you for some time, you know." Dekker shook his hand and gave him a quizzical look. "Ever since the episode with Lord

Geoffrey Stapleton, I've wanted to meet the man who exposed him."

"Yes, sir, but he was only one part of a larger scheme."

"To be sure, Mr. Dekker, but Lord Geoffrey was a particular embarrassment to the Crown and, especially, the House of Lords." C took a seat opposite Dekker and continued. "I spoke with Lynch regarding the predicament you find yourselves in, and I assure you, we stand ready to help. Whatever this new attack is, we too want to stop it before it spreads."

"Jim…Mr. Lynch, thought you might be able to assign a liaison for my visit to Egypt." Dekker struggled with the niceties of protocol.

"Yes, Mr. Dekker, and I have the perfect agent in mind: sharp, experienced, and a full-blooded Egyptian. I've asked her to join us." At that moment the office door opened and a beautiful woman stepped in. "Mr. Dekker, may I introduce Agent Hannah Ahmed."

Hannah took Dekker's hand with a firm grip and a soft smile. She was in her mid-30s, her long dark hair was pulled back from her face and collected on her neck in complicated plaits intertwined to create a pleasing braid. Adam sensed in the expression on her oval face that she considered herself his equal. Her eyes were disarmingly blue, an odd combination for someone of her lineage, he thought. She wore a business-style jacked over a matching skirt, and like the agent who escorted him to this floor, sported stylish yet sturdy shoes. It was clear she was accustomed to carrying a weapon, but hers, by regulation he assumed, must have been left outside with the receptionist.

"I am pleased to meet you, Mr. Dekker." Her accent suggested a sophisticated education, Eton or Cambridge, and Adam thought it quite pleasing.

"As am I, Agent Ahmed." He chastised himself for noticing her beauty, but he couldn't help it. Where Kelly had been an all-American girl, Hannah was striking and exotic. Like Kelly, however, this agent applied a minimum of makeup—a little eye liner and only a hint of eye shadow. But unlike Kelly, this woman had a hardness to her, an aloofness, and she exuded a sense that she was in charge. Dekker decided that, despite her appearance, this was not a woman to be trifled with.

"May we begin?" The chief looked at his watch. "I have fifteen minutes."

Dekker began a rapid briefing for C and agent Ahmed. He summarized key points from the information analysis meeting in Washington and outlined the roles each of the agencies was to play.

"And what was your role in the meeting, Mr. Dekker?" asked Hannah.

"I am an operative for NCTC, and my superior wanted someone with field experience in a room full of information-gathering gurus."

"Why am I here, sir?" Hannah posed the question to C, but Dekker answered.

"Because I plan to focus my attention in Egypt, and I'm told you have experience in that region." Hannah looked from her superior to Dekker, then nodded her understanding. Dekker continued. "The drone's unexpected target, a camp of about twenty people, was in the Sinai. The video feed from the drone showed a site that was vaguely military, an orderly setup protecting a central tent that proved to be ammunition storage."

"Why hit a small camp? Surely it wasn't a threat," said Hannah.

Dekker asked C for a map of the area, which the chief called up on a large-screen monitor on the wall. Dekker stepped to the monitor and pointed to a spot. "Here is the strike point. You can see it is well positioned for a move into Egypt proper. I think whoever was in this camp was going to infiltrate. The question is: who would do such a thing?"

"Other factions competing for recognition?" offered C.

"Or notoriety," said Hannah.

"Why would someone, whatever his technical skills, strike that particular camp? After all, they could have just as easily been Bedouin moving through the area for all anyone observing them from a distance could tell. No, it was not random. There was a reason, a very good reason, for that strike. I just can't figure it out." Dekker sat back waiting for a response.

"You may be on to something, Mr. Dekker," said C. "I suppose it is worth a look." He turned his gaze to Hannah.

"Yes, sir, I'll go," said Hannah. "I can be ready in the morning."

"I was hoping we could catch the evening flight to Cairo," said Dekker. "The clock is ticking and we don't know how they did it or why or when they will decide to do it again."

"Right, then. We'll leave tonight."

THE AFTERNOON WAS busy for both Hannah and Dekker. There were telephone calls to be made, contacts to be alerted, and most importantly, transportation to a remote and difficult area of the world to be organized. Hannah was a little annoyed this American could cause her to drop everything and go back to Egypt. *But it isn't all bad*, she thought. *It will be good to again touch the soil of my home, my Egypt.*

She did as much as possible from London, but because much of this trip required face-to-face negotiations, and not a little finesse, most of the details would be worked out upon arrival. She loved such personal-level interactions and the sense of victory that came with each successful agreement, and the more she thought about this trip the more she longed for the clean smell of the desert, the expansive blue sky above and the sand beneath her feet below.

"This will be a little vacation," she said to no one. "A quick trip to my Egypt to do some reconnoitering, enjoy a dinner or two at the fabulous restaurants in Cairo, and then back home."

A taxi ride took Hannah to Heathrow Airport where she found Dekker waiting at the gate for British Airways flight #156 direct to Cairo.

"We're just about to board. I was worried you wouldn't make it."

Hannah looked up at the flight display and said casually, "The flight doesn't leave until 5:45. We have plenty of time."

"You're right about plenty of time, but I'm thinking about the five hours in the air we can use to get in sync on this thing." Hannah just shrugged and waited for the desk attendant to call their row for boarding.

DEKKER SAT QUIETLY during takeoff and then decided on a new approach with the SIS agent. "Hannah, may I call you Hannah? I think we got off on the wrong foot back at SIS headquarters. May we start again?" His appeal was so sincere and self-effacing Hannah had to give in.

"You are right, Mr. Dekker. I was a little miffed about being forced to drop everything to escort you to my Egypt."

"That's an interesting way to put it, 'my Egypt' the personal possessive. And by the way, please drop the 'mister.' Just Dekker will do."

"All right, Dekker, and yes, you may call me by my given name. As to my possessive phrasing, as you so expressively put it, Egypt is much more than a government or lines on a map to me; it is the sacred land where my ancestors lived for many thousands of years. I trace my lineage back to the era of kings, *Muqawqis*, before the time of Mohammed and the incursion of his Islamic Caliphate. Today you cannot distinguish Egypt from any other Arab nation, but there is still a remnant of the true Egyptians there—a heritage of which I am most proud."

"Wow, that's a little more information than I expected. I didn't mean to insult you."

"There was no insult. I get possessive about my land, my Egypt. I suppose it comes from my father, who was a professor of Oriental Studies at Oxford. He instilled a love for my heritage and my land. I apologize for coming on so strong."

Dekker went silent for a moment, trying to remember another who shared this same sentiment about Egypt, the same sense of possession. The name was right on the tip of his tongue but Hannah interrupted.

"So we have both apologized and forgiven. Can you tell me more about your plans?"

As they discussed how to proceed, Dekker was surprised at how well connected Hannah seemed to be, both in the government and in the general population, especially among the criminal element. She told him she had scheduled a meeting with the Commander-in-Chief of the Egyptian Air Defense Forces, to be followed by a less formal but no less important meeting with a smuggler trading in black market goods.

"The lieutenant general will give us the official clearance we need to go snooping around the Sinai," said Hannah, "but Kassis will be our ground asset. He knows how to move through the system and find information the military could never provide."

"I am impressed, Hannah."

She seemed to shake off the compliment and produced a map of the region they would search. "Let's talk about how we will approach this investigation."

CHAPTER THREE

THE FLIGHT PASSED QUICKLY AS Dekker and Hannah focused their discussion on logistics and communications. It wasn't until the airplane's wheels bumped on the runway that Dekker looked out his window. "A quick five hours. By the way, I made reservations for us at the Ramses Hilton." Hannah nodded her approval. "And maybe you'd like to get a late night snack. They have a great Indian restaurant."

"That sounds good, but I am much too tired. Let's just get to the hotel and meet for breakfast in the morning."

As a taxi took them through the city, Hannah pointed out landmarks and monuments of particular interest. The pyramids were awash in light and Hannah gave Dekker a quick history lesson.

"The pyramids were not tombs for the Pharaohs, you know. Many now believe they were some sort of amplifier or spiritual center."

"I know a little something about that," said Dekker, remembering his experiences with the Flows and the struggle with Abaddon.

"The official age of these pyramids is put at about 3,500 BC, but there is growing evidence they were actually constructed long before that time, a theory I personally subscribe to."

My Egypt indeed, Dekker thought.

Their route took them along the Nile River, past shops and stalls still brightly lit and open for business. "Shops stay open quite late here," said Hannah. "The people rest during the heat of the day and reopen for business as the sun is setting." Dekker sat quietly, enjoying the late night bustle of the city. He wondered for the hundredth time what the hacking of a drone had to do with these people.

After checking in, Hannah went directly to her room, but Dekker was not ready to sleep. Now that he was in Egypt he felt a greater sense of unease. He knew that his sensitivity to the Flows enhanced his natural "danger" sense, and being this close to the pyramids made the Flows all the more influential on that sense. He wandered through the hotel lobby and found himself at the Sherlock Holmes Pub, a traditional English setting that was warm and inviting. Taking a seat at the ornate and heavily polished bar he ordered a pint and munched on local pistachios while sorting out his feelings. In the end he had no answers because there were no clear markers for him to follow. He finished the beer and went upstairs to his room.

The morning dawned bright and clear, although Cairo was already blanketed with a layer of pollution reminiscent of Los Angeles in the 1960s. Dekker met Hannah in the hotel's Terrace Café which offered an interesting array of buffet foods. Hannah took a light breakfast of fresh juice and pastries while Dekker went for a full English breakfast.

Their conversation was light and Dekker was curious about Hannah's background. "How did you come to be such an historical expert?" Hannah placed her muffin next to the fruit on the small plate before her and looked at Dekker. *What an interesting man*, she thought. "Like my father, I majored in Oriental Studies. I suppose my interest, my imagination, was kindled from an early age. I wanted to know and understand who my people were, how they lived, how they loved, and how they died."

"How does a scholar get to SIS?"

Hannah paused, not certain how much she should share. *But somehow, this man's openness almost draws it out of me*, she thought. "I actually started with the Security Service, MI5. I came to the attention of SIS and have been there for the past five years."

"That tells me how but not why," said Dekker.

Hannah looked away briefly and then turned back to Dekker. "My mother was killed in an IRA attack. I was twelve and a deep anger grew in me toward those who would take innocent lives for no good reason. I made it my business to understand who those people were and when I finished my schooling I took a position with MI5 in the Counter-Terrorism Protection Division. By then the IRA was no longer a threat. They had been replaced by Islamic fundamentalist terrorists."

"And with your heritage and background, you fit right in," observed Dekker.

"Yes, I did, even though it was mostly men in the division."

"Were you handicapped because it was a male-dominated environment?"

"At first I felt that way, but I soon discovered that, being a woman, I could move through certain groups unnoticed, which proved to be my greatest asset. I uncovered an al-Qaeda cell planning to strike the underground. We arrested them all, and my superiors gave me a medal."

"That's some story," said Dekker.

"That is also the reason I came to the attention of SIS, and, well, the rest is history."

"It's almost eight o'clock," said Dekker. "We need to get to the Air Defense Forces building. People start work early here." He scooped up the last of the food on his plate, signed the check, escorted Hannah to the front, and hailed a taxi. It was a short ride, hardly fifteen minutes, but Dekker could imagine the traffic congestion later in the day. They arrived at the ministry complex, a group of large buildings occupying the corner of a wide boulevard. Hannah walked confidently up the red brick entry and waited for Dekker to pay the driver and catch up.

Inside the large lobby Dekker saw a number of people waiting while others took impromptu meetings. Hannah approached the reception desk, announcing herself and who she was meeting. Dekker stood mute at her side. This was, after all, her show. They followed the receptionist's instructions and took a lift to the seventh floor where another receptionist invited them into an office. They were greeted by Lieutenant General Al-Moniem Al-Terras. Following light conversation in English, the general learned of Hannah's heritage and asked after her family. After briefly filling him in on her family and ancestry, Hannah moved to the purpose of the meeting.

"General, I'm sure you know about the drone strike in the Sinai." General Al-Terras nodded and Hannah continued. "Mr. Dekker wishes to investigate the site and determine why this happened. I am accompanying him to provide a local liaison for his inquiries."

"We do know about the incident. It seems it was a US drone, Mr. Dekker."

"It was, sir. However, the drone was way off course."

"Yes, I was informed shortly after the incident," said Al-Terras.

"Of course, general and I've been sent to find out why this happened," replied Dekker.

"I would normally tell you killing Egyptians is very serious business, but in this case reports tell us they were foreign nationals, Syrians mostly, so our concern is less who was killed than a bombing by your drone could happen at all." Hannah jumped in to the conversation.

"We would like to ask for permission to travel into the area, under your authority, of course, to investigate. We will provide you a full report after the fact." General Al-Terras studied the pair sitting before him, apparently gauging if there was some non-stated objective to their request. Satisfied they were being honest about their investigation, he gave his consent and called in the secretary, instructing her to prepare the appropriate documents. With the meeting over, the general stood, thanked the pair for their consideration of the Egyptian government, and wished them luck.

"That went smoother than I thought," said Dekker when they were in the next room.

"That is because C already contacted General Al-Terras," said Hannah.

They waited a few minutes while the secretary assembled documents, placed them in an envelope, and handed the packet to Hannah.

WHEN THEY WERE once again on the street, they hailed a taxi and were taken to a café near the Ministry of Culture.

"This is where I've arranged to meet Kassis," said Hannah. Dekker found a table on the sidewalk and ordered two coffees. In a few minutes the small cups of the thick, strong coffee appeared, and they waited. Hannah seemed unconcerned with the passing time as she sipped coffee and watched the procession of humanity swirling around them.

After half an hour Dekker could stand it no longer. "So where is this Kassis? We could be waiting all day."

"I'm sure you know the pace in this region is much different than the clock-driven culture of England or America." Admonished, Dekker sat quietly, waiting.

An hour passed when Hannah sat up, her attention captured. "What is it, Hannah?" Dekker looked around for some sign of trouble.

Hannah made a small sign with her hand, and seemingly from out of nowhere a dark-complexioned man took a seat next to Dekker. "Miss Ahmed, you are more beautiful than ever," said the newcomer.

"You are too kind, Kassis," she replied.

"Your message said something about trouble in the Sinai. How may I help?"

Dekker inspected the man, noting his dark good looks, his long hair and short beard. He sensed the man could be dangerous. Kassis was dressed in Western clothes but Dekker could easily imagine him in a traditional Thobe robe.

Kassis was given a broad account of the situation with an emphasis on the need for secrecy while investigating the now decimated camp. Kassis nodded his understanding, but he obviously knew there was more to this situation than the pair was telling him. The money they promised to pay him eased his curiosity and he agreed to take them into the desert.

"Do you have travel documents?"

Hannah offered the papers given them by General Al-Terras and waited for Kassis to look them over. He gave Hannah a nod, handing back the documents.

"When do we leave?" Dekker asked.

Kassis looked at his new clients and waved an arm in a broad gesture. "No time like the present. Don't you agree?" A small van sailed around a corner and stopped directly before them. "And here is our transport." He opened the sliding side door and invited them into the van. "If you please, Miss Ahmed, Mr. Dekker."

THE SEVENTY-FIVE mile trip was scenic if uneventful. They traveled through towns along the Nile, all of them green with groves of date palms and fields fed by the annual inundation. After crossing the river, however, the countryside became arid and unforgiving. Hannah thought of it as the crucible that forged the ancient Hyksos into the fighting force that conquered Egypt during the Intermediate period when Manetho recorded, "During the reign of Tutimaos a blast of God smote us." But Egypt learned from the defeat and returned to drive the invaders away. Hannah gazed out the window as she reflected on the ancient history of her people and lamented what they had become.

Kassis leaned over the front seat, removed his wide-brimmed hat and wiped his brow. "So far there has been no trouble, but the camp is a few klicks ahead and I expect some sort of guard detail." No sooner had he spoken than two vehicles emerged from behind a sand dune, blocking their way. Kassis swung around and peered through the windscreen. "Ah, I see we have a greeting committee. Please give me your papers." Dekker and Hannah passed a look between them but said nothing. Hannah was confident, however, as was Dekker, all would go well. After all, they had papers from General Al-Terras.

Kassis stepped out of the van and began speaking with the men. While Literary Arabic was the official language, Kassis knew most people spoke Egyptian Arabic and he addressed the soldiers now facing them in that language. His distance from the van made most of what he said unintelligible, but Hannah was able to catch a few words.

"What's he saying?" Dekker asked.

"He's telling them we're on a mission for General Al-Terras."

"Are they good with that?"

"Yes, and they seem satisfied with the written orders."

Kassis returned to the van and instructed the driver to continue. The soldiers made way for the van to pass. "They say the camp we are looking for is just ahead, but they warned of bandits in the area."

CHAPTER FOUR

THE DRONE ATTACK WENT PERFECTLY. Kamenwati was stunned at the ease with which he reached half a world away and took control of the drone operator, fogging his mind and ordering a new location for the attack. He laughed and congratulated himself, but then he felt the spirit speaking to him.

You have done well, Kamenwati.

Thank you, Master.

The immediate threat is stopped, but there is still much to do. Officials will try to find you. You will wait for my next move. Never forget this has been my doing. You are simply the means to accomplish my goals.

Of course, Master. I do not forget but it was just so simple. I had no idea such control was possible.

Remember, the control is mine.

Kamenwati felt the Abaddon spirit withdraw, and he relaxed. His experiences with the spirit were always dangerous, and leveraging its power without giving up his own identity was a struggle. But for now he felt invincible, like a king, or even a god. Leaving his private quarters, he went outside and down to the lagoon where he bathed and refreshed himself. Lounging on a cushioned couch under the shade structure, he allowed Rahotep and another follower to bring him a tray filled with fruits. He acknowledged his followers with a nod. "Master, you look different," said Rahotep.

When Kamenwati looked up, Rahotep felt his master was gazing into his soul. He also noticed a soft glow around Kamenwati, the remains of his encounter with the Abaddon spirit. "I have dealt with a threat to our Egypt, and now I must prepare for the inevitable search."

"How will you do that, Teacher?" Rahotep did not understand what Kamenwati meant by dealing with the threat, but this did not seem the time for questions about that part of his plan.

"I will make this island disappear," said Kamenwati.

Rahotep opened his eyes wide in wonder but said nothing. He bowed slightly and left Kamenwati alone.

STILL IN THE afterglow of his experience in the Flows, Kamenwati lay quiet, his consciousness still adrift in the sensation of invincibility. Without warning he sensed something, not danger exactly but that something menacing approached. He sat up fully focused, attempting to locate the source of his perception. He could not pin it down; it was too elusive or perhaps too well masked.

The threat was non-specific, as was normal within the Flows, but his sensitivity raised an alarm. He called for his guiding spirit but received no reply. For whatever reason the Abaddon spirit was absent and he felt strangely vulnerable.

With his mood disturbed, Kamenwati left the lagoon.

In the large front room of his complex, he called for his followers, who quickly gathered.

"My friends," Kamenwati began, "I want you to know that today we have struck a blow for our Egypt, perhaps the first step toward the new era so long hoped for." Looks of surprise passed between the gathered men and women. "There was a new threat from the Caliphate, a vanguard assembled in the Sinai. Today I struck at that group, obliterating their camp and scattering their ashes to the wind." This pronouncement evoked a loud cheer from the group.

Rahotep, with a wide grin on his face, spoke for everyone. "How Teacher? Did you send a plague on them?"

"No, this was an entirely new use of Magick. It is a way to control not only men but also to direct their machines. While in Germany, I encountered a new power, one that, among other things, allows me to influence both men and machines." Kamenwati gazed across his assembled followers, a satisfied look on his face. "I seized control of an American drone operator and directed him to destroy the Caliphate infiltrators."

An awed silence fell over his followers, but after a few long seconds, Rahotep spoke out. "Greatness will be ours again!"

The group echoed the cry, repeating it several times. Kamenwati allowed them to enjoy the moment and then quieted them.

"Yes, my friends, greatness will be ours once again; but not without a struggle. The Americans are sure to launch an investigation, but they will not be able to discover how they lost control of their machine. I have had a premonition, which is not yet specific, of a coming threat to our sanctuary and our cause, but it is a danger we will deflect." He looked over his small group of loyal followers and swelled with pride.

"There are two things we must do: use this victory to recruit more of our brethren, the true Egyptians, and at the same time stop the American investigation." Murmurs of agreement flowed through the group. "I need six of you to infiltrate the Caliphate infiltrators campsite in the Sinai and be on-hand to observe any investigation." He looked directly at Rahotep. "Find anyone asking questions and eliminate them."

Rahotep and five others immediately stepped forward and Kamenwati nodded his approval. "You will be dispatched at sunrise. Meanwhile, all others are to begin reaching out to the larger community and bring them into our fold."

INFILTRATING THE DRONE strike site was even easier than Rahotep expected. The few locals around the sites were fearful the hand of Allah would strike again from above, and the local officials were not equipped or trained to deal with the devastation found in the camp. This made Rahotep's offer to sift through the debris, for a price of course, a welcome opportunity to let someone else do the work.

Rahotep was pleased the local police, who believed at any minute another bomb might be dropped, stayed far away from the site which allowed Rahotep to follow Kamenwati's instruction to misdirect the investigation.

A few days later there was a flurry of activity among the local police; they crowded into their two vehicles and left in a hurry.

"Someone must be coming," said Rahotep to his men. "Be ready. You know the plan should these people choose to stay." The others nodded their understanding.

One hour later a plume of dust kicked up along the road leading to the now devastated camp. A van with a rooftop cargo rack filled with sacks and boxes came to a dusty halt before the site where the central tent used to sit. Now there was nothing but a burned-out hole in the ground, the black tendrils of the explosion spreading perhaps one hundred feet outward from a central point. The driver and another man emerged from the front while a woman and an obviously foreign man stepped out the sliding side door. Rahotep looked closely at the strangers and was surprised that the woman appeared to be Egyptian, perhaps a true Egyptian, and yet her clothing suggested something else.

The driver was no threat, only a hired man with no interest in the mission. The man who seemed to serve as guide had "thief" and "mercenary" written all over him. The foreign man standing next to the woman was another matter. Rahotep sensed something unusual about him, an intangible quality he associated with his master. *Who is he, and how did he become involved?* Rahotep stepped forward, introducing himself as a humble local and giving a false name, Aziz.

"Why are you here?" Hannah asked.

"Searching for weapons, no doubt," said Kassis.

Rahotep/Aziz gave a hurt look at the reprimand. "Surely the police told you we were pressed into service to clean this place." He looked back at his men. "We had no choice," he lied. Turning to the foreigners with an open look on his face he asked, "How may we help you, *effendi*?"

Kassis was still suspicious, but Hannah took over. "Can you tell us what happened here?"

"I cannot say for certain. You see, we were traveling through the area…" He waved his arm in the general direction of the low hills in the distance. "We saw a great light and heard a blast that shook the earth. We were frightened at first, but when no more explosions were heard we decided to investigate. The camp we had seen from a distance was completely destroyed and we judged they were rebels with a great deal of weaponry, all destroyed by a mysterious explosion. We were afraid to be caught in the camp of rebels, but the police came and questioned us. They realized we knew nothing and pressed us into service to sift through the debris and bring them any evidence we might find."

The foreign man stepped forward. "Did you find anything?"

"No *effendi*, nothing. Just burned out earth, a few tattered tents, and a few simple cooking utensils. There were, however, many bodies to be buried."

Dekker looked to Hannah, who in turn looked to Kassis. "We should inspect more closely."

"Why bother? We can see what happened," said Kassis.

Dekker stood silent, looking over the site and then fixing his gaze on Aziz. *If that really is his name.* "There's more going on here, and this Aziz is somehow connected with it."

"How could you possibly know that?" Hannah asked.

"Call it a sixth sense. He is not what he seems and he knows something." They watched the local men shuffle back to the shade of a tent they had erected outside the blast zone.

"Okay, so how do you want to proceed?"

"We give them what they expect. We'll look around." Dekker went to the center of the blast zone and bent down, doing his best to appear to be investigating. Hannah got into the game as well and spent time looking at odd bits of debris, but in reality they watched the men under the tent, especially the leader.

The day dragged on and the heat grew; Kassis and the driver erected a small tarp for shade. Dekker and Hannah retreated to the shade of the tarp, maintaining the "inspection" ruse by continually holding up bits and pieces of junk.

"Their leader's eyes haven't left us for a minute, even when we came over here for shade," said Dekker.

"Do you think he knows you are suspicious of him?"

"I am certain of it. He's just waiting for us to leave."

Kassis stood and looked to Hannah and Dekker, and then to the setting sun. "Are you ready to leave?"

The driver took down the tarp and the group climbed back into their van. Kassis nodded to the driver who put the van into gear and drove away.

In the camp, Rahotep stood, satisfied the suspicious strangers knew nothing. "They will return to Cairo, file their reports, and go away." He was in fact trying to convince himself that was the end of any outside investigation but knew it would not be that simple. He motioned to his men who gathered up their camels and set off into the evening, not knowing Dekker would be following from a distance.

IT WAS NECESSARY to convince Hannah and Kassis that the band of men needed to be followed. Hannah seemed to understand after a moment, but Kassis was resistant. "Why do you want to follow those nomads?"

"They are not simple Bedouin," said Dekker. "They had a finer look to them, almost un-Arab." Hannah agreed with Dekker. "After you brought your suspicions to my attention I looked more closely. They dress like desert people, but their manner is different, as are their features. They are not so darkly complected, and their hands have not seen rough work."

"Whoever they are, they were not in the camp to help us," said Dekker. "They were watching us, and now I want to return the favor, see where they go and who they report to." With all parties in reluctant agreement, Kassis instructed the driver to pass the police checkpoint and find high ground where they could watch for the six men. It was dark when the van stopped atop a small hill. Dekker instructed the driver to move the van off the crest. "We wouldn't want to give them a silhouette." Dekker settled down with a pair of field glasses Kassis brought along, scanning the valley below. A partial moon rose, washing the barren land in a soft, cool glow that aided in Dekker's search.

It wasn't long before the line of six camels came into view. "They're heading south," said Dekker. The others took turns looking at the group through the binoculars.

"There is a ferry across the Suez about ten miles from here," observed Kassis. "I will wager they are heading there."

Dekker, looking again through the binoculars, was silent. He was reaching into the Flows and to the men below, probing. He sat back and handed the field glasses to Kassis. "Yes, you are right. They're headed for the ferry and we must reach it before they do."

"The road takes us a little out of the way, but with the van we should have no trouble reaching the ferry before them. After all, they're on camels," said Kassis.

"Thank goodness for that," said Dekker. "Let's go."

DEKKER SPENT THE entire trip looking through maps of the area. "This doesn't make a lot of sense," he said more to himself than to the others. "Assuming they're heading for the ferry crossing, where does that leave them? It's nowhere near Cairo and it takes them in the opposite direction of other Arab capitals." His rhetorical question went unanswered. Hannah was deep in her own thoughts. She was certain the men in the camp were ethnic Egyptians. Why in the world were they in that place? What were they looking for? What was going on? There were no answers to her conundrum and she was frustrated with her inability to unravel this mystery. Next to her Dekker shifted back and forth between maps and satellite photos, his own frustration apparent.

"I'll bet we're chewing on the same problem, Mr. Dekker." He looked up, a little startled at the sound of her voice.

"I'm trying to imagine where in the world these guys are going. We could easily lose them in the southern desert after they cross the Suez."

Hannah crossed her arms tightly around her torso. "I think they are ethnic Egyptians, and I'm wondering what is really going on here."

The van arrived at the queue point for the ferry. A number of trucks were in line already, despite the hour. The driver turned off the motor and sat back to nap while they waited for first light and the ferry. The others couldn't sleep and watched the great dark forms of container ships pass along the canal, each with its own destination somewhere in the world.

At sunrise a loud whistle sounded, signaling the ferry was setting out from the western bank of the canal. In a few minutes the van driver sat up straight and started up the engine, and the drivers of the trucks in the line started theirs as well. Dekker looked around for the men on camels but saw none. "Damn. They haven't made it yet." Kassis opened his door in the front and stood on his seat, leaning out the door to gain elevation.

"Wait. I think I see them." Kassis leaned back in with some excitement. "They've just come to the end of the queue, which means they will cross just as I predicted."

"And I'm worried about losing them in the open desert. This van is fine on groomed roads, but the open desert is quite another thing."

The driver perked up at Dekker's comment. "Yes, sir, you are right. My van is good, but not for off-road driving." He gave Kassis a look that seemed to say, *Don't even think about asking.* Kassis sat back down, his enthusiasm obviously blunted.

Dekker looked first to Hannah and then to Kassis. "Let's first see what they do and then work on Plan B."

CHAPTER FIVE

THE MYSTERIOUS AZIZ AND HIS band left the ferry well ahead of the motor vehicles. It was the custom to let people with livestock debark first, a practice developed from previous incidents where anxious drivers struck or killed a horse, donkey, or camel. The ensuing entanglement with the local authorities could stop the ferry's operation for hours and cost the operators a good deal of money. So, in the interest of good commerce and good sense, livestock went first.

By the time Kassis' van rolled off the ferry the camel-mounted men were gone. They drove around looking for them, but without success. The van driver had no desire to pursue them and was just as happy they were gone. Kassis sat in stoic silence, accepting the situation. Whatever the outcome, he would be paid. Dekker and Hannah were not so favorably disposed. Each looked frantically out the side windows, checking every street they crossed. They had said nothing for a long time when Kassis suggested they stop to ask a few locals what they might know. Dekker agreed and they parked outside the souk located around the staging area for the ferry.

The open air market was a rambling collection of tents, tables, and carpeted areas with people milling about, inspecting fruits, woven goods, hammered metal pots, and food stalls. Kassis moved into the tangle of humanity like one born to it. Surprisingly, Hannah was not far behind and seemed equally comfortable in the confusion of the souk. Dekker was able to keep up only by bulling his way through the crowd, keeping Hannah's red headscarf in sight. When he caught up, Hannah and Kassis were deep in conversation with an old man sitting on a pile of woven rugs. He was nodding and gesturing toward his goods. Kassis was beginning to lose patience when Hannah placed a hand on his arm. She spotted Dekker coming through the crowd.

"Dekker! Come over here." Hannah's tone was insistent and Dekker made his way through the last barrier of people. "I need you to buy something, anything. The old man won't tell us where the men on camels went unless we buy something." Dekker looked around for the cheapest item in the stall and spotted a rather nice head wrap. "Will this do?" Hannah nodded and asked the old man how much for the head wrap. Kassis got into the action as the first price given was unacceptable, but after a few rounds of back-and-forth, an acceptable price was reached.

"Give him one hundred Egyptian pounds," said Kassis. Dekker made a mental calculation and realized it only amounted to about thirteen dollars. He peeled off the notes and handed them to Kassis who gave them to the old man. The old trader inspected the money, then eyed Dekker, looking for any sign of deceit. Finding none in his eyes, the old man began speaking while waving his arms around in a circle. He seemed ready to rid himself of these people, and he stood, pointing through the tangle of souk vendors. Kassis and Hannah thanked the old man and headed in the direction indicated while Dekker did his best to wrap his new purchase around his head and follow.

When they broke through the final line of vendor stalls they were faced with a scattering of ramshackle houses built from leftover lumber, plywood, tar paper, and asphalt rolls. Beyond the shanty village was open desert.

"This is where the old man said they went," said Hannah. Dekker could only stand mute with the bitter taste of defeat in his mouth.

"Well, we know what direction they went," said Kassis. "What now?"

Dekker turned and faced Kassis and Hannah. "Kassis, I want you to stay here with the van and see what you can find out about those men. Hannah and I will rent a four-wheel-drive and do a little reconnoitering."

Two hours later, after finding a Hertz rental office, the group split as planned. Kassis returned to the souk to question vendors and the ferry operators. Dekker and Hannah took their rented Range Rover around town to the spot behind the souk where the six men had taken to the desert. Dekker drove a short way into the open land and stopped.

"Why are we stopping?" Hanna asked.

"I need to find some tracks that will show the direction they took, and I don't want to mess them up with this vehicle." He got out and took a few steps in front of the Range Rover. He turned back to Hannah. "You stay there. I'll be finished in a minute."

Hannah did as she was told, watching as Dekker bent over the bisque-colored ground looking for signs. He wandered to the left, then stopped and walked to the right. He followed this pattern several times, each pass being farther out than the last. Hannah watched the strange ritual for about thirty minutes, thinking Dekker was wasting his time just as he suddenly stood up, walked a few paces forward, and then back. He looked at the Range Rover and beamed, holding a thumb up in the air. He jogged back and jumped in, wiping perspiration from his forehead.

"I found tracks, Hannah. They went in that direction," he said, pointing to the south-southwest. "The tracks are still fresh, although a little muddled because they're traveling in a straight line, one behind the other."

"What is out there?" Hannah asked. Dekker consulted a map and shook his head.

"Nothing, so far as I can tell." He got a faraway look. "But still, there is something. I can sense it."

"You can follow your nose for a couple of hours, but then we turn back," said Hannah. "I don't want to get stuck out there in the dark."

Dekker nodded his acknowledgement and put the sturdy vehicle into gear.

RAHOTEP WAS PLEASED to be going home. Instead of following the canal to their island, he cut off a major portion of the journey by setting out across the open desert. His men followed in silence, each appreciating the harsh, stark wilderness for its beauty. Rahotep knew that only a true Egyptian could appreciate the land as he and his companions did. *From the fertile Nile Valley to these open and unpopulated lands, it all works in harmony, one balancing the other and each filling the soul with its own comfort.* His reverie was broken by a strong feeling. *Are we being pursued?* It was certainly a feeling of someone with power searching. Stopping his companions Rahotep looked behind and concentrated on this feeling. He was using the Flows as his teacher instructed.

He realized the feeling, this sense of someone searching, was still far off, perhaps as far as Suez. After gathering his companions to him, they discussed a strategy. "We are being followed," said Rahotep. The others looked around, as if they had ridden into an ambush. "No, brothers. Our pursuer is not here yet."

"Do we set a trap?" asked one.

Rahotep thought about the question for a moment. "No." The others looked questioningly at him.

"I fear a trap would be sensed by this man long before we could spring it. I believe our best strategy is to scatter and confuse the trail." The group agreed and remounted their camels. "No two of us will take the same path We will meet at the deserted village on the shore opposite our island in two days."

The group scattered and disappeared into the vastness of the desert.

KAMENWATI FELT THE quiet in his sprawling seigneury. Most of his followers were absent following his command to gather new recruits. The stillness was comforting and he found the ambience peaceful. He lounged on a couch in the porch area open to the Nile and luxuriated in the soft breeze that always seemed to blow, and he relaxed into a light meditative state.

Moments later he sat up with a start, realizing someone was using the Flows to search for Rahotep and his companions. He was confused about the source. *Could it be the Icelander, Galdur, or the meddling Salim, guardian of the Flows?* He could not imagine they had any interest in his affairs. Besides, they had no knowledge he was even alive. No one knew. Kamenwati injected himself into the Flows in a way that assured a low probability of detection. It was most important he keep his identity secret and feared even this most surreptitious of probes might result in his discovery, but his men could not be discovered.

Kamenwati concentrated on Rahotep and set a passive deflecting shield around the company. He sensed them scattering, making his deflection easier because it reduced the overall footprint of the invisible shield, but it also increased the amount of concentration required to shield six subjects going in different directions. As he sat in ever-deepening concentration he wondered how persistent this unknown follower would be. He sat very still, concentrating until he became aware the sun was setting. His sense of the presence faded, a suggestion the pursuer failed to find his men and turned away.

Unlocking his body from the position held through the afternoon, he stood and stretched his arms, but his problem was not solved. Whoever followed Rahotep was sure to begin again and he needed a plan for such an eventuality.

DEKKER DROVE THROUGH the afternoon trying to concentrate on the feeling of presence that grew stronger as he and Hannah travelled deeper into the desert. He realized his sensitivity was heightened by proximity to a Flow line and the nexus point existing in Giza, at the pyramids. The open desert, largely devoid of life, made the strength of his probe that much greater. Hannah, searching with the binoculars for signs of the fleeing men, had no idea her new partner was engaged in a hunt of a different order.

As they travelled, Hannah stole glances of her companion. He was large and quite fit; he kept his dark hair a little long and slightly unkempt; he had keen eyes and a sharp wit. She decided he was attractive, not movie-star appealing, but handsome in a rugged way. He had stayed in the background while she took charge with General Al-Terras and Kassis, and he even kept his thoughts to himself at the site of the drone strike. *Yes*, she thought, *Dekker is a man who has seen much and is comfortable with himself. It makes me want to know more.*

She stole another glance at his strong profile, concentrating on...*what*? He seemed focused on the desert in a way she did not understand. His course was unwavering and he seemed certain of their direction. She turned back, lifting the binoculars to her eyes. *I trust this man*, she thought. *More than that, I like him.* Hannah's feelings surprised and confused her. "It's getting late," she said nodding toward the setting sun. Dekker reacted oddly. He pulled the Range Rover to a stop, stepped out and looked intently at the horizon.

"They're gone," he said, climbing back into the Rover.

"What do you mean, gone?" Dekker looked at Hannah, her eyes questioning.

"I've lost them. Besides, I promised we would return before sunset." He turned the Rover around and headed in the direction they had come. Hannah sat back trying to understand what just happened.

They travelled back in silence, but Dekker's mind was in high gear. He just experienced something he had not encountered since Krugerschloss in Germany: a masking that blocked his ability to discern the location of the men he followed. Perhaps someone more experienced, like Galdur, could penetrate the veil; but the fact that there was protection for these men told him a great deal and also raised new questions. *Who still has powers like this?* The Abaddon organization was completely dismantled after Krugerschloss, and the only practitioners of Magick he knew about were the remnants of the priesthood in ancient Babylon and under the direction of Galdur's friend Salim. *They certainly would not be doing this*, he thought *protecting these men.*

So who else is left out there? Dekker had no answer, and he was getting too tired to focus. He would think about this again in the morning.

AS DEKKER, HANNAH, and Kassis gathered for a light breakfast of baked cakes, dates, and thick coffee, Dekker had a new resolve. It was now time for him to take the lead, especially given his realization of what force was used to seize control of the drone operator. "Kassis," he said, "I think our contract is complete. You've been very helpful, and I am grateful, but it is time for you to return to Cairo." Their guide nodded his understanding and took a last sip of coffee. "In that case, I bid you farewell. Thank you Miss Ahmed. This has been a most interesting trip." He stood to leave as Hannah, stunned, looked sharply at Dekker.

"No, Miss. Mr. Dekker is correct. I have completed the task for which I was hired and it is now time to go." Hannah sat speechless. "May I drop you two somewhere?"

"Thank you, Kassis, but no. We've got a few things to wrap up here, and then we'll be on our way back to England."

"As you wish," said Kassis, but reaching the door, he turned. "And good luck."

Hannah had the good sense not to question Dekker in front of Kassis, but now she spoke sharply to him. "Why did you send Kassis away? He's very knowledgable about what goes on in this area and is known among the locals."

Dekker considered his answer and then offered only the barest of explanations. "The fewer people who know about this the better."

"What do you mean? Kassis already knows what we're doing."

"He doesn't know what's really going on, and frankly, neither do you."

"Are you going to send me back to London, then?"

He looked into Hannah's eyes, gauging her resolve. "No, because you are an experienced field agent and because of your heritage." He looked around the crowded café. "Let's get out of here. I've got a story to tell you that I don't want overheard or repeated."

With a mystery thus offered up, Hannah had no choice but to go along with Dekker.

CHAPTER SIX

DEKKER TOOK HANNAH BACK TO the Range Rover and set out on the road following the Nile. Once they had passed out of the city proper, Dekker began telling his story. "I went through an experience a few years ago that changed my view of the world, my way of thinking, in fact." Hannah nodded in tacit understanding. "You probably know my background in the Army Rangers and later working for the NCTC."

"Your counterterrorism organization I know about, but there's not much information there. That you spent time in the Army is news to me, but not surprising after watching you for the last few days."

"I was successful in the Rangers because I had a natural ability to sense things, to 'see around corners' as Jim Lynch used to say. I left the service and ended up in New

Mexico, and I reconnected with Lynch while investigating an espionage case at Los Alamos Laboratories. It was during that case I learned of a shadowy and unknown global organization answering to someone called Abaddon. The incident at the Labs was one I later discovered was connected to a plot to collapse all the major world economies."

"And this was all the idea of a single madman?"

"Incredibly, yes it was. The event was many years in the planning, and we uncovered the plot and defeated Abaddon only at the last minute."

"I never heard about this incident, even in the SIS."

"You wouldn't have heard about it. Knowledge of the incident was never shared beyond the few people directly involved."

"How did this change your worldview?"

Dekker was silent for a moment, trying to compose a narrative that would make sense to the SIS agent. "I discovered I have a sensitivity to something called the Flows and I was introduced to the ancient practice of Magick."

Hannah gave him a skeptical look. "You mean like hocus-pocus?"

"No, Magick with a K, and it's not like that at all. It was, or is, a way of interacting with the world without relying on technology."

"Do you mean these people are Luddites?"

"Not at all, but practitioners of Magick study an entirely different way to manipulate what people do and think. It's a way of harnessing invisible forces to influence events, effect change in material conditions, or present the illusion of change. It sounds crazy, but I've seen it firsthand."

"So how does this Magick have any bearing on our drone situation?"

"It has to do with the Flows." He looked around as if he could see the phenomenon. "The Flows are like rivers of energy crisscrossing the globe, going from point-to-point, creating a web encircling the world. I was taught some of the basics of Magick by an old Icelander, himself a deep practitioner of Magick and a believer in the Old Truths; and I'm now able to operate in this non-physical environment." Dekker's passion for the subject was beginning to intrigue Hannah. *Could this possibly be true?*

"Someone who is enlightened and operates in the Flows can be located, and the men we were following were definitely part of that brotherhood. I sensed it first at the strike site, and then more strongly when we saw them from the hilltop as they were leaving. When we found their tracks I knew for sure, and I began tracking them, not with my eyes but with my senses."

"You said 'we lost them' out there. What was that all about?"

"That was the moment I knew someone intervened, a powerful practitioner able to mask their presence with a Word of Deflection."

"Okay. Who and where will we find him?"

"It doesn't work like that, Hannah. The man or woman, I suppose, could be literally anywhere in the world, or at least anywhere near a Flow line."

"Then why are we out here in the desert again?"

"It goes back to my last encounter with Abaddon. I was captured in Maryland and flown to Strasbourg, France, and from there held on a barge. That's where I met an Egyptian named Kamenwati, himself a practitioner like my friend Galdur; but he wanted Abaddon's power. I thought about this drone situation last night, and the only one I know with both the power and the means to pull this off is that Egyptian, Kamenwati."

"I'm not sure that is logic so much as a big supposition," said Hannah.

"Perhaps, but the possibility that Kamenwati is involved is worth looking into, don't you think?"

"I guess so, but where do we find this Kamenwati?"

"That's the problem. I don't exactly know. He mentioned his home was on an island in Egypt, and I took that to mean an island in the Nile. I don't have any more to go on than that, and so we're going to drive along the river and see what we find."

"That doesn't sound very scientific. How would you ever know which island was his? You know, there are many islands above the Aswan dam."

"I believe I can sense where he is if we get close. I'm counting on that, and I'm also counting on your knowledge of the language. My Arabic is sketchy."

"You are a strange man, Adam Dekker. On the surface you are cool and calculating, a very rational man; but underneath, you have an odd sense of spirituality."

"Is that bad?"

"It is strangely consistent with the ancient beliefs of my people."

Dekker nodded and drove on.

KAMENWATI RECEIVED THE report from Rahotep. After scattering, the companions reunited near the island compound. Their master nodded when Rahotep told of the strange feeling he had from the man tracking them. "I think he was using the Flows."

"He was," replied Kamenwati. "It was only my Word of Deflection that protected you and the others from discovery." Rahotep offered words of thanks and departed.

Kamenwati knew more scrutiny was coming, and he mentally reviewed the events in Germany. When he considered the former Abaddon host, Kambrian, he remembered his manic focus on an American. That was it! The American, Dekker, the man he made a deal with, the man who somehow expelled the spirit from Kambrian. *Of course! How could I be so blind?* Seizing an American drone would of course generate an investigation, but he never imagined the intelligence agencies would link him to the activity. None of them could have known the source or nature of the attack except for Dekker.

"How very clever to involve Dekker in this," he said to the empty room. He would have to take defensive measures, much like those used by his predecessor, to hide his island. There was nothing to be seen from the banks of the river, but from the river itself was another matter. He needed more strength to deflect notice of his home base. He needed power only the Abaddon spirit could provide. He went to the special meditation spot in his office, a collection of large pillows on the floor with a large mosaic tile sculpture on the wall behind. Practicing the familiar routine, he slipped into a deep meditative trance and summoned the spirit of Abaddon.

Did all go as planned, or do you reach out for some other reason? The spirit asked.

Master, I am pleased to tell you the plan went perfectly. Those operating the drone device had no idea what happened or who took control. Also, striking the Caliphate interlopers seems to have crushed any plot to control Egypt.

Yet there is something troubling you.

Yes, Master, there is. A group of foreigners visited the camp.

This was anticipated.

They found nothing but later followed my team when they left the site. There was one among them who is schooled in Magick, in the Truths, and in the use of the Flows. The searcher quit only when I covered them with a cloud, causing me to suspect he is not a deep practitioner.

And who is it you suspect demonstrated these talents?

A man you will remember from Germany, the American. Dekker. The spirit was silent for a moment and then lashed out at Kamenwati.

You will find this man, this nuisance, and stop him. If you do not or cannot you will suffer the same fate as your predecessor.

Taken aback by the threat, Kamenwati replied, *I will find and eliminate him, but I ask your help to keep a cloud around my island. He will eventually remember our previous encounter and seek me out, and I need your strength to shield this place.*

It is done.

With the knowledge his island was shielded from discovery, Kamenwati set about laying a trap for his American adversary. "I already have the perfect device to strike him. I only lack his location."

He searched deeply in the Flows but could not locate Dekker. "He will show himself, and when he does, I will be ready to strike."

THE RANGE ROVER came to a halt along the banks of the Nile River. Dekker looked across the water to the open desert opposite, wondering how many generations had traveled this same route. He reached into the rear seat and took a small zippered case from the canvas messenger bag. He took out the small earpiece and the pocket-size base unit.

"What in the world is that?" Hannah asked.

"This is a satellite phone," responded Dekker.

"You're kidding."

"No, but the technology is something of a secret. So keep it to yourself."

"SIS needs to get one of these," said Hannah.

"Give me a minute, then we can return to our search."

"Some search. Only open desert all around."

Dekker stepped away from the Rover and activated his sat phone. He promised Jim Lynch to call in every forty-eight hours with a report, and it was time to check in. He gave a full report on their findings in the Sinai and the suspicious group from the camp. "You are continuing to track them?" asked Lynch.

"I only need one more day. I just want to satisfy my curiosity," said Dekker.

"Fine, but then I want you back here to work with the military intelligence investigation."

Dekker signed off and returned to Hannah. "I have orders to wrap this up and get back home."

"Right away or do we have a little time?" asked Hannah.

"We have another day, and then we return." Dekker looked perplexed. "I need some help on this," said Dekker replacing the sat phone to its case and stuffing it back into the messenger bag. "Give me a few minutes."

A small stand of date palms stood on the riverbank and Dekker walked to their shade. Hannah watched as he sat against one tree and seemed to gaze across the river. She thought his actions odd, but then he was an unusual man, she reminded herself. After half an hour, Dekker rose and walked back to Hannah, who had waited patiently in the Rover.

"Is everything all right?"

"Yes, and I've enlisted the help of an old friend."

COMMUNICATING THROUGH THE Flows is not like using a telephone. Images and feelings are the language of the Flows, and interpreting a message requires skill and experience. Galdur was pleased to hear from Dekker, and he shared Dekker's suspicion that Abaddon, or some version of him, was behind the drone incident. Galdur shared his friend's misgivings that this was a new method of attack from an old enemy, promising to probe more deeply.

After ending the connection Galdur stepped onto the porch of his cottage nestled against a cliff in the remote northern region of Iceland near Dalvik. The wooden porch supported a green sod roof that blended with the environment, making the cottage all but invisible to the casual glance. Looking across the small valley he alone inhabited, the Icelander recalled his involvement with Dekker and Abaddon.

It began with the death in Scotland of an American official Dekker was assigned to protect. Yet it was no ordinary killing. The assassin used the tools of Magick, and Dekker saw it all but did not understand what he experienced. Soon after, Dekker met and befriended Ulrig, a deep practitioner and longtime friend of Galdur, who began opening Dekker's mind and senses to the world of Magick. But Ulrig was killed before he could explain much, only managing to tell Dekker before he died that he would find answers in Iceland.

Galdur and Dekker did connect in Iceland and went on to find and confine Abaddon, but the confinement did not last and Abaddon was freed, setting up a new contest between the opposing forces. In the end Dekker was the one who confronted and bound the spirit that is Abaddon, casting it from the host and into the void. "But now Dekker believes spirit has returned, something I hoped would not happen during our lifetimes," Galdur said aloud only to the sky.

He stepped back inside his cottage and sat in a large overstuffed chair before the fireplace. "I must consult with Salim on this matter." Salim, the leader of their order and protector of the Flows, was instrumental in the final defeat of the Abaddon spirit and would be in the best position to know if the spirit had returned. Galdur slowed his breathing and shut his eyes, slipping easily into a light trance. He sent out a call to Salim's location in ancient Baghdad and waited only a few minutes before the familiar presence joined him. Galdur wasted no time with pleasantries, launching immediately into a synopsis of Dekker's communication.

If the spirit has returned, said Salim, *we have a new fight on our hands. The Abaddon spirit wants nothing less than control of the world and all mankind, and he will have hatched new schemes to achieve his goal.*

Agreed, my brother. That is why I called you, so that you might monitor the Flows for any unusual activity. Should you discover anything, please let Dekker and myself know. With that the session ended and Galdur felt confident of his old ally's help.

THE FLOWS ARE similar to electricity, energy but on a wider, deeper scale and moving continuously from point to point around the world. The Ancients knew of the Flows and understood how the power moved, and they knew how to use it for their own purposes. It was from this understanding of the tidal forces of the Flows that Magick was born. The art was practiced by a select few who learned how to use Magick to influence people and events. They also learned that Flow lines could be split and then set out to build nexus points at key locations around the world. The practice of Magick and the knowledge imparted to its initiates were known as the Old Truths and became a closely guarded secret, one held by priesthoods controlling the common people through its use.

Belief in the intangible power of Magick slowly gave way to the demonstrable power of technology. The conquest of the known world by the Romans in 300 BC was the death knell for Magick as a system of interacting with the world, of trusting invisible forces rather than the technologies being introduced by the Romans. A remnant of the ancient priesthood held on, however, living outside the new order that marched forward with ever greater technological feats. Pockets of believers could be found in various countries, and over time there was discontent with technology's influence on the world. When a man arose promising to return Magick to its rightful place and restore the ancient Brotherhood to a position of authority over men and events, he was able to gather virtually every Brotherhood cell to himself and his version of Magick. The man called himself Abaddon.

Many years later when Abaddon was captured and placed in stasis, a Merlin Box, a shudder went through the Flows and the Brotherhood came out of a long, dark period of oppressive control. Kamenwati felt the shift in the flows and spent a great deal of time understanding the impact of Abaddon's loss. He held a dream of his own, a dream not so dissimilar from that of Abaddon: the restoration of his Egypt and true Egyptians, men and women who would drive out the Arab invaders and return to the guiding principles of the Old Truths. So Kamenwati set out on a plan to resurrect Abaddon, to bring him back from stasis, and use his power to achieve Kamenwati's own dream. But his plan was ruined by an unlikely American and helped by renegades from his own Brotherhood.

Then it all changed. The spirit inhabiting Kambrian's body for more than a century was expelled and found Kamenwati. The moment the spirit attached itself to Kamenwati it began soothing him with quiet words and the promise of great rewards. Devastated by the defeat in Krugerschloss, the Egyptian mystic enthusiastically embraced the spirit of Abaddon, and a new era was born. The spirit knew the old idea of collapsing the economies of the world was no longer an answer. He needed new schemes and new ideas, and Kamenwati was just the man for his purposes. Kamenwati's jingoistic attitude regarding Egypt would fit nicely into the Abaddon spirit's larger plan. The spirit would draw Kamenwati in by attacking a band hiding in the Sinai and then extend the assault to all the technologies keeping people from acknowledging spiritual rule. His rule.

Kamenwati was in his meditative state when he felt an odd energy source from somewhere near. In the Flows he was accustomed to, and ignored, radio waves traveling though the atmosphere, but this one was different. He discerned the signature of Abaddon's adversary, Dekker, along with a peculiar radio signal. "That's it! That is how I will target him."

Kamenwati turned his attention to the drone operators in the United States.

CHAPTER SEVEN

SERGEANT BAINES LOOKED AT HIS control console with dismay. Fear grew as he watched himself punching buttons and toggling his joystick. It was an odd feeling, seeing oneself from outside and unable to stop his own actions. *It's happening again*, Baines realized. He watched helplessly as the UAV launched from the Bahrain base, its payload intended for targets in Iraq, instead flew west.

Captain Dunn, exonerated of having any responsibility for the last event on his watch, was back on duty as well. He did not notice Baines' state or the redirection of his drone. Dunn only took notice when the nose-mounted camera showed the aircraft firing its missiles at a vehicle in a small valley. He punched the comm line to the sergeant and shouted, "Baines!" Dunn had a sickening feeling the phenomenon was happening again, and once again, Sergeant Baines was the target. Even before relieving Baines of duty he called his commander.

"Sir, it's happening again. A drone was launched from Bahrain heading for targets in Iraq, but somehow it struck a target in the Sinai. Sir, it's just like before."

"Hold your post while I make a call," ordered his commanding officer.

Sergeant Baines was confused and slightly disoriented when Dunn came to his operating post. He had no explanation for the captain or himself. He didn't want to go through the interrogation he experienced after that last incident. He heard nothing, of course, and so did not know if they found out what, or who, was behind the event. He couldn't help wondering. The captain was in an animated conversation with an officer who earlier rushed into the operations center. The new officer reached for a red button on the captain's console and pressed it. A klaxon sounded, triggering red lights spinning in the ceiling. The unit was in lockdown.

A full company of men rushed through the doors, some taking up guard positions while the rest surrounded Sergeant Baines' station. It seemed everyone asked questions at the same time and Baines sat helplessly trying to respond to all of them. Dunn stepped through the crowd, shifting attention to himself. He tried fielding questions, but each answer seemed to elevate the passions of the ever-growing group of officers.

After thirty minutes of squabbling, the group settled down, understanding that neither Captain Dunn nor Sergeant Baines could account for this new incident.

"Do we have any idea of its objective?" asked a full-bird Colonel.

Captain Dunn looked quickly to Baines, then back to the Colonel. "Yes, sir, but it doesn't seem to make sense. It struck a single vehicle in a remote area of the Sinai."

DEKKER DISCONNECTED HIS call, turned off his pocket base unit, and was about to return to the Range Rover when he felt a probing, not a call but more like a passing presence. He stopped to consider the implications when his "danger alarm" began sounding in his head. The alarm had served him well over the years and he wasn't about to ignore it now. He looked into the bright, blue sky for...what? His instinct told him the danger was approaching from the sky, but he saw nothing.

"Hannah, we need to move. Right now."

"Sure, but why the rush?" Dekker made no reply and started the Rover. Hannah, caught up in his unease, jumped into the passenger seat as the Range Rover began moving, barely getting inside before the vehicle leaped forward.

"Dekker! What is going on? You could have killed me."

"Sorry about that, but we've got to find some cover, and quickly." She looked around the barren wilderness, and other than low hills, she saw nothing that even approached cover.

They were on the east side of the Nile heading south and were only a few miles past the Valley of the Kings on the opposite shore, but it was barren, rough country. Despite the rugged terrain, Dekker set off at a high rate of speed, the tires kicking up a cloud of dust. He looked from left to right as they rocketed over the rough desert floor. "There must be something…" Dekker said to himself. With occasional glances upward he pressed on.

Hannah's concern was now growing with each passing minute. "Dekker, what are we doing? You are taking us out into the desert, not following the Nile."

"We are trying to find somewhere to hide this car and ourselves."

He was following a dry wash when Hannah pointed out the window. "How about over there?" Hannah indicated a cliff face on their left. Dekker swung the Rover in the direction she pointed and headed for the hills.

It turned out the cliff face masked a shallow valley, and Dekker thanked Hannah for her direction. Driving into the valley, he searched for anything that might hide the Rover. He spotted a tumble of rocks along the left hand wall. Bringing the Rover to a stop, Dekker inspected the space between the rocks and the cliff wall. "It looks like we can squeeze in."

He told Hannah to fold in the sideview mirror as he did the same to the one on his side, and then he eased the Rover forward. There was a metallic shriek from the left side as the Rover squeezed into the slot. "Hertz isn't going to like this," he said.

With the vehicle settled between the low rock wall and the hillside Dekker felt they were hidden. "Only one more thing to do," he said. "Let's get out."

"Out? How do we do that? There isn't an inch between the door and the rocks," said Hannah.

Dekker crawled over the seat and into the rear where he opened the hatch. Stepping out, he asked Hannah, "Coming?"

Hannah climbed out of the Rover and stood next to Dekker. "Okay, what now?"

"We cover the Rover with dust, like this." He scooped up a double handful of the thick dirt covering the valley floor and tossed it over the roof of the Rover. "Camouflage." Hannah, understanding what he was doing, joined in, and soon they had the roof and hood surfaces covered in dirt.

"This is good," said Dekker. "Now we need to find somewhere for us."

The Range Rover was blocking the narrow gap, and so they walked out and around the rock formation and entered from the other side. They walked along the canyon wall, poking and prodding at any anomaly in the surface. "You know, back home in New Mexico the ancient natives built homes into hillsides like this."

"My ancestors dug tombs," replied Hannah.

"Do you suppose this hill might have an excavation?"

"It's doubtful. We are too far south for any tombs. Besides, this is the wrong side of the Nile."

Dekker continued along the cliff side, stopped, and then reversed his track a few feet. Stooping, he wiped loose dirt from a flat stone. Hannah noticed his interest. "Did you find something?"

"Maybe...I'm not sure." He wiped more dirt away to reveal a flat stone about three by four feet set into the wall of the hill. Hannah crouched beside him, her curiosity piqued, and helped clear the edges of the stone.

"This certainly looks manmade," she said.

"It may be nothing, but if it is the entrance to some sort of chamber, this could save us."

"We'll need tools," she replied.

Dekker stood and looked at their Rover. "Yep, and I think I know where to get some." He went back around and opened the Rover's rear hatch, lifting a cover over the spare tire. Grabbing a tire iron, the jack, and a flat pry bar, he hesitated before closing the rear hatch. "I'd better grab this, too." He stuffed the tiny sat phone into a leg pocket on his cargo pants and returned to Hannah.

"Excavation tools have arrived!" Hannah gave him an appreciative look. "Let's get to it," he said.

Using the archeology skills developed searching ancient sites in New Mexico, Dekker carefully outlined the stone. Next, he took his pocket knife and inserted the blade between the dressed stone and the cliff face, probing for obstructions. He continued looking to the sky at regular intervals, searching for any indication of danger.

"Why do you keep looking up?" asked Hannah.

Dekker stopped his probing and faced the SIS operative. "I think we have a drone coming our way, and other than hiding, I don't know how to escape it."

"How do you know that?"

"As I told you, it's a skill. And I sensed someone probing when I made the sat phone call."

"I guess I don't understand the logic. Just because you felt one of those Flow things, how does that equate to a drone strike on us?"

"Satellite phones emit radio wave energy that can be perceived within the Flows. Most of those waves are like low-level background noise and you quickly learn to ignore them. But this time someone was looking for me and found my location by following the sat phone signal. It would have been easy, given there are no other users out here. My guess is the mastermind behind this drone business has gone back for another. After all, no one was able to identify the source of the first hack and so why not risk another."

"No one except you, Dekker."

"Right. No one except me, and that's why I believe a new attack is coming. Here, help me with this stone. It doesn't seem to have anything behind it." He handed the prybar to Hannah and pointed to the upper right side of the stone seal. He took the tire iron and inserted the flat end at the opposite side of the stone.

"Carefully now, ease into the cracks. Push against the wall, not the stone itself. We don't want to damage it."

At first the stone sat much as it had for presumably thousands of years, but by moving their tools down the cracks on either side they began to see success.

"Dekker, I think the stone moved a little!"

"Easy, Hannah. We want to pull this out in one piece. Even if there is only a small hollow behind it, we have to be able to put this stone back in front of us."

"Infrared sighting. Right. I almost forgot."

The pair continued their task and soon both succeeded in separating the stone from the wall. With a soft *hiss* they realized the seal between stone and wall was broken and the work went much faster. In a few minutes the stone was entirely free, and Dekker went to Hannah's side, inserting his tire iron about a foot above her pry bar.

"We open it very slowly this is the most delicate part."

Dekker and Hannah pushed against the wall, their tools now the fulcrum. Slowly the rock moved outward and Dekker was forced to adjust his stance before continuing. In small steps they moved the stone outward on one side to a point where they could climb in behind.

"Enough," said Dekker. "Let's have a look." He pulled a small Maglite from his breast pocket and shined it into the void behind the stone. "Now, that's interesting…"

Hannah leaned over his shoulder and saw stairs carved into the rock, stairs leading downward. She and Dekker looked at one another, surprise on their faces.

"It sure looks like a tomb," said Dekker. Hannah nodded her agreement. At that moment they heard a buzzing sound, a drone aircraft, and it wasn't far away.

"That's our cue. Follow me."

They squeezed behind the stone, and Dekker handed the Maglite to Hannah, motioning for her to train the beam on the stone. Dekker then sat and wrapped his fingers around the open edge and began pulling. There wasn't much to use as leverage and it was only sheer muscle power that moved the stone inward inch by inch. Standing behind him, holding the light steady on the stone, Hannah admired his strength.

"How are we going to open this again?"

"Easy," said Dekker. "We are going to use this jack to push the stone out."

"How clever you are, Mr. Dekker."

"Let's sit here and listen for a moment. Besides, I can use the breather."

KAMENWATI SAT VERY still. Deep in the Flows, he focused on his objective: the drone operator in America. Soon he was seeing what the operator saw: a video monitor with a feed from the drone's nose camera, a distinct cross mark at the center of the monochrome image. Kamenwati was pleased the young operator seemed fixed on the monitor. "This makes him all the easier to control."

The images he was receiving through the Flows varied from murky to clear, depending on the man's level of concentration, but the Egyptian was able to follow the drone's progress across the open desert of Saudi Arabia. Exercising his new powers, he directed the drone to the American's location in Egypt. He sensed confusion around the operator, who tried to activate the drone's self destruct mechanism. It was a thought Kamenwati easily turned aside.

As the unmanned aircraft approached the location of Kamenwati's target, he was suddenly confused. "Where is Dekker?" The target area was deserted. "He can't have gone far." Noticing a set of tire tracks heading southeast, he pushed the drone operator to follow. After a short distance the tracks became faint and then nonexistent due to a change in surface from dirt to hard shale. He watched as the aircraft continued when the trail began once again, now heading into a dry wash leading into the cliffs beyond. "I have you now, Dekker."

The drone's altitude dropped, the airspeed slowed, and Kamenwati saw faint tracks leading toward the cliff wall. He scoffed disdainfully when he saw Dekker's attempt to hide his vehicle between some standing boulders and the cliff side. Despite the camouflage attempt, he saw the vehicle wedged into a spot Dekker could not escape. "I suppose you are cowering inside, hoping I won't see you."

The aircraft was running low on fuel, but it did not matter to Kamenwati. With a thought, he caused the drone operator to activate the armament. In this instance, the drone carried a single missile along with anti-personnel guns. He first strafed the location, tearing the vehicle apart, and then had the aircraft swing around to unleash its missile. The explosion created a white overlay in the image lasting nearly ten seconds before resolving into a scene of complete devastation. The vehicle was obliterated along with most of the boulders that once held it in place. The cliff face also showed effects from the blast, a large portion having slid down to cover much of Dekker's vehicle.

The unmanned aircraft was now running on fumes, but Kamenwati did not care. His enemy, Abaddon's enemy, was gone and he was free to begin the next phase of the plan: striking Western interests from Turkey to Europe, and even in America.

Kamenwati emerged from his trance with a euphoric feeling. He stood, stretched his tight muscles, and signaled for Rahotep. When Rahotep arrived he was pleased to find his teacher in such a good mood.

"Rahotep, please assemble your men. I want you to verify Dekker's death."

"As you wish. When will we leave?"

"Immediately."

CHAPTER EIGHT

THE BUZZING OF THE DRONE grew louder and Dekker knew the Range Rover had been spotted. He looked at Hannah apologetically. She stood stoically, training the Maglite on the stone door. "I hope this will be enough," she said. Moments later they heard the chatter of the drone's Gatling gun and the Rover's metal roof being ripped apart.

Hannah turned to Dekker with a wry look on her face and quipped, "I imagine Hertz will truly not like this."

The firing stopped as abruptly as it began and Hannah made a move toward the stone door; but Dekker grabbed her arm and held her back. "Wait. I don't think it's over yet." A huge blast outside knocked them both to the floor of the little cave and clouds of dust blew in from the poorly sealed door. It was several minutes before they could see though the now settling dust or hear one another speak. Dekker stood and saw they were both covered with a layer of bisque-colored dust, only their eyes breaking the powder coating.

"This must be what it feels like to be mummified," said Dekker. Hannah was still having trouble getting the ringing in her ears to stop and could only shrug. Still holding onto the Maglite, she trained it on the stone door.

"Dear Lord," she said. "It looks like we are trapped."

Dekker stepped to the stone and put his shoulder to it. It would not move. "Must be something blocking it out there."

Hannah stood next to him, her intelligent blue eyes questioning. "What are we going to do?"

Dekker could see she was not panicked, a quality he appreciated at that moment. "We've got the jack, but with the door fully closed, I'm not sure there is any way to get leverage." He idly traced the left edge of the doorway with his finger.

"What about this way?" Hannah asked, shining the light on the stairway.

"Lead on," Dekker replied while slapping the dust off his clothes.

They were careful on the stairs since these too were covered with dust blown into the entry alcove. With one hand on the wall for stability they descended in silence. "This is quite amazing," said Hannah after a few moments. "We are on the opposite side of the Nile from the Valley of the Kings, and quite a distance as well. There really shouldn't be a tomb here."

"And yet, here we are," said Dekker.

As their descent continued, the new layer of dust thinned. "How far down are we?" asked Dekker.

"I've been counting stairs, and right now we've gone down one hundred and two," said Hannah. "I'd say, at about six inches for each stair, and I'd say we're approximately fifty feet below ground level. And look. It seems our stairs end ahead."

Another dozen steps brought them to a landing where they faced a blank wall. "Is that supposed to be here?" asked Dekker.

Hannah shook her head. "I don't know."

THREE THOUSAND FIVE hundred miles away, Galdur looked up sharply, sensing a new presence in the Flows. "Not a new presence," he said, "rather, an old one, Abaddon." He resisted the impulse to make himself known, instead letting the spirit move without obstruction. He observed the spirit's movement until it joined with a familiar aura. "Kamenwati. I might have known." He turned his attention away and summoned Salim, who responded within moments.

My brother, I have news. Galdur showed Salim his efforts to follow the Abaddon spirit and the joining to Kamenwati. Salim was silent for a full minute and Galdur thought he might have withdrawn from the Flows, but his friend was only thinking.

It seems the spirit has found a new and willing home in our old friend Kamenwati.

Galdur agreed. *It was Kamenwati who released Abaddon from the stasis, foolishly thinking the ashes of the incubus would give him control over the spirit.*

The ashes gave control over the man Kambrian, but not the spirit, responded Salim.

That was Kamenwati's downfall. But somehow he escaped Krugerschloss and made his way back to Egypt.

And came under the spirit's influence, conveyed Salim.

What new scheme is the spirit implanting in Kamenwati's soul? What does the Egyptian hope to gain? Galdur asked.

Perhaps the answer is in the attack you told me about, the one you suspect was carried out by a practitioner.

This time it was Galdur's turn to be silent, putting the pieces together. *You are right, Salim, and I believe we have found both the source and the influencer of these events.*

Where is Dekker? Salim asked.

Our last communication indicated he was headed to Egypt, to the site where the attack took place.

He may have awakened a formidable and determined opponent in Kamenwati, and now with Abaddon's influence, who knows what will happen?

Galdur was silent and a deep concern came over him, not only for his friend Dekker, but for the world.

DEKKER TAPPED ON the stone wall facing them while Hannah inspected first the left and then the right side of the wall. "It looks like a dead end," she said. Dekker continued tapping the center wall with his closed Leatherman knife.

"Doesn't it strike you as odd that tomb builders would have dug all the way down here and then stopped?"

"Maybe the patron ran out of money," said Hannah.

"Or he fell out of favor," Dekker added.

"What is it you are looking for?" Hannah asked.

"Maybe nothing, but if I learned anything from archeological sites in New Mexico, passageways are often concealed." His light tapping continued, now on the left side of the wall. This time his knife produced a chip that flaked off the wall. Hannah did not notice and continued her inspection of the right side of the chamber. Dekker opened the blade of his knife and pried off more of the surface, revealing it to be a half inch thick plaster-like substance. "I think I've found something," he said.

Hannah picked up the Maglite XL200 she had placed on the floor in its widest light setting and lowest power consumption. She spun the bezel of the flashlight to focus the beam and increase its brightness, training it on the section of wall Dekker was working.

"What is it?"

"Hard to say. Hand me that pry bar, would you please?" Hannah handed the instrument to Dekker. "Thanks."

Dekker gently worked the edge of the bar under the exposed plaster and pushed. A large piece of the wall broke away, falling to the floor. "This looks promising."

In a few minutes Dekker and Hannah were standing before a rectangular outline set into the stone. "It's a door!" Hannah exclaimed. "How do we open it?"

"Based on the entrance above, I'd say we need to pull it out." Dekker handed her the prybar and picked up the tire iron. They set the Maglite on the stairs and began the long, slow process of extracting the stone door from the wall.

As they dug Hannah questioned Dekker. "Who sent that drone?"

"I'm not certain, but I have a good idea."

Hannah nodded in understanding. "Does he believe we're dead?"

"I'd say yes, which, if we can find another way out of here, will be an advantage."

The speculative talk continued with each offering theories about their current plight and hopes for what would be found beyond the door. Once the frame was fully revealed they sat on the dusty floor and began working their tools deeper into the creases between the door and the stone wall. Inch by inch, and with coordinated pushes, Dekker and Hannah moved the stone door until it stood just forward of the opening. Dekker stood and inserted his tire iron behind the stone door, then levered the door outward with all his strength. The stone moved slightly and Hannah joined in with her prybar, adding her force to Dekker's effort. They stopped to catch their breath after several minutes.

"I don't suppose these ancient tombs come equipped with water fountains," quipped Dekker. Hannah gave a small laugh. "I didn't think so." They returned to the door and resumed work.

It took two more hours and increasingly frequent breaks to slide the one side of the stone door wide enough to allow passage. Hannah retrieved the flashlight from the stairs and asked, "How long will this operate?" Dekker, ready to squeeze through the narrow opening, tried to put Hannah at ease.

"It should go more than two hundred eighty hours on the low setting. We've been in here for maybe four hours, so we'll be fine."

She looked appreciatively at the black aluminum tube, thankful for the invention of the LEDs this flashlight used. She handed the light to Dekker as he made it through the opening, and with her smaller form, moved through more easily than Dekker.

"I believe this is a *mastaba*, an ancient tomb for the wealthy," said Hannah. "Which makes sense because we are across from the Valley of the Kings where Tutankhamun, Ramses, and many other kings were buried. This area has many of the same qualities, and the wealthy of ancient Egypt would want to be in proximity to the divine departed."

"What does that mean for us?"

"Well, it means the design of this tomb, while smaller than a royal tomb, should include the same characteristics like an air passage."

"Do you mean there is a way out of here?"

Hannah nodded.

"Fabulous. How do we find this passage?"

"Let's press on into the main chamber and see what we find."

They moved through a passageway lined with clay bricks. Dekker commented on the lack of wall paintings; Hannah shrugged and continued on. They emerged from the tunnel and found they were at one end of a rectangular chamber. The chamber walls were plastered and covered in painted murals. "Happy now?" Hannah asked.

Across the room was a pedestal with a sarcophagus covering the greater part of the wall. "It looks unspoiled," said Hannah.

Dekker swung the flashlight around, intent on finding an exit. Then he walked to the sarcophagus, inspecting the setting closely.

"What are you doing?" Hannah asked.

"This thing covers most of the wall, and between the pedestal and the sarcophagus, stands about five feet tall. I'm wondering if this doesn't cover another corridor."

"It is possible. The traditional design almost always included an alternate tunnel or air passage."

Dekker continued feeling around the edges of the platform. "It's flush to this wall, and I'm certain it weighs two or three tons."

"Isn't that about the weight of a car?" Dekker got her point and went back to the stairs and gathered their tools, including the jack.

"If we can make enough room between the pedestal and the wall, the jack should be able to move this." Dekker began with the pry bar, striking about three feet above the ground between the platform and the wall. He added the tire iron about a foot below and, gathering himself, pushed.

"Nothing's happening, Dekker."

"Give me another try." He set to pushing the bars once again. Hannah could see the strain was great. His arm and shoulder muscles bunched tightly, and his face turned red. The platform moved! "You're doing it," said Hannah.

A few more minutes of hard pushing moved the sarcophagus and its platform about six inches from the wall. Dekker slid down to a sitting position. "This thing is heavy."

"Yes, but now you've got room for your little jack," said Hannah, handing the device to him. Dekker placed the jack between the wall and the pedestal at the top of the platform. He hefted the tire iron that was now bent into a slight curve and inserted it into the jack.

"Here goes." Holding the bottom of the jack he pumped to seat the screw-driven device and let go as it settled firmly into place. Inch by inch the pedestal began moving.

"I can see a corridor," said Hannah. "Just a little more and we can get in." Dekker responded by increasing his efforts with the jack until it reached its full extension.

"That's all, Hannah. Let's see if we can squeeze through." Dekker took the flashlight and led the way into the opening behind the platform, Hannah following closely.

The corridor was perhaps five feet high and three feet wide, requiring both Dekker and Hannah to stoop as they walked. It was especially difficult for Dekker as he had to keep his six-foot, two-inch frame bent in an uncomfortable position, forcing a slow and arduous walk. They stopped at regular intervals so Dekker could sit and relax his constricted muscles. Despite the rigors of walking through the tunnel, he never lost his humor. "I guess I'm a little taller than the average ancient Egyptian." Hannah laughed at his self-effacing joke and found herself once again admiring the American.

The small corridor came to an end, and once again they faced a wall. Sitting on the floor with his feet solidly on the opposite wall, Dekker began striking the rock surface while Hannah held the light. The surface was rough fill, not a solid slab like the entry way, and so Dekker's efforts were quickly rewarded. First a small hole opened, pouring light into the cramped corridor. "We've done it, Dekker," said Hannah. "We're going to make it out of here." He continued working the wall and soon had an opening large enough to pass through.

The rays of the sun were long, casting a golden glow over the terrain. "I don't think I've ever felt so alive," said Hannah.

"I don't mind telling you I was concerned back there. I thought we might be buried alive. And you're right," said Dekker looking across the dry, mountainous landscape. "It is like being reborn." Hannah looked back at the hillside and shuddered.

"The sun's beginning to set, so we better get going," said Dekker.

"You're right," said Hannah who set off purposefully.

Dekker looked with admiration at the British agent, saying to himself, "She's got courage."

RAHOTEP AND HIS two senior associates, Nebwawi and Sabu, travelled more than two hundred miles overnight, arriving at the second drone strike location at first light. They began by reconnoitering to be sure there were no government troops, and they were rewarded with an empty canyon. "It appears we are the first here," said Rahotep. "We begin with the destroyed vehicle, and then if we have time, we find the aircraft." The trio drove into the narrow canyon and located the bombed-out Land Rover.

"Nothing could have survived this," said Nebwawi. "There doesn't seem to be much point in looking for bodies. They would have been blown to pieces."

"And they are buried under tons of rock," said Sabu.

"Nevertheless, we will look," said Rahotep. The three men spread out over the blast area and began sifting through the rubble. After half an hour of searching it was clear there was nothing to find and Rahotep became uneasy.

"What is the problem, Rahotep? Is this not good to see the American's transport totally destroyed?" Sabu asked.

Rahotep shook his head. "No, this is not good. Even if the remains were scattered, we should still find some sign of him: blood, bone, or clothing."

"What does it mean?" Nebwawi asked.

"It means there is a strong possibility the man escaped, but I do not know how or where."

Nebwawi stood atop a rockfall from the cliff face. "Perhaps he jumped out but got caught in this landslide." Rahotep walked to where Nebwawi stood and considered his theory.

"Yes, that is possible." Rahotep stroked his bearded chin. "But we do not have the equipment or the manpower to move these boulders for proof."

"It is not possible the man got away," said Nebwawi. "He is entombed as surely as our ancient kings."

Rahotep turned around and climbed back out of the narrow gap, now filled with rocks from the cliff above. "Come. We will search for the little aircraft and bring it back to Kamenwati. He wants no evidence left for others to find."

THE SUN SET behind the hills, casting a warm amber glow across the rugged terrain as Dekker and Hannah made their way around the mountain that was nearly their tomb. Stopping for a moment they looked back at the horizon now aglow with the final rays of the sun and deepening blue sky above. "This is my Egypt," said Hannah. Dekker nodded and turned to continue their hike.

"It's going to get cold when the sun is down, so we need to make it back to the Nile. I think it's about ten or twelve miles."

"And when we get there, then what?"

"I hope to hitch a ride." Hannah was becoming accustomed to Dekker's sense of humor as well as his ability to get out of tight situations. They turned and set off toward the Nile.

Dekker did his best to keep a pace of about three miles per hour, but the terrain often made sure they did not move at anything close to that fast. Their path was anything but straight as they were forced to detour around hills and through wadis. After three hours they finally reached the only road that would take them toward the Nile, and after a short while, they flagged down an old pickup headed for the Luxor Bridge.

The old man driving the truck asked why they were out in the wilderness at night. Hannah, answering in Arabic, told him they had been exploring and their vehicle broke down. "You must need water," said the old man. "There's a jug behind the seat."

"At least there's water," said Dekker, trying to force a cheerful tone.

"I don't think you want to drink that water," Hannah replied.

"Oh, you unbeliever! Look what Mr. Wonderful can pull out of his sleeve." With a flourish Dekker produced a blue straw-like item. "Behold, a water purifier."

Hannah was astonished and took the one-half inch wide tube. She inspected the tube carefully, noting the interior stuffed with filtering. "Where in the world were you keeping that?"

"Standard field gear. I didn't think about it until we reached the Nile." She inserted the tube into the murky brown water in the jug and took a long sip.

"Good…Thanks for the filter." She handed him the jug and filter tube.

Later, with their thirst slaked, they saw the Luxor Bridge in the distance and beyond, the lights of a town. "I think that may be Ad Dabiyyah," said Hannah. "Perhaps we can catch another ride there."

"Catching a car to Cairo won't be easy," said Dekker. "I was thinking more about a river voyage in a *fallucca* carrying cargo down the Nile. We'll have to wait for sunrise, but I'm certain boats will pass by and we'll hail one." He asked Hannah to instruct the old man to drop them off at the bridge.

They waved to the departing pickup driver, tired but thankful for the ride. They then walked down a slight slope through the greenbelt lining the Nile and sat against a tree.

"I'm so tired that just sitting here feels good," said Hannah. She sat back and was immediately asleep. Dekker took a moment to look at her. Even covered in dust she was attractive, and he once again wondered at the feelings stirring inside him. He sat back and looked at the blanket of stars above, thought of Kelly, and went to sleep.

The sun peeking over the horizon woke Dekker. Hannah was curled in the crook of his right arm, having moved into a more comfortable, and warmer, position in the night. He was stiff from the ordeal in the tomb and gently moved Hannah, who woke slowly. Dekker stood to stretch his tight muscles, and stroking his cheek, he realized he needed a shave. "It's a shame a razor isn't in the standard field kit," he said.

"How about a toothbrush? Anything like that in your famous field pack?" Hannah asked. Dekker shook his head and helped her stand. "Let's see who's going down river."

Not far upriver they found a small fleet of traditional *falluccas* preparing to cast off. With a little sweet talk from Hannah and the promise of American dollars from Dekker they found a willing boatman. "I can take you as far as Faiyum, about one hundred kilometers from Cairo. That is where I deliver my cargo," said the ship's master in Arabic.

Hannah nodded her understanding and replied in the same language, "What is your name?"

"I am Ahmed."

"This is good, Ahmed. We will travel with you."

Sitting comfortably on cotton bales, they watched the warm morning glow spread across the river. Hannah soon went back to sleep. Dekker pulled out his compact satellite telephone kit, turned on the base station, and inserted the earpiece. It only took a minute for the phone to triangulate off satellites, and Dekker placed a call to NCTC.

Once connected he asked for Jim Lynch and was quickly put through. "Dekker! Where have you been? You missed the last contact time and I was worried."

"It's a bit of a story, but the digest version is that we went through another drone attack..."

"Do you mean *you* were attacked?"

"Yes, and Hannah and I were buried in a tomb."

"We knew about the second drone. Like the first, there was nothing anybody could do, except watch helplessly while it blew up a car." Lynch grew concerned. "Was that your car, Dekker? Are you two unharmed?"

"We're fine. A little tired and dirty, but no worse for the wear. And yes, that was my car. By they way, would you have someone contact Hertz? I'm afraid the Range Rover won't be returning to Suez."

"That sounds a little too close for comfort. Where are you now?"

"We're on a *fallucca* sailing from the Luxor Bridge toward Faiyum. I figure if someone is looking for us, they won't look on the river."

"You never cease to amaze me, Dekker."

"Thanks, Jim. Now let me tell you what I've found about this case." Dekker recounted their movements from the inspection of the initial strike site to his dismissal of their local guide, Kassis, and following tracks into the desert.

"I wasn't following the tracks as much as trailing a feeling. Then the feeling was gone, or more accurately, blocked, and I realized we were in trouble. I'd been thinking about the drone disappearance, and I have a theory." Lynch listened patiently. "During our last encounter with Abaddon, I met an Egyptian named Kamenwati. He was on the platform with Abaddon."

"I remember very well, Dekker. Go on."

"In all the excitement Kamenwati disappeared."

"And I recall in your report you said to forget about him."

"I did, and that was a mistake. I think the Abaddon spirit went straight to him, made himself at home, and is now helping the Egyptian cause mischief."

"Like stealing a drone? That's a little more than mischief."

"Jim, this is an entirely new twist on the Flows. Even Galdur knows nothing about it, and I think the signal to control these drones is coming through the Abaddon spirit, to Kamenwati, who is carrying out the order."

"Say you're right, Dekker. Why did Kamenwati attack a band in the desert?"

"I'm still working on that, but you can be sure there is a reason and an objective far beyond that one strike. After all, look how he attacked me; he doesn't want his methods or plans discovered."

"Does Kamenwati believe he killed you?"

"I think so. At least, that's what I'm hoping."

"I want to put Dennis on this from our end," said Lynch. "If there is a way to identify how Kamenwati is making this happen, Dennis is the guy who can figure it out."

"I agree, and it's a good idea. Oh, another thing. Would you mind calling C in London and request an extension of Hannah's assignment with me? There's a deeper subtext here, and given that there is a cultural and political component specific to Egypt, she may be the key to understanding what is going on."

Dekker signed off and placed the tiny satellite phone back in a pocket. "Damn handy thing, this phone."

CHAPTER NINE

THE FELUCCA MOVED SMOOTHLY DOWN the Nile, alternately passing population centers and broad, green fields. Hannah woke after two hours and stretched her aching muscles. "Welcome back," said Dekker. "I didn't want to disturb you." Hannah sat next to him and gazed across the countryside. "I always forget how beautiful it is here. How long did I sleep?"

"A couple of hours. We passed a town a little while ago. There was a bridge."

"It was probably Nagaa Hammadi."

Hearing the name, Ahmed nodded his head vigorously. "Nagaa Hammadi and Qena," he said in Arabic.

"Thank you, Ahmed," said Hannah in the same language. "He said we passed by Qena. We'll be coming to

Sohag soon. You'll recognize it by the serpentine course of the Nile. Beyond that we'll reach Asyut, and then there is a long empty stretch of about one hundred fifty miles before we arrive in Faiyum."

They sailed on through the day, reaching Asyut late in the afternoon. Ahmed indicated they would dock for the night and Dekker perked up. "That's great! We can stretch our legs and see what the town is all about."

Dekker and Hannah walked up one of the many narrow streets, finding themselves fighting their way through teeming crowds. "I can't believe how many people are out," said Dekker. "It's not surprising," replied Hannah. "About four hundred thousand people live here."

"And here I thought this was some sleepy little town. It's more like a metropolis." Dekker had a sudden thought. "Isn't today Friday?"

"Yes, it is."

"And it's sundown. Why aren't these people in the mosque?"

"Assiut has the highest concentration of Coptic Christians in Egypt, and their Sabbath is on Sunday."

"Are you a Copt?"

"By birth, yes. Although I am not a strict follower."

"I guess I've never really known a Copt before. I mean...That came out wrong. I'm sorry if I offended you." Hannah laughed. Dekker thought the laugh sounded nice, and her face lit up too which he liked even more.

Embarrassed, Dekker kept his mouth shut and continued moving through the crowd with Hannah directly behind. He spotted a café through the throng and steered for an empty table. As they sat a short man in a white *galabia*, the traditional full-length garment with wide sleeves, arrived to take their order. Hannah asked for two coffees and the man scurried away.

"This is an ancient community and in many ways, these are my people," said Hannah. Dekker looked at the passing crowd but said nothing. "We share a sense of history, a connection to an unbroken past going beyond the seventh century invasion of the Arabs."

"You mentioned that before. Can you tell me more?"

"Copts hold to the concept of Pharaonism, the belief that the Coptic culture is derived from the pre-Christian Pharaonic culture and not indebted to Greece. It gives all Copts a claim to a deep heritage in Egyptian history and culture."

"So you don't see yourselves as Egyptian?"

"On the contrary. We see ourselves as true Egyptians, a non-Arab race reaching back thousands of years." She took a small sip of the thick coffee and set off on a new tack. "Did you know that Gamal Abdel Nasser was from Asyut? He led the coup that deposed King Farouk and established the Egyptian republic."

"I had no idea. I suppose you revere him…"

"Not really. Nasser's nationalization severely impacted ethnic Copts." Dekker was again silent, and after taking a couple of sips of coffee himself, tried a new line of conversation. "It certainly is hot here," said Dekker.

"Asyut is famous as the driest city in Egypt, but wait a while. Once the sun is fully set, the temperature will drop." She looked at Dekker and had another thought. "Would you like to see Asyut in hieroglyphs?"

"You can write in hieroglyphs?"

"It was one of the things my father insisted I learn as a young girl, but I only remember a few names and places. This is the glyph for Asyut." She took a small spiral notebook from a pocket and began drawing.

"Wow. I'm impressed," said Dekker.

"Did you know that the shield of Recami, an ancient king of Upper Egypt, was discovered a few years ago and is now on display at the University of Asyut?" Dekker shook his head. "You really are a wealth of information, Hannah."

"Would you like to see another? I can render Faiyum, too." Dekker nodded and she went back to work in her notebook. "There. At least I think it's right."

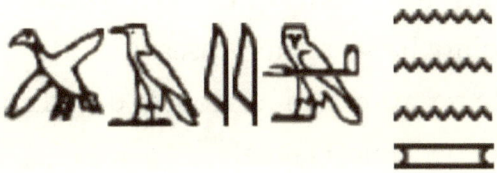

"It has many of the same elements, like the duck and the eagle," said Dekker. "But it has more elements. Is that because it is a larger city?"

"No. It has more characters because it is an older city and the hieroglyph tells us more about its location, that there is an oasis, and that the greenbelt along the Nile exists only on the west bank. The east is barren."

"That's a lot of information for a name," said Dekker. Hannah closed her notebook and took another sip of coffee. "It's beginning to get dark," she said. "We'd better start back to the boat."

Ahmed greeted them as they returned to the boat. He pointed out the area on deck he had prepared for them among the bales of cotton.

When they were lying upon makeshift pallets with the canopy of brilliant stars above, Dekker was once again deep in thought. "Something on your mind?" asked Hannah. Dekker propped himself on one elbow. "I am troubled by the drone attack in the Sinai. Why there and why that target? I mentioned my suspicions about Kamenwati and his connection to Abaddon, and the more I think about it, the more certain I am that he is behind the attack. It's the motive for the attack that stumps me. Was it simply a test run of this new capability he seems to possess?"

"He certainly had no trouble duplicating the attack and aiming it at us," said Hannah.

"No, he didn't, and that is where I hit the logic wall. During my encounter with Kamenwati in Germany, he confided that he was the one who resurrected Abaddon."

"Why in the world would he do that?" asked Hannah.

"He felt Abaddon could be controlled with a talisman he possessed, the ashes of an incubus. He was looking for a means to appropriate Abaddon's power, but I never knew exactly why." Hannah listened closely to this previously unknown history as Dekker continued. "When I killed Abaddon I thought it was all over, and I told the others with me not to pursue Kamenwati because I believed he got what he deserved. But I badly misjudged him, and I'm usually good at reading people."

Hannah sat up and studied Dekker's face. She could see the deep concern over his miscalculation etched there. "You could not have known," she said.

"I should have known. It should have been stopped right then, and I'm the only one to blame."

"Didn't you say he was a 'deep practitioner' of this Magick you talk about? Isn't it possible you were deceived?" Dekker looked at her and thought about his journey through all this business of Magick, the Flows, and Abaddon. He had to admit that, while he did possess skills, he was far from experienced and could easily have been misled. He turned his head away from Hannah, the truth of her words stinging him. *This is no time for a pity party*, he thought. *What's done is done.* "You're right, and I'm approaching this from the wrong angle. What do we know about Kamenwati?"

"He's Egyptian," said Hannah.

"Yes, but what kind of Egyptian is he?" Hannah considered his question. Dekker continued, "Let's consider the man: he does not follow Islam and is, in fact, a follower of a much older order, one rooted in the ancient history of this land."

"He is an ethnic Egyptian then, just like the Copts in this city," said Hannah.

"If you had the ability to turn back time, to change history and alter what happened to Egypt fifteen hundred years ago, would you?"

"That's a crazy question, Dekker. What happened with the Arab invasion was as much a product of the times as any political weakness in this one."

"I know it's crazy, but humor me. Would you alter history to preserve your ethnic control over Egypt?"

Hannah stopped to consider how she would answer. "Given your hypothetical, I would answer yes." She took a hard look at Dekker, her eyebrows bunching together. "Are you saying Kamenwati can change what happened?"

Dekker shook his head. "No, not exactly; but knowing the depths of his narcissism, his emersion in Magick, and his newfound alliance with the Abaddon spirit, I'd say he might see the emergence of a cleansed Egypt as a nation that would once again be the greatest power in the world."

"You can't think that...It's too wild, and besides, the world is a very different place than it was in the seventh century."

"You're right, it is wild, but is it any wilder than Abaddon trying to take over the world by collapsing all national economies and propelling mankind into a feudal society ruled by a priest class?"

"Are you telling me *that* is what was going on in Germany?" Dekker nodded. "Then I suppose it isn't so wild after all. How do we find him and stop him?"

Dekker deliberated for a moment before replying.

"You said Asyut has the largest concentration of Copts in Egypt. Even more than Alexandria?"

"Yes."

"If you wanted to recruit new followers, where would you look?"

"I'd begin in Asyut!"

"I think we should take our leave of this vessel's good master and set up somewhere in town." Hannah saw the wisdom of his thinking, and at sunrise she made their apologies to Ahmed, who was sorry to see them leave but appreciated Dekker's full payment for the trip even though they were debarking early.

A FEW INQUIRIES soon brought Dekker and Hannah to a retired Nile Cruiser permanently moored on the riverbank and displaying an ornate sign reading *Partner Tut Hotel*. They entered the three-deck ship through a canopy-covered café and restaurant. Beyond, on the boat, a small registration desk, manned by a pleasant young man dressed in a business suit, suggested this was one of Asyut's finer hotels. Another restaurant occupying half of the top deck, large windows looking out on the Nile on one side and the city on the other, were unexpected additional amenities. The roof of the top deck was a lounge and recreation area, complete with a swimming pool. Hannah was impressed. "This is quite lovely," she said with a slight emphasis on the word *quite*, which for a Brit meant she was impressed. Dekker saw the hotel/ship as a convenient place to begin their investigation. There was adequate space for planning, and it was conveniently located on the riverbank.

After renting rooms, Dekker and Hannah met in the outdoor restaurant. They were both hungry and attended appreciatively to their meals. As they finished eating, Dekker looked around. "You know, I think this hotel, or ship or whatever it is, will work well for us." Hannah nodded her agreement as she sipped on a glass of fresh orange juice. "We need a strategy, a plan of attack. Any idea how we can locate a man who in all probability isn't here?" Dekker asked.

"There are a number of things we can try. How's your Arabic?"

"Rusty at best. I haven't used it in years. That's why I've been relying on you, but for the most part I've been able to follow what you've said to people."

"Good. Let me give you a few questions you can use."

"Let 'er rip, professor!"

After tutoring Dekker for an hour Hannah confessed she was done in. They rose from the table and walked in silence to their rooms which were located across from one another on the second deck. "G'night," said Dekker. Hannah nodded in response and watched the American enter his room. She closed her eyes and imagined… "Now, stop that, girl! What are you thinking of?" She stepped into her room and closed the door. There was a simple tub behind a drape and she decided a bath was just what she needed. "After all, I haven't properly bathed in two days."

She filled the tub and found a small packet of salts that she opened and poured into the flow of water, releasing a wonderful fragrance. Slowly stripping her clothes, she placed them into a plastic dry cleaning bag for the maid to take in the morning. She stood before the full length mirror on the wall, pirouetting and admiring her body, wondering what a certain Mr. Dekker would think. "Stop it, you shameless so-and-so."

Slipping into the warm water felt luxurious, and she let out a long sigh. At first she basked in the water, the aroma of the salts filling her lungs. Then, taking a bar of soap she began covering herself with silky bubbles, caressing her arms, legs, and belly. All the while she continued to imagine Adam

Dekker's hands doing the caressing. Her hands moved to more private parts, and with eyes closed in her daydream, rubbed and stroked with increasing intensity. Her breathing became rapid and a soft groan escaped her lips, and then, without warning, she climaxed. "Oh, my God!"

Hannah, a little embarrassed, sat up in the bathtub. "That's never happened before." She stood and stepped out of the bathtub, her skin warm and pink, and she once again thought about Adam Dekker. "What is different about this man?" She began toweling herself dry. "He's not a self-absorbed prig, for starters." She moved back through the curtain and sat on the end of her bed. Stretching her hand out over the duvet cover, in her imagination she saw a strong body atop her own, lovers lost in the moment.

Dropping the towel to the floor, she climbed naked into the cool sheets and almost immediately fell asleep, her dreams filled with images of her imagined lover.

DEKKER CLOSED HIS room door, sorry to leave Hanna for the evening. His SIS partner was surprising on many levels. At first meeting she came off cool and all business, but it wasn't long before he saw more. And learning about her heritage and interest in Egyptian history gave her an altogether different aspect. And then there was the whole affair out in the desert. "She's tough and doesn't scare easily. I like that."

As Dekker sat looking out his cabin window facing the city, he drifted into a half-sleep. He was still seeing the crowds of people moving like a tide through the streets, but in this half dreaming state the cityscape dissolved into an ancient city, a crossroads for commerce up and down the Nile. The people were all clad in *galabia,* the white full-length garment with wide sleeves, and some carried large baskets on their heads. His imagination had taken him far back in history. He stopped when he saw, or thought he saw, a woman walking down the dusty street in his direction. Unlike everyone else in the crowded road, she was not in white; she wore a brilliantly colored robe that wrapped around her body. It was hard for him to distinguish the color. *It must be many colors,* he decided. The cloth wrapping the woman was filmy, and the way it wrapped around her showed off her curves. He still could only see the top of her head, and he silently wished she would look up. And, as if in response, she raised her face and looked directly at him. It was Hannah Ahmed! But this was not Hannah the hard SIS agent; this was a woman whose beauty radiated and seemed to reach out and grab him. No, it enfolded him. He closed his eyes, relishing the feeling.

When Dekker opened his eyes the vision was gone and he was a little sad. He rubbed his temples trying to understand what was going on. It didn't take him long to put it into words. "I like her. I like her company and I like her independence. And she intrigues me." He tried to regain the dream state he enjoyed, but it would not come. "Maybe I'm just a fool. These thoughts of Hannah must be because of the extreme situation we just went through." In his heart, however, he knew it was far more than that.

Dekker went to bed but his dreams kept him restless. It was an odd combination of images. A dark, wild face seemed to fly out of the dark and dive on him, and then the face was replaced by the dark-haired beauty on the imagined ancient street of Asyut. That street became a dark stone staircase leading down to the depths of Hell, and that transformed into Hannah's face sitting across from him at dinner. The dreams were disturbing, and he awoke just as the sun was about to rise.

He went to the drape across the bath area and, pulling it back, saw there was only a tub. *I'm not much of a bath kinda guy.* He went to the sink, grabbed a washcloth, and filled the sink basin with hot water. "I guess a GI shower will have to do." He quickly sponged himself off and found a clean shirt in his bag.

Opening his room door, he looked across at Hannah's door for a moment, and then closed his door. "It's too early to disturb her," he said aloud, and he went down to the café fronting the Partner Tut. He was pleased to find a Times of London on a side table and settled in with a cup of coffee and the paper.

One hour later, Hannah entered the café and, looking around, found Dekker at a far corner table reading a newspaper. As she walked toward him, she couldn't help but remember the fantasy from the night before; and she was surprised by a tightening in her lower abdomen. She squeezed her eyes closed, opened them and took a seat across from Dekker. "Good morning, Adam." It gave her pleasure to call him by his first name.

Dekker lowered his paper and was surprised by how pleased he was to see Hannah. "Good morning to you. Did you pass a good evening?" Hannah smiled. "May I order something for you?"

"Tea please, and perhaps a croissant."

Dekker signaled a waiter and placed Hannah's order. "So, what is the order of the day?"

The pot of tea arrived and Hannah poured a cup, and then sipped delicately. She nodded to herself and placed the cup back on the saucer. "I think we need to cover as much territory as possible."

"Agreed," said Dekker.

"Since you do not read Arabic, I will go to the university library and research the ancestry of our mysterious Mr. Kamenwati."

"That sounds a little boring."

"That is why you will begin canvassing the local cafés and practice your new found speaking skills."

CHAPTER TEN

DENNIS ALLENDE, CHIEF OF THE Forensic Information Investigation Unit for the NCTC, listened while his boss, Jim Lynch, laid out Dekker's theory about the lost drones. "You remember Kamenwati, I assume," said Lynch.

"I sure do. He was the guy who resurrected Abaddon and caused all that trouble, especially for Dekker. I wanted to look for him after Abaddon died, but Dekker said no. I guess he was worn out from the ordeal."

"That's correct, but right now you are probably the only other person who understands what kind of power this Kamenwati is capable of wielding." Lynch walked around his desk and sat on its front edge. "I want you to design something that can detect whatever sort of signal he is using to control those drone operators and find a way to repulse future attacks."

"I'm not sure where to begin. I understand a little of what Dekker and Galdur told me about the Flows: they're like rivers of energy moving around the world, and people with the proper training can access the Flows. They tried to teach me, but my rational mind couldn't let go of the tangible realities of our world. Intangible is a little difficult for me."

"Dennis, if these Flows are in fact energy, can't you devise an instrument that will detect them?"

He thought about the question for a moment and then had an epiphany. "Yes, you're right! If it's based on electromagnetic energy there must be a way to read it." Dennis stood and left Lynch's office in a hurry.

Lynch smiled as he watched his young genius rush out of the office.

BACK IN HIS office in the basement of the NCTC, surrounded by banks of computer equipment and exotic instruments, Dennis was energized. Lynch's suggestion was so simple. *I need to learn about brainwaves, and in a hurry.* He began with a survey of information on the Internet. He found a number of articles on brainwave frequencies. He was most interested in the brainwaves in the Theta range, 4 to 8Hz. "That could be the frequency Kamenwati's using," he said. Following a link through several pages, Dennis found a physicist from the 1950s who published a paper stating the Earth behaves like an enormous electrical circuit. The physicist, Winfried Otto Schumann, postulated there is a cavity defined by the Earth's surface and the inner edge of the ionosphere, which is about thirty-five miles above the surface, and that void carries a vertical current flow. Shumann's resonance theory holds there are standing electromagnetic waves that exist in this cavity. "If there are EM waves, I can measure them!"

Dennis discovered the US Navy was doing most of the research in ultra-low electromagnetic waves, and he decided to start there. "I need to speak with scientists who know what they're talking about." Since most of the ultra-low EM work related to submarines, Dennis focused on a physicist in New London, Connecticut who was happy to receive him.

"Wonderful. I can be there tomorrow morning," he said to the physicist, Dr. Herman Goddard. He went back to his computer and booked a commuter flight to Groton-New London Airport.

The next morning, Dennis boarded the Delta Airlines flight to New London. Since he had been in New London during the episode at Ravenswood, he was familiar enough to rent a car. He drove across Interstate 95, exiting toward the Navy base and his meeting with Dr. Goddard. After passing through the security checkpoint, he followed directions to a plain building with a small sign that read: Research Center. Dennis parked, entered, and introduced himself to the Navy seaman seated behind a reception desk. The young enlisted man made a call and instructed Dennis to wait for an escort to Dr. Goddard's office. He didn't have to wait long, and he was surprised when a very pretty young civilian arrived to accompany him.

After being shown to Goddard's office and dispensing with the introductory pleasantries and bona fides, Dennis got to the reason for his interview. "Dr. Goddard, I was asked by my director to develop a means to interfere or deflect certain electromagnetic wavelengths we believe have been behind a serious breach in national security."

"My goodness Mr. Allende, that is an impressive and ominous opening. I'm not certain how I can help, but the fact you are here suggests you may already know."

"Yes, I think I do. The Navy leads the world in ultra-low frequency research, and I need to understand it in a hurry."

"Your security clearance is…"

"I have a Top Secret clearance," said Dennis.

"Very well, Mr. Allende. What do you want to know?"

"I reviewed brainwave frequencies and came up with a list of the full range, from Gamma down through Delta. As I understand it, each of these can be blocked or hindered with an EM field that is properly tuned to the necessary frequency. I am most interested in the Theta range since that seems to be where an individual can still be conscious but susceptible to suggestion or control."

"In general, that is true. Theta is the range normally associated with daydreaming or losing track of time," said Goddard.

"I also found a bunch of articles on the Schumann Resonances," said Dennis.

Goddard nodded. "Schumann's work in the early 1950s was actually foundational to the Navy's pursuit of EM research on generating ultra-low waves and transmitting them. Schumann's theories on standing waves and the notion these waves interconnect and cover the Earth was, in certain circles, revolutionary. We have used his resonances as one part of a broader program for communicating with our submarines around the world."

Dennis leaned forward for emphasis. "My problem is twofold: how to identify EM activity at a specific frequency, and then, how to block , or at least deflect, the signal."

"That is an interesting problem, and we can work on it, but there is another man I suggest you see. I don't even know if he is still alive, but a scientist who used to be at Los Alamos Laboratory was the leading researcher in resonance theories. His name is Horace Rimmer." Dennis almost jumped out of his chair with excitement.

"I know Dr. Rimmer, and he is very much alive." Goddard was startled by Dennis' statement.

"How in the world do you know Dr. Rimmer?"

"It's a long story and it involves some strange experiences." Goddard gave him a quizzical look and then returned to the matter at hand.

"Well, let's arm you with some design ideas you can take to Rimmer for further research." Dennis was pleased with the direction his inquiry had taken. After all, it was Rimmer's work in gravity resonance that began everything that happened during these last years. Rimmer might be just the person to help him design a device to block the effect of the Flows.

DENNIS SPENT THE entire day with Dr. Goddard and one of his engineering colleagues, sketching out a device that might intercept EM waves in the Theta range. "Now, blocking a specific wavelength is a little more difficult," said Goddard. "It's not as simple as wrapping your head with tinfoil. The specific wavelength requires an entrainment solution."

"What is that?" Dennis asked.

"Brainwave entrainment," explained Goddard, "is a process of using outside stimuli like sound, light, or an electromagnetic field to influence brainwave rates, which in the process, affects the mental state. I assume you are trying to protect individuals, not buildings or bases."

"I'm not entirely sure. I am looking to protect people, but we may also need it on a larger scale. We simply need to have a solution, and quickly."

Goddard looked at the young man with compassion. "I'll continue to work on this problem, but I suggest you go to Rimmer and get his input as well. Perhaps we can collaborate."

Dennis thanked Dr. Goddard and left with the preliminary sketches and calculations he hoped would be a solution to stop the attacks. *Finally, something I can sink my teeth into instead of the ephemeral realm of mysticism.* He called the office and informed his assistant that he was taking a flight to New Mexico.

His next call was to Horace Rimmer, who was delighted to hear from the young computer expert. "Of course we can meet, Dennis. What is this about?"

"I'll explain it all when I get there. I'll see you midday tomorrow."

With new arrangements made, Dennis took a seat in the airport lounge. *I think we've got a fighting chance against Kamenwati.*

HORACE RIMMER GAVE Dennis a warm welcome with much fussing over his long trip to visit him. "My boy, you look wonderful and have grown into a fine man. Tell me, is there a young woman in your life?" Dennis blushed and looked down, not wanting to show his embarrassment. "There is someone I've been seeing for a while, Dr. Rimmer, but that isn't why I'm here." Dennis walked into the living room of Rimmer's traditional adobe style house, admiring the rough exposed logs in the roof, the white plastered walls, and the beehive fireplace in one corner. In a semi-circle in front of the fireplace and doors leading to a back patio was a large sectional couch with an antique Spanish table in front.

Dennis took a seat and accepted Rimmer's offer of refreshment. The elder scientist rattled around in the kitchen. After gathering ice in two glasses, he filled them with Coke. He presented one glass to Dennis and sat down to hear what the young computer expert had to say. Dennis told him of the stolen drone and the search by the various intelligence agency technical experts for how it was accomplished. "Dekker is involved as well. He went to Egypt to inspect the strike site. But that's not all. He was specifically targeted by another stolen drone."

"Oh, my goodness. I pray he is safe," said Rimmer.

"He is, but just barely. When he called headquarters, Mr. Lynch, convinced the attack was somehow connected to Abaddon, took me off my line of inquiry. He asked me to design a device to identify the specific brainwave frequency being used and find a way to block it. My research..." He handed Rimmer several sheets of paper. "Led me to the belief the target brainwave range may be Theta. It also led me to New London, where the US Navy has been conducting most of the serious research into ultra-low EM transmission. I interviewed Dr. Goddard, the head of their research department, who helped me map out a basic approach to my problem; but then he said I should see you."

"Why me?" Rimmer asked.

"He said you have done the most work in resonance theories. As you can see in these papers, Dr. Goddard's focusing on the Schumann Resonance as a possible solution. I knew of your experiments with gravity resonance..."

"That is a long and unhappy chapter reaching all the way back to World War II, and frankly, it's something I'd rather forget."

"I'm not looking to open an old wound, Dr. Rimmer. Your inquiries into resonance, not only in gravity but also in sound, light, and electromagnetics make you uniquely qualified to help me."

Rimmer sat back and looked through the papers Dennis had given him. He quietly studied the documents while Dennis patiently waited. "I met Schumann once, in the mid-50s I think. He was a remarkable theorist." He read some more and finally put the papers down. "Yes, I see where Goddard is going with this."

"He spoke highly of you," said Dennis. "Can you help me?"

"I think the best approach will be through brainwave entrainment," said Rimmer.

"Dr. Goddard mentioned that, too. Here…" he dug out a few more pages from his messenger-style shoulder bag, "I almost forgot about these." Rimmer accepted the new sheets, looked them over, and nodded in agreement.

"I see he agrees on the broad approach, and in response to your question, yes I think I can help you." Dennis let out a sigh of relief. He knew, if there was anyone able to figure out where these attacks were coming from, it was Horace Rimmer. "Come. Let's go to my workshop out back."

The pair went through the rear doors and down a short stone-paved path to a small outbuilding.

CHAPTER ELEVEN

DEKKER AGREED TO BEGIN CANVASSING local cafés with a simple question in Arabic: do you know Kamenwati? The canvassing was boring, but he was able to sample coffees at each stop, so there was some benefit. Hannah started her investigation at the Asyut University library where she could begin research into Kamenwati, or at least the families in the area claiming ancient ancestry.

Entering the surprisingly large facility Hannah felt a little sorry for Dekker, having sent him off alone with minimal linguistic skills. *Still,* she thought, *he might stumble on something well before I can finish in this library.* She entered through the main lobby into the dense array of stacks holding books and scrolls going back many centuries. Letting out a sigh she said, "Here we go," and headed for the card catalogs.

Dekker had just completed a visit to his fifth café with no luck questioning the owner or waiters, and he decided a change in tactic was in order. "If I were going to join Kamenwati's little army, where would I go?" He looked up the street lined with multistory buildings that housed various businesses. All of the buildings had street-level storefronts selling goods: fabrics, rugs, tinware, copper pots, clothing, leather goods, and much more. "That's where I'd be, shopping for supplies." He began working the shops, going from one to the next. Although he saw a number of interesting items, he was still batting zero as late afternoon approached. He remembered his agreement to meet Hannah back at the hotel around five o'clock and was just about to give up, when a young boy tugged on his sleeve. The boy repeated, "Kamenwati," over and over.

"Kamenwati?" Dekker asked. The boy nodded vigorously and then took off around a corner with Dekker following. The boy was leading him down a narrow alley between buildings, an alley filled with trash and debris that slowed him down, but not the boy. He emerged on another street, one not as wide as the street he came from. The alley continued on the other side, and the boy was standing at the alley entrance, waiting for Dekker. When the boy saw the tall foreigner, he turned and disappeared down the next alley. Dekker followed as fast as he could to the other side of the street, but then he slowed his pace when he entered the dark alley. He began to get suspicious of the boy. *Where is he leading me, and why?* Now moving at a walking pace, Dekker reached out with his senses, his "danger alarm" as he called it, but detected nothing. He nevertheless slowed his pace even more and looked all around for any sign of danger. He'd lost sight of the boy, but there was only one way through the alley, forward, and so he pressed on.

The alley made a turn up ahead and he noticed higher piles of refuse lining the walls. Walking with as much stealth as possible now, he rounded the corner and came face-to-face with three men, all armed with knives, simple straight blades about seven inches in length, that they held in menacing postures. Dekker began backing up but stopped when he felt the presence of more men behind him.

"Boys, there's no need for violence." As he spoke he spun around and pulled the composite pistol from the holster at the small of his back. The armed men stopped their advance, wondering how this foreigner managed to produce a weapon.

It seemed a long time passed in the tableau, Dekker holding off a circle of knife-wielding assailants with his odd weapon, frozen. The extended pause was broken when one attacker lunged toward Dekker, his knife held straight out. Dekker avoided the strike by spinning out of the line of attack and delivering a roundhouse kick. His defensive move struck the attacker on his side, sending him crashing into the alley wall. The others held back for a moment after the besting of their leader, but then gathered their courage and moved in on

Dekker. Surrounded, he did not see a man raise a club and strike him from behind. Dekker went down, unconscious.

The group gathered around the prostrate figure, full of congratulations for one another. Their leader, dazed against the wall, stood and walked over to the motionless foreigner and sneered. He gave an order and the others quickly restrained Dekker's hands, and lifting him by the arms, they dragged him into a dark doorway at the end of the blind alley.

HANNAH LOOKED AT the time on her smartphone and worried. It was well after five o'clock and Dekker still had not appeared. After knowing him only a few days, Dekker did not seem the type to miss a meeting time unless something was wrong. She got up from the table in the open-air restaurant and walked in the direction she had last seen him going. *We agreed he would canvass the coffee shops, and so that's where I'll begin.*

She finally found a café proprietor who remembered the large foreigner. "Yes, I spoke with him," he said in Arabic. "He was looking for someone, but I can't remember who."

"He was asking about a man named Kamenwati," she said.

"Yes, that is the name."

"And…"

"I didn't recognize the name. He thanked me and left the café."

"Did you see where he went?" The man thought for a moment before replying.

Pointing up the street, he said, "I think he went that way." Hannah thanked the man and continued her search. "At least I'm going in the right direction," she said aloud as she left the café.

After three more café inquiries, Hannah decided her search method was flawed. "It seems he was getting nowhere fast on this café inquiry. Now where else would he look?" She looked up and down the street, which was now dark with occasional pools of light cast by shops and cafés. Trying to channel what Dekker would or would not do was impossible. "Back to the hotel," she said.

In her room at the Partner Tut hotel she developed a new plan. She placed a call to SIS in London. The time difference was only an hour, but she knew headquarters never slept anyway. She waited for the distinct *clicks* of the connection to the secure line she had called, which was followed by a mechanical sounding voice. Hannah identified herself, giving her code words to the person on the other end, and waited once more. A new voice came on the line and Hannah explained what she needed. "I am on detached duty with an American NCTC agent. He is carrying a next generation satellite telephone, and I need to track it. Will you contact his organization and ask them to locate Adam Dekker via GPS and send the coordinates to my phone?"

"Certainly, Agent Ahmed. We'll need a few minutes to set this up."

"Thank you."

Thirty minutes later her cell phone gave a familiar *ding* and she opened her message app. The message was from an unidentified source, but she looked with satisfaction at the coordinates on the screen. She wrote the numbers on a hotel notepad and opened Google Earth, entering the longitude and latitude coordinates in the search box. The image zoomed in to Asyut in a densely congested section of buildings. She switched to a street level view and panned around the area of the coordinates to get a feel for the location. Hannah zoomed the image out to a higher view, tagged the location, and then tagged the Partner Tut.

She put the phone down and considered her next move. She witnessed Dekker in action while they were buried in the tomb and knew he was not easily surprised or captured. *Whoever has him must have set an ambush. Now, how do I infiltrate and extract him...* She left the question unanswered and went to a small pack in her dresser drawer. Opening the drawstring, Hannah pulled out tightly rolled dark fabric. She spread the form-fitting top and bottom pieces on her bed and then unwrapped a full head mask from the bag. She went back to the closet for a pair of black soft soled shoes. "The perfect attire for an evening out on the town," she said with a small laugh. She left the hotel with a light cotton shirt over her dark clothing so as not to arouse suspicion. The fanny pack

146

hooked around her waist completed the illusion of a tourist going out for the evening.

As soon as Hannah came to the blind alley she had seen in the satellite image, she took off the cover shirt, wrapped it carefully, and placed it in the fanny pack. Then she put on the full head mask. "A proper little ninja now," she said.

Hannah double checked the mapping program to be sure of her location before turning the cell phone off. "It won't do to have interruptions." Moving down the dark alley, she seemed to merge with the dark shadows. She came to a rusted metal door set into a stone wall, tested the handle and found it securely locked. Digging into her fanny pack again Hannah pulled out a small coil of silver-white wire. She wrapped the magnesium fuse around the door handle and used a small lighter to ignite the hanging end of the fuse. She looked away, shielding her eyes from the blazing white light emitted by the fuse that burned at 5,600 degrees Fahrenheit. It was over in an instant and the door handle fell to the ground with a clatter. The handle was still much too hot to touch, and so Hannah kicked it away with her foot and pressed her shoulder to the door. Despite the weathered look of the metal door, the hinges were well oiled. *Someone wants this place to look abandoned*, she thought.

The interior of the building was dark and a layer of dust covered the floor. Using a small UV flashlight, Hannah saw a trail through the dust as if something had been dragged.

She switched off the light and moved lightly through the dark until she came to stairs leading to an upper floor. Hannah froze in place when she heard someone coughing. *It came from above,* she thought. Hannah stepped lightly on the outside of each step, not wanting to signal her approach with a creaking board. Fifteen stairs delivered her to the upper floor where she crouched and looked around. There was the faintest glow coming beneath a door. Drawing closer, Hannah heard low murmuring, a discussion in Arabic. Pressing her ear to the door she realized someone was about to leave. She looked around for somewhere to hide but the hallway was bare. Pressing herself against the wall, she could only hope her dark form blended with the dark of the hallway.

The room door pushed outward, covering Hannah, and she breathed a sigh of relief. The man leaving was giving instructions to someone in the room. *Is there only one guard inside?* Only one muffled voice acknowledged the order to watch "the man." *That can only be Dekker,* she reasoned. The man leaving grabbed the edge of the door and swung it closed as he walked away, lighting his path with a flashlight. He descended the stairs. She stood listening for several minutes, mentally tracing the man's exit from the building. There was apparently another door in the building because he did not leave by the alley door. *That's a good thing,* she thought. *If he'd seen the damaged door he would have raised an alarm.* Again, turning her attention to the door she continued listening for some indication of how many were inside. She heard some movement and then a slurred voice. "Where the hell am I?" It was English...*it is Dekker!* A voice responded in Arabic and Dekker's anger grew. "What are you saying? Don't you speak English?" An angry response was punctuated with the sound of someone striking Dekker and Hannah used that moment of distraction to enter the room. She acted on instinct alone, assessing the situation with a glance and moving on the man standing over his heavily restrained prisoner.

Dekker saw a masked figure enter the room over the shoulder of his jailer. The person moved with amazing speed and agility, striking the guard first in his right kidney and then a killing blow to his larynx. He dropped in a heap at Dekker's feet. The masked savior landed in a crouch and surveyed the room carefully, looking for other threats. This was the only guard.

Hannah stood and pulled off the black mask, shaking out her dark hair. "Come on, Dekker, let's get you out of here." She produced a small folding knife from her fanny pack and cut the bonds on Dekker's hands and feet.

He stood groggily and Hannah had to help him balance. "Drugged?" she asked.

"Yeah. How'd you find me?"

"Later. First let's get out of here."

She helped Dekker down the stairs, out the alley door, and back to the street where Hannah put her white cotton shirt back on. Dekker was feeling better with each step, and by the time they arrived at the hotel, he was moving unaided.

They sat in the cool evening air on the upper deck that was, at that hour, almost empty. Hannah went to the bar and brought back a wet towel along with a straight-up Scotch whiskey. Dekker took an appreciative drink and leaned his head back as Hannah cleaned his cuts and bruises. "Pretty," she said. Dekker grunted, indicating his assent not only to her comment but also her ministrations. After more wiping, Hannah stood back. "There. I think we've got it all."

"May I have another of these?" Dekker asked, holding up his glass. She took both the glass and the bar cloth back to the bartender and returned with a fresh glass of whiskey. Sitting across from him, Hannah was ready to hear his story. "Well, it seems you had a much more exciting day than I. Tell me about it."

"The beginning of the day was boring enough, going from café to café with no luck at all. I was going to pack it in, and then I realized I was asking in the wrong places. I was visiting the shops along the street when I was approached by a boy who kept saying *Kamenwati*. He took off down an alley and I followed until I ended up in a dead-end spot surrounded by a group of knife-wielding men. I pulled my pistol and held them off, but only for a short time. They rushed me and someone hit me from behind." He rubbed a sore spot at the base of his skull. "I don't remember much after that; I awoke in the room where you found me tied up and on the floor. There were several men standing around me, all talking at once. I heard them mention the name Kamenwati and point to me, and then one of them came over and forced a drink down my throat. I guess that was the drug that knocked me out. I awoke disoriented and they administered another dose. The next thing I knew, you are bursting into the room." He gave Hannah a grateful look. "By the way, thanks for getting me out of there."

"I guess we're even then," said Hannah. "You got me out of that tomb if you remember."

"I do, but you entered a room not knowing how many were there. That's dangerous and you should have called for backup."

"There was no time. I heard the parting order of another guard leaving, and he told the one watching you to get ready to leave at midnight. I figured there was no time like the present, and so I acted."

"You were terrific," said Dekker. "I know why SIS values you as field operative. By the way, how did you find me?"

"When you didn't show up here at the hotel, I retraced your route through the cafés. I found someone who remembered you, and he aimed me in a direction. But I realized there was no way to find your new path, and so I came back here, placed a call to SIS, and they communicated with your people in America, who sent me a GPS location for you."

"GPS? Where was the tracker?" Dekker realized the answer to his question before he finished asking. "The sat phone, of course." He searched for the compact device in his cargo pants pocked but came up empty. "That was a good move." He looked a little dejected. "I'm only sorry I lost both the sat phone and my gun." Hannah reached into her hip pack. "You didn't lose the gun. I picked it up before we left that room. The guard had it in his belt. The phone wasn't there." She handled the piece carefully, testing its weight and balance. "It is very light. What is it made from?"

He took the pistol and placed it back in the holster at the small of his back. "A composite material hard as steel but only a fraction of the weight, and it's undetectable to airport scanners."

"How deliciously James Bond," she said with admiration. "How may I get one of those?"

"I'm afraid this is a prototype. Dennis, one of the technical whizzes in NCTC, outfitted me with the piece. It also fires special ammunition that can pass airport surveillance."

"James Bond indeed," said Hannah. She sat back and crossed her arms. "So, now what? We seem to have lost our only lead."

"Not necessarily. Someone in that group has my sat phone, as you discovered, but even turned off it can be tracked. That's a little insurance Dennis built into the device."

"Clever," said Hannah. "So we simply ring up your people and ask for directions?"

"Something like that. Let's get some sleep. Tomorrow promises to be busy."

CHAPTER TWELVE

KAMENWATI WAS PLEASED WITH REPORTS coming in from across his Egypt. Followers dispatched to recruit new believers seemed to be striking a nerve among those of the ancient ancestry. Alexandria was a target community, having historical prestige no less than Cairo, and its proximity to the capital city afforded it greater influence in government affairs than others. No less important to his appeal was Asyut, an ancient city with a large non-Arab community, precisely the people Kamenwati wished to join his True Egyptian cadre.

In secret meetings, Kamenwati's evangelists conveyed a simple and compelling message, offering an alternative to their present second-class citizenship in the form of an intoxicating mix of jingoism and prophecy: "It is we who should be leading, and now is the time to gather our strength and prepare for what is coming in the name of our Egypt!"

Not all reports, however, were positive. Spies were beginning to infiltrate cells, which was, however, an expected development that Kamenwati's followers dealt with in the harshest terms. What Kamenwati overlooked was the report of someone in Asyut asking about him, a report that would come to haunt his future plans. But for now, pride and ego were being fed both by the positive reports coming in and the Abaddon spirit.

You are doing well, Kamenwati. Very soon you will retake Egypt and reclaim its position in the world, and soon thereafter, your power will be felt throughout the Earth.

How will I reach out and control the world, Master?

You will reach out to the remnants of the Brotherhood and re-establish their presence, and influence, in key nations. Kamenwati nodded to indicate his understanding.

I see your plan, and I can remain on this shielded island, directing action as I will.

Not as you will. As I will. Do not forget: it is I who gives you power, and it is I who can take it away.

Kamenwati sat in silence, stewing in anger and fear as the spirit withdrew. *Do I not have great power and learning in my own right?* He had to acknowledge his newfound abilities came as a result of joining with the spirit, and he knew the spirit could crush him in an instant, extinguish his life and all he hoped for, but he chafed at the spirit's commands. He had to find a balance between obsequious subservience and absorbing as much power as possible. "One day I will be able to cast off the spirit of Abaddon and follow my own ambitions." It was a heady thought and fed his growing narcissism.

KAMENWATI'S FOLLOWER AND the leader of the True Egyptian group in Asyut inspected the small package given him by a new disciple. The little rectangular box was clearly designed to hook onto a belt; the clasp on one side was proof of this. There was a single cord for charging the box, but there were no other cables or input points. He turned the mysterious device over, rubbed it, smelled it, and shook it. The leader knew it must have some purpose, if only because it came from the foreigner captured earlier in the evening, but he had no idea of its function.

His thoughts were interrupted by the young man. "Sir, we are assembled and ready for instruction." The leader waved the youth off and stood to prepare himself, placing the mysterious device in an inner pocket of his robe. "I will return to this later."

The assembly of followers, about fifty men and women, waited in respectful silence for their leader. He entered the room and stood before the group. "My people, it is time for each of you to take the next step toward the realization of our cause. I am only a messenger, sent by a great man and fellow True Egyptian. He is bringing back the traditions of our past and wields unimaginable power. It is to him you must pledge your allegiance and your life. In return you will be protected and his power will reach out to drive off our enemies." He paused and looked at each person in the room, his gaze penetrating the very souls of the assembly. "My master, Kamenwati, has the ability to wield the ancient powers once belonging to the Pharaohs and the chief priests. He is privy to the Old Truths that governed this world but have been lost to time. I know this sounds strange, but I assure you it is all true. I have seen the power and felt the potency of his presence. Kamenwati will lead us back to a position of superiority over our land, our region, and even the world." A hushed silence fell over the assembly, and the leader waited. A man stood, lifted his hands, and proclaimed, "I will follow Kamenwati!"

The dam burst and, in quick succession, everyone in the room stood to proclaim allegiance to Kamenwati. A smile crossed the leader's face and he allowed the excitement to continue for several minutes before settling the people. "Now, my friends, we will talk about assignments for each of you." The meeting continued for some time as he received each in attendance, discussed their background and talents, and assigned them an appropriate task. It was a long evening but in the end he had the makings of a true movement in Egypt.

During the excitement he forgot about the device in his cloak pocket.

EGYPT TIME IS six hours ahead of Washington, DC and so Dekker and Hannah had only a couple hours rest. They met early in the main parlor where a seating area in the far corner offered the privacy needed to place their call. Using Hannah's cell phone, Dekker dialed a number he memorized long ago. He waited for the connection and was pleased the signal was so clear. He asked to be connected with Jim Lynch, and the receptionist connected him to Lynch's assistant, Marilyn, who connected him immediately to her boss.

"Dekker, this is a little unusual. You weren't scheduled to call for another day."

"I know Jim, but there's been a development here and I need some help from home." He told Lynch of his capture and Hannah's brave rescue, and then he admitted the loss of his satellite phone. "It was the GPS on the sat phone that gave Hannah the coordinates of my captors, and shortly after getting the information from you, I was left with only one guard. One of the others found the phone in my pocket and took it away."

"That is not good, Dekker. It's an expensive piece of experimental equipment."

"Right, Jim, but I need to talk to Dennis and get a new location for the phone. We believe it will lead us to the location of Kamenwati's cell here in Asyut."

"Dennis isn't here at the moment. As a matter of fact he is meeting with Horace Rimmer." Dekker couldn't imagine why Dennis wanted to see his friend and former father-in-law, but he didn't have time to question Jim further. "Can someone else ping the sat phone and give me its location?"

"Certainly. We'll put the location on a cloud server in a few minutes so you can retrieve it."

"And I'd like to have regular updates, say every hour, to confirm whether it's stationary or on the move."

"I will make that happen."

"Thank you, Jim." He disconnected the call and filled Hannah in on the particulars. "Now we wait."

"I'll go back to the room. I want to collect a few items we may need," said Hannah. She returned in ten minutes attired for a walk through town: tailored khaki trousers, white cotton blouse from the evening before worn over a gray camisole, light boots, and her hip pack. She held up her cell phone for Dekker to see.

"It looks like they've set up the file drop. Let's find a hotel computer and see where your mysterious captors are hiding." They inquired about a computer at the Partner Tut front desk and were directed to the business office, which was hardly more than a closet off the lobby. Dekker entered, typed a web address into the browser, and waited. He had to go through an identification interface, followed by an authentication page. Once in, he searched for the proper folder, which Dennis' department had conveniently labeled, *Dekker_Egypt*. There was only one document inside, time-stamped five minutes earlier. He wrote down the GPS coordinates and backed out of the server site, taking care not to leave anything either on the desktop or in the browser cache.

He then stepped out of the room and nodded to Hannah. They returned to the lounge and Hannah entered the coordinates into her smartphone mapping program. "Got it. They seem to be on the outskirts of the city in the direction of St. Katherine's Monastery. It's a little too far to walk, so we'll take a taxi."

Out front they found a small taxi stand, and Hannah gave the driver instructions in Arabic.

"He must have a death wish," said Dekker, holding on to a strap while the taxi swerved and rocketed through traffic. "This is fairly normal for Egypt," said Hannah.

They rode on in silence, watching the city move rapidly past their windows. The driver turned to ask Hannah a question about their destination. Dekker was horrified because the driver was not looking where his taxi was going. Hannah answered him and the driver returned to his proper position behind the wheel. "What was that about?" Dekker asked.

"He wanted to know if we are going to the monastery. I told him we wish to visit the church of St. Katherine which, I believe, is coming up ahead." The taxi came to a sliding halt in front of a modest Coptic church. After Hannah paid the driver, they stood on the front steps watching the taxi disappear in a cloud of exhaust. Dekker was glad to be free from that rattling death trap.

After consulting her map program, Hannah looked across the road. "That direction, two streets away." They headed in the direction indicated on the map. "We're close. It's telling me the destination is on the left." Dekker took her arm as they walked. "We should look like a happy couple out to enjoy the sights of the city," he said. Hannah offered no protest, and in fact, enjoyed the close contact.

They stopped in front of a two-story structure hardly distinguishable from every other in the area. They pretended to consult a guide book that Dekker had picked up in the hotel lobby, turning pages and acting confused. They walked first to one end of the building, then to the other, all the while pointing in various directions as if they were searching for their destination. There was no movement from the building and no one came out to inquire about their business.

"It sure looks deserted," said Dekker. Hannah nodded her agreement and then turned to Dekker with a question. "What is your plan?"

"It's still early. Let's go over to that *bakal*," said Dekker, indicating a store across from them. "We can sit at the little table out front and watch for activity." Hannah agreed and led the way across the road to the tiny convenience store. Taking possession of the single outside table, they spread their props and settled in to begin surveillance.

TWO HOURS OF waiting, a falafel for both, and their surveillance paid off. Two men approached the building and stopped at the entry door. They looked around to be sure nobody was watching and, using a key, entered. Dekker stood and walked into the store, paid for their food, and returned to Hannah. "Ready?" She stood in response, her eyes now steely. "I guess you are," said Dekker.

The road was now busy with traffic. Picking their way across, they made it to the building entrance. "Shield me," said Hannah. Dekker complied, standing in such a way that Hannah's lock picking would not be seen. In a few moments she stood, replacing the small tool in her hip pack. "Ready?" Dekker looked around, much like the two men who had entered previously, and followed Hannah inside.

It was dark. The few windows had been painted over and so allowed little light to filter through. The floor was covered with broken furniture, old boxes, general trash, and a thick layer of dust that was disturbed in several places. "It looks like a homeless squat," said Dekker, and Hannah responded with "um-hm."

With a hand signal from Dekker, the pair separated left and right. Hannah moved with silent grace, Dekker noted, a talent well-suited to her profession. He was once again impressed with the British agent and was strangely reassured by her presence.

They completed the circuit of the main floor, meeting at the broad staircase leading to the second level. A questioning look from Dekker was answered by a negative shake of Hannah's head, her meaning clear: nothing here.

They looked up the stairs and then back to one another before starting up. They reached a landing and found the floor configured much differently than below. The stairs continued to the third and final floor of the building, but the second level led down a hall with rooms, offices presumably, lining one wall. Dekker crouched and drew his pistol from the holster at the small of his back. Hannah did the same except she withdrew a small Beretta BU9 Nano from her hip pack. Dekker nodded his approval of the 9mm pistol but wondered what happened to the SIS preference for Walthers. *Maybe it's all a myth,* mused Dekker.

They moved silently down the hall, both alert for the smallest indication of danger. They reached the end of the hall and were presented with another hall running left and right. Hannah mimed her question: which way? Dekker looked in both directions and pointed down the left corridor. Hannah spotted what caught his attention, a faint glow of light beneath one door. With Dekker taking the lead, the pair moved to either side of the door and listened. A murmur of voices could be heard but no clear words.

Dekker leaned close to speak into Hannah's ear. "I'm going to check the next room. You stay here and watch the door." Hannah pulled back, shaking her head.

"How about you watch the door and I investigate the next room?"

Dekker smiled, realizing she was not a woman accustomed to taking the back seat. "How about we both take a look?"

The next door was unlocked, and Dekker turned the handle and pushed the door inward. When there was sufficient space, Hannah slid through the narrow opening, and a moment later her hand appeared, beckoning to Dekker to proceed. At that moment the door they left only moments before opened, spilling light across the hallway. Dekker jumped into the room, now grateful they both left that door. Dekker was about to close the door when Hannah stopped him, leaving it slightly cracked. She stood at the crack, listening. They heard the first door close and people conversing.

"Well?" asked Dekker.

"It was two men. One, the leader I think, was giving orders to the other man."

"What kind of orders?"

"Not to put too fine a point on it: orders to find you."

CHAPTER THIRTEEN

RAHOTEP AND HIS TEAM RETURNED to the island refuge ready to report on their firsthand observation of the drone strike. Kamenwati sat comfortably in the pavilion below the main house watching the gossamer drapes flowing in the Nile's gentle breezes. He did not invite Rahotep, Nebwawi, or Sabu to sit.

"Report," he ordered.

"Sir, we went to the location you gave us and found evidence of a large explosion. A vehicle was crushed under tons of rock loosed by the rocket's impact." Rahotep looked to the others for support. "We tried to dig through the rubble, but the task was too great without tools or a considerable number of men."

Nebwawi continued in their defense. "There is no way a man could live through such a landslide. The American is buried as eternally as any Pharaoh." The three men stood uncomfortably waiting for Kamenwati to respond.

"We did retrieve the remains of the aircraft," offered Sabu, the third of their company. "It sits before the house, ready for your inspection." Kamenwati looked directly at Sabu, his penetrating gaze reaching deep inside and frightening him.

"Dispose of the device in the desert. I do not want it found." Turning his attention to Rahotep he continued, "And I hope you are correct about the American. Now leave me." Rahotep and the others made a slight bow and went back up to the main house. Kamenwati stood and stared at the eternal river, silently congratulating himself for eliminating Adam Dekker. Sweeping his garment behind, he walked purposely up to the house, ready to give his own report to the Abaddon spirit.

When he reached his private quarters Kamenwati settled himself into a comfortable meditation position. He moved smoothly into the Flows and reached out to his guiding spirit. In a few moments he felt the familiar yet brutal presence join him. *"Master, there is good news: I have eliminated the American as you desired, and I have established new followers throughout the country."*

The spirit remained silent, confusing Kamenwati.

"Surely this is a welcome report…"

Welcome, yes, but not nearly enough. You have learned new skills and now I wish you to use them on a much broader scale. You will reach out and reassemble the ancient Brotherhood in Germany, England, and America.

"How will I accomplish such a task?"

As you have done in Egypt: send trusted representatives to each nation. Let them restore the Brotherhood and then, using the Flows, establish your authority.

"What then?"

They will become your spearhead into the military communities. They will sew distrust and dissension. They will steer the world toward war.

Kamenwati was stunned at the spirit's plan. *He isn't interested in restoring Egypt*, he thought. *This spirit wants to pit East against West and destroy both in the process.* Uncomfortable with such a plan, he struggled to find a way out; but think as he might, there was no alternative. He must obey the spirit.

"As you wish. I will send Rahotep, Sabu, and Nebwawi," he said out loud.

There was a sense of satisfaction emanating from the spirit as it withdrew from Kamenwati, who felt anything but satisfied. He called for his young assistant to summon Rahotep and the others.

It was several hours before the three men appeared before Kamenwati, explaining they were disposing of the drone aircraft as ordered. Kamenwati nodded his understanding. "And you buried it?"

"No sir, not completely," said Rahotep. "We stopped as soon as we received your order to return. But do not fear. It is in a place that will not implicate us."

Kamenwati stood and addressed the men. "I have an important assignment for each of you. Tomorrow, at daybreak, you will travel to Germany, England, and America. You will find people whose names I will give you, brothers in our cause, and you will reassemble their organizations. I will establish my authority through the Flows." The three men looked at one another with expressions of surprise and confusion. Kamenwati paid them no attention but handed each a piece of paper identifying their contacts.

"Rest well, my friends. Tomorrow you begin an important journey. Farewell."

"MY BROTHERS, IT is a great honor to be given responsibility for rebuilding organizations for our teacher and master, Kamenwati," Rahotep said to his two companions as they looked up from their papers, their question obvious.

"How will we find these people, and if we do find them, how can we persuade them to join our cause?" Sabu asked.

"All of the men listed here," Rahotep said lifting his paper, "have been elders in the ancient Brotherhood, a network of people committed to the Old Truths, and are experienced in power of the Flows. It is my belief they will find you." This answer seemed to temper the others' misgivings.

"It seems I am going to Germany," said Sabu referencing his paper.

"And I to England," said Nebwawi.

Looking at his paper once again Rahotep spoke to his two old friends. "And I will be going to America to Washington, DC."

The next morning Kamenwati's emissaries departed for their respective destinations. Sabu headed for Krugerschloss in Germany's Black Forest, the scene of Abaddon's defeat and Kamenwati's rise. Nebwawi set out for England, to the Salisbury plain near Stonehenge and the late Lord Geoffrey's estate. Rahotep, the most senior of the three, was tasked with reassembling Origen's followers, now scattered throughout the Washington area since the discovery of their headquarters in the Maryland suburbs. Each of the three men knew they faced challenges fulfilling their assignments, but all had assurances from Kamenwati that he would send messages ahead to expect their arrival.

Sabu and Nebwawi had the easier assignments since the Brotherhood groups in both locations were still largely intact if presently disorganized. They would be able to meet the leaders and quietly begin reassembly of the cells in both Germany and England. Rahotep was not so lucky. When Origen fled the Maryland estate, he left behind a staff whose loyalty was betrayed and the group disbursed in bitter disappointment. Interestingly, it was Origen's previous "clients" who gave Rahotep his first victory. Origen's client list included politicians, bureaucrats, and military personnel, and none knew of the events in Germany. They were not troubled by the long silence of their patron, and when approached by Rahotep, they assumed there was a change in leadership, a belief Rahotep did not discourage.

After contacting most of the old client list, Rahotep found Sammy, a young foot soldier who had been adrift since Origen's disappearance. "You know," said Sammy at their first meeting, "I went out to the Patuxent River estate a while back and other than being empty, it looked normal."

"Was there any surveillance? A parked vehicle or individuals walking around?" Rahotep asked.

"No, it was quiet. The estate is at the end of a road and there aren't any close neighbors."

This gave Rahotep an idea. "Do you suppose we could get back in?"

"I don't see why not, and as I recall, we left it furnished and the security system intact."

"The security system could be a problem. Do you know if the FBI left it engaged?"

"I'm sorry but I don't know. I wasn't there when our business was discovered." Rahotep looked closely at Sammy. "Do you know about the Flows?" Sammy looked bewildered and hesitated before responding. "I know about them. Some of the other guys talked about how Origen was always 'consulting' the Flows. But more than that, I can't say."

"Were your people schooled in the use of a power that you probably think of as supernatural?"

"Now that you mention it, weird stuff happened sometimes. I couldn't explain any of it, and neither could most of the security staff. We all sort of accepted it and the good fortune that seemed to come from the strange stuff, you know, like cash bonuses."

"So none of your colleagues knew where the 'strange stuff' originated?"

"No, sir. We were all part of a consortium. We took orders and did our jobs."

"Interesting. Can you get in touch with any others?"

"Yeah, I think I can. Probably about half a dozen or so."

"Perfect. Now, take me to the Patuxent estate."

THE ESTATE HOUSE was at the end of a rural road and completely surrounded by forest. "This is an excellent out-of-the-way location," said Rahotep. "Let us see if it is as deserted as you claim, Sammy." They drove around to the side portico and stopped.

"Here it is. A little overgrown, but in pretty good shape." Rahotep nodded and took three steps up to the landing at the side door. He tried the knob but found the door locked. He looked back to Sammy, his face questioning. "They keep it locked up, but I'm hoping they don't know about the set of keys we kept outside." He led Rahotep to the back, across the overgrown lawn area, to the edge of the woods where a small shack stood. "This is where we used to store garden tools, but this shelf is a compartment." He used a pocket knife to pry open a piece of board forming a false wall behind the shelf. In a moment Sammy held a rectangular metal box. After opening the box, he held up a set of keys on a ring. "Here they are, sir," he said with pride.

Sammy and Rahotep went back to the house, to the rear stairs leading up to a door. "Our security office is inside on the left," Sammy said while opening the door. He let Rahotep enter first. When they entered the security office Sammy was sorry to see all the equipment gone. "This used to be filled with monitors and motion detectors," he said sadly.

"Let's move on," said Rahotep.

They continued touring the estate house, covering the main floor and then the upper floor. "What is in the basement?" Rahotep asked.

"Just storage and the heating system," replied Sammy.

They returned to the main foyer and stood before the front door. Sammy hesitated before opening it. He was looking at a partially opened closet door, remembering the man who was held inside. "This is where it all started, where Origen had the government man, and after that everything began to unravel."

171

Rahotep stepped over and closed the closet door. "Today begins a new chapter. I want you to collect as many of Origen's followers as you can find. Bring them here for a meeting in one week. Meanwhile, I will arrange to purchase this property."

Sammy took care to lock the doors as they left, then handed the keys to Rahotep.

CHAPTER FOURTEEN

DENNIS LOOKED WITH ADMIRATION AT Horace Rimmer, whose hands were rock-steady as he delicately manipulated knobs mounted below a series of small monochrome video monitors. Rimmer was preparing yet another test to isolate the specific frequency used to incapacitate and control the UAV operators in North Carolina. Earlier tests were unsuccessful, but he consoled Dennis by reminding him Thomas Edison failed hundreds of times before creating the lightbulb.

"Okay, Dennis, come here and sit down." The young man went to the chair beside the wall of equipment.

"What are we trying now, Dr. Rimmer?"

"We are going to use something called binaural beats in a brainwave entrainment experiment."

"I know about brainwave entrainment from Dr. Goddard, but I'm afraid I don't know about beats," said Dennis.

"Beats allow you to perceive frequencies far below the normal range of human hearing. I've been reviewing the Schumann Resonance you so cleverly identified as a possible source of power for the Flows. As you found in New London, the fundamental Schumann mode is a standing wave in the Earth–ionosphere cavity with a wavelength equal to the circumference of the Earth. The only way to test the different Theta wavelengths is to subject you to their effect. Can you handle that?"

"I am ready and willing. Let's do it."

"Let me tell you what will happen so you are not taken by surprise." Dr. Rimmer lifted his fingers from the large analog dials and pulled up a stool across from Dennis. "The Schumann Resonances are quasi-standing electromagnetic waves. They are not present all the time, so they have to be 'excited' to be observed. The waves aren't caused by anything internal to the Earth, like the crust or core. Schumann postulated they were related to electrical activity in the atmosphere, particularly during times of intense lightning activity. They occur at several frequencies between 6 and 50 cycles per second, specifically at 7.8, 14, 20, 26, 33, 39 and 45 Hz. So long as the properties of Earth's electromagnetic cavity remain about the same, these frequencies remain the same."

"What does that mean?" Dennis asked.

"The higher resonance modes are spaced at approximately 6.5Hz intervals, a characteristic attributed to the atmosphere's spherical geometry. The peaks exhibit a spectral width of approximately twenty percent due to damping of the respective modes in the dissipative cavity. The eighth partial lies at approximately 60Hz, and that coincides nicely with Theta 1, but the space between Theta 1 and Theta 2 is of the greatest interest."

"Uh, Dr. R, I'm not sure I follow all of that."

Rimmer looked affectionately at the younger man. "Let me simplify: these sub-frequencies I mentioned are sometimes called Epsilon, Lambda, and Sigma, and are the subject of some dispute within the scientific community. Nevertheless, it is within these small frequency variations that I hope to find the signal that will induce the ganzfeld effect."

"What is that?"

"A condition first described by Arctic explorers as an altered state of consciousness brought about by blizzard conditions where they saw nothing but white, regardless of where they looked. I will recreate this effect by using sound, specifically pink noise, fed through those headphones." He pointed to headphones and blackout mask sitting on the table next to Dennis. "This will create a 'sonic blizzard' resulting in the same altered state of consciousness as a literal blizzard."

"How dangerous is this?"

"As long as you don't wander off and fall into a crevasse, you will be fine. One more thing, Dennis." Rimmer grew serious. "There is another corollary that may come into play. I'm not sure if you will sense it, but perhaps you will."

"And that is…"

"There was scientific research in Beijing, China, a study of natural healers. They found that the most powerful healers were able to emit a strong infratonic, or low frequency sound, from their hands. They developed what was called an Infratonic Qui Gong Machine, or Infratonic QGM, to study the phenomenon. They found the infratonic sound emitted from average individuals was only a hundredth as strong as that of a deeply studied healer."

Dennis had a confused look on his face. "Dr. R, sometimes I feel like a first-year physics student when you talk."

"I'm sorry, Dennis. I get lost in a subject and tend to lecture. Let me put it this way: this Infratonic QGM may point to the actual method used to seize control of a man's consciousness…and a drone aircraft."

Needing no more encouragement, Dennis picked up the headphones, attached a pulse clip to his index finger, and placed the sleep mask over his eyes. "Fire it up, doc!" Rimmer placed an electrode cap on Dennis' head, stepped over to the control console, and flipped a switch. With a clipboard in hand, he began the experiment.

At first Dennis listened to the pink noise, a steady *hissing* sound that was uncomfortably loud. He tried humming in the same frequency to counteract its effects, but he soon gave up. After a few minutes, he seemed able tune out or ignore the noise, settling into a strangely calm condition. He had no idea how much time passed after that for there was no point of reference. His mind slowly lost focus and finally went into a daydream-like trance. He no longer knew where he was, whether he was standing, sitting, or lying down; and he really didn't care.

Rimmer watched the monitors carefully, noting changes in Dennis' brainwave activity. With precise movements, he nudged the electrode signals slowly through a narrow frequency range from Epsilon to Sigma. He made notations with each frequency stop and checked the Infratonic effect output from Dennis' finger clip. Other than his subject being in a complete daze there was no significant activity until he reached 5 Hz where he noticed a distinct jump in Dennis' cognitive functioning and his index finger began fluttering up and down. He adjusted the frequency, lowering the signal to 4.5 in increments of .05 Hz, and interestingly, the effects diminished with each change of frequency. He worked the frequency back upward and decided 4.9 Hz was the point the effect was strongest.

Slowly reducing the pink noise being fed to the headphones, Rimmer allowed Dennis to return to consciousness. After a few minutes he was pleased to see his young subject sit up straight and remove the sleep mask. "How long was I out?"

"Not too long, perhaps half an hour."

"It seemed a lot longer." Dennis looked directly at Rimmer, posing the question at the top of his mind. "How did I do? Did you find the brainwave frequency we're looking for?"

Rimmer smiled and held up the clipboard. "We certainly did, Dennis. Now the problem is devising a mechanism to block, deflect, or otherwise defeat future attacks."

"Is it possible?" Dennis asked. "I mean, we're not talking about putting tinfoil hats on everyone, are we?" Rimmer chuckled.

"Yes, it is possible to block the waves, Dennis, but no tinfoil hats. This is not dissimilar to the early days of radar, and later stealth technology, when we looked for a means to defeat radar. We will approach this problem in electromagnetics in much the same way. Now, give me some time. I've got work to do."

THE VISIT BY the young NCTC representative gnawed on Herman Goddard's mind. The Schumann Resonances that so interested Mr. Allende were somewhat out of his normal arena of inquiry, and because the Schumann Resonances held true only in the atmosphere and Goddard's work was underwater, deep underwater, the influence of such electromagnetic waves was not within his purview. Nevertheless, Schumann's research had led to the Navy's present work in sonic properties, and in fact, Goddard had researchers working for him who were currently testing a new underwater sonic torpedo focusing a shaped burst that, so far, was able to destroy targets several thousand yards from the firing point. It all worked within the same general principles, and the more the researchers on the team informed him they were about sonic wave features that applied both below water and on the surface.

Goddard wondered how Allende's meeting with Rimmer had gone. Was there some hope he could find an answer, or was it all a dead-end? He decided his group should look into this problem, too. It was a fascinating hypothesis and one deserving some attention. He picked up his telephone and punched a button connecting him to his administrative assistant. "Carol, will you round up Kurt and Joe and have them meet me in an hour?" Goddard hung up and sat back in his chair pondering Dennis' problem anew.

An hour later Kurt Cheetham and Joe Linden, both Ph.D. engineers working in Goddard's department, entered the office. They dressed like engineers: business suits somewhat ill-fitting, white shirts with the top button undone, and out of fashion ties slightly loosened. They greeted Goddard collegially as they took seats before his desk. Goddard opened the middle drawer and pulled out a copy of the preliminary sketches and calculations he had given to Allende. He explained the basic questions raised along with Dennis' interest in the Theta range. Both men studied the papers given them, nodding and making notes on their electronic tablets while Goddard summarized.

"I told the NCTC gentleman we would look into his problem, and that's why I called you in. I don't want you to stop on the sonic torpedo project, but I think you can squeeze in some time on this."

"Does this have a project number?" Cheetham asked. Goddard shook his head.

"Not yet. This is very preliminary, and depending on what you find, I might be able to take it to the level of an official project." His two subordinates looked to one another, shrugged, and stood, telling their boss they would work on it.

Goddard thanked the pair and closed his office door.

AFTER SENDING AN email to the base commander alerting him to the new inquiry and assuring him there would be no impact on the sonic cannon project, Goddard placed a telephone call to NCTC. He went through several transfers but eventually reached Jim Lynch, the Deputy Director. Once identifying himself to Lynch, Goddard got to the purpose of the call.

"Mr. Lynch, I had a visit from one of your people, a Mr. Allende."

"Yes, he informed me of his intention to meet with you, Doctor."

"He was quite passionate, and in a hurry, something about a stolen UAV."

"We've been trying to keep a lid on this thing, but Dennis was correct, a drone was stolen. Actually, two were seized. He did some research and found interesting avenues of investigation in brainwaves."

Goddard agreed. "I found his hypothesis interesting and worked on some preliminary ideas for him. I also suggested he find the man who did more work in resonance theory than anyone I know: Dr. Horace Rimmer."

"Rimmer!" Lynch's surprise was genuine.

"That's how Mr. Allende reacted. I take it you know Rimmer as well."

"Oh, yes, and I assume Dennis went to New Mexico."

"Yes he did, and in a great hurry. Is this as critical as he said?"

"It is, Doctor, and we have to stop this…this…I don't even know what to call it. This hack, I guess is accurate enough, before we lose control of our entire UAV fleet."

"I understand, Mr. Lynch, and to that end I have begun researching the problem more deeply here."

"I appreciate your help, Doctor. The more minds we have working on this, especially those with your particular knowledge and experience, the better."

"Thank you, Mr. Lynch. I wanted to let you know we are working on the problem, but I still believe Dr. Rimmer is the best bet for a solution."

Goddard ended the call and went back to work on his primary project, the UnderSea Sonic Torpedo, or USST. He wondered if there was something in the USST research that might also answer the NCTCs problem. The Navy's work developing a focused underwater sonic weapon had revealed that, under certain conditions, such weapons could work on the surface. He looked at the documents given to the two engineers, closed his eyes to facilitate concentration, and considered how his torpedo device might be modified. After several minutes he opened his eyes and reached for his phone to call Cheetham.

"Kurt, I have an angle for you to pursue."

CHAPTER FIFTEEN

DEKKER COULDN'T IMAGINE HOW KAMENWATI'S people discovered that he escaped the missile attack or how they figured he was in Asyut. And then he remembered the satellite phone. "It seems the signal tracking works both ways." Hannah gave him a confused look. "I think they found me through the sat phone, or at least it allowed them to deduce someone with special knowledge was on to them."

"You may be right, Dekker. Do we follow the man sent to find you or the leader?"

"We need to retrieve the sat phone," he said.

"And we need to know what these people are trying to do," said Hannah.

Dekker considered their situation for a moment and then came to a decision. "We split up. I'll get into that room while you follow the other guy to see what he's up to." Hannah nodded and peeked out the door.

"The hallway is clear," she said. "Let's meet up at the bottom of the stairway in, say, fifteen minutes." Hannah stepped through the doorway, stopped and turned back to Dekker. "Good luck."

"See you in fifteen," he replied as Hannah disappeared without a sound. By the time Dekker reached the door and looked out, Hannah was already gone. *She moves quickly*, he thought.

Standing at the adjoining door, he listened. He did not hear voices but did hear someone moving around, as if the occupant was changing clothes. He was reluctant to reach out in the Flows for fear he would himself be detected, and instead he relied on his own senses and continued listening. After a few minutes another door inside opened and closed. Dekker opened the hall door just a crack, and confirming the room was empty, pushed it fully open. After checking one more time up and down the hallway, he entered the room.

As with the room next door, this was a simple office, more like a reception room with a door in the rear wall leading to another office. Dekker noticed a round meeting table with several chairs. The walls were empty except for a coat closet on his left. Moving quietly to the rear office door, he once again listened. There was some low talking, but it sounded like one side of a discussion, a telephone call. The man was speaking Arabic, and much too fast for Dekker to follow, but he detected a sense of urgency in the man's tone.

The conversation ended, but there was no sound of a handset being replaced. *A cell phone*, thought Dekker. The handle to the inner office door turned. Dekker, who had not heard any footfalls in his direction, moved quickly to the coat closet and hid inside just as the inner office door opened. He didn't have time to completely close the closet door and hoped he would not be discovered. The man in the office was distracted with the papers he was stuffing into a soft leather folio, looking down as he organized his material and then moved through the outer reception area. Dekker observed the man: slight and light-skinned, his dark beard neatly trimmed. He wore no robe, which was a little unusual. Instead he wore a Western-style loose fitting white shirt and trousers. Dekker watched the man leave the room and realized that, since he was not wearing a robe, he was not going out of the building. He stepped out of the closet and looked back inside. He saw a garment hanging on the rear wall: a white cotton robe. Dekker patted the robe and discovered something in an inner pocket. He reached in and removed a small case, his sat phone. Breathing a sigh of relief, he closed the closet door and opened the reception room door leading to the hallway, spotting the man from the office turning the corner. With a few quick steps he followed as quietly as possible.

He watched the man ascend the stairs to the third floor. After a few moments at the stairway, Dekker heard the man's footsteps receding, stopping, and going through a door. Dekker quickly mounted the steps to the top floor where he found a double door, the sort found in larger conference rooms, and if he knew anything about such rooms, there would be a service hall in the rear. Following the wall past the double doors he came to a single door with a sign written in Arabic. He couldn't read the sign but assumed it said "Service" or something similar. He opened the door and found a dark hallway. He took out his Maglite and spun the bezel to the narrowest beam. Broken dish carts, long abandoned, littered the hall, along with a few bent aluminum trays. At the end of the hall was another door providing access to the main room. This door was not entirely closed, which allowed Dekker to both see and hear what was happening. He observed a group of perhaps twenty men and women listening closely to the white-shirted man. He only understood a few words and wished Hannah were with him, but then someone asked a question. He addressed the man standing before them as Leader, and the Egyptian responded with a few words that included one he knew: Kamenwati.

Moving back up the service hall, Dekker thought about the implications of what he had heard, confirmation of Kamenwati's connection to the leader and the others in the room. Dekker had the terrible feeling the Krugerschloss template of control and manipulation was being duplicated. He checked the time and realized he had been almost twenty minutes and Hannah would be waiting. He descended the stairs, taking care to check that no one was about at each landing. When he reached the ground floor Hannah stepped out of the shadows, concern on her face.

"I was worried you had been discovered," she said.

"Sorry. I followed the leader up to a third floor meeting room. It looked like he was lecturing to a group of men and women, but I couldn't understand most of what he said. What I did get was a clear reference to Kamenwati."

"Are they trying to find us?"

"I don't think so. I believe this cell has been here for a while and the leader has been organizing people into a working group."

WHILE DEKKER FOLLOWED the leader, Hannah had moved like a ghost down the hall: no sound of footsteps, no rustle of clothing, no indication of her pursuit. The man she followed had no idea she was there as he descended the stairs, secure in the knowledge this building was occupied entirely by his people. Hannah had stopped at the top of the stairway, flattening herself against a wall in the shadows, observing the man. He moved without hesitation out of sight to the right.

She glided down the stairs, holding close to the wall until reaching the last step. Looking around the corner she saw the man exiting the building from a small door leading into an alley. Hannah had stepped quickly to the closing door, catching it just before it latched. Breathing a sigh of relief she waited a moment before continuing the tail. Hannah looked around and found a piece of rebar. *This will work nicely*, she thought, placing it on the ground to prevent the door from fully closing, and then stepped into the alley. She noted her target go to his right after leaving the building, so she went that way as well, following the alley until it opened onto a street. It was a narrow and crowded street, teeming with pedestrians and smoking, honking autos.

Hannah had stepped out as if nothing were amiss and blended in with the crowd. She spotted a café across the street where her mark had taken a seat with two other men. It took some doing and a couple of hair-raising near accidents, but she managed to cross to the café and took a just-vacated table close to her mark. The three men were deep in conversation, their tiny cups of thick coffee untouched. Hannah ordered a glass of fruit juice and leaned back in her chair, just as a hot and tired lady might. In reality, she was positioning herself to hear the conversation behind her. Even with her proximity, the three men were leaning in close and speaking softly, but she was able to catch enough to get the general drift of the conversation. Her mark, a man named Walid, was giving his two associates instructions. She couldn't figure out what the instructions were, only that they were specific and detailed. Hannah thought she heard Walid say something about another group in Alexandria and the importance of coordination.

The men sat back in their chairs, the formal part of the meeting apparently complete. Each lifted a cup to the others, nodded, sipped, and stood to leave. Hannah had sat forward so she wouldn't be suspected of eavesdropping and waited for the three men to leave. She checked the time and saw she could just make it back to the rendezvous with Dekker. There wasn't much information, but perhaps it would mean something to her American partner.

When she was again at the staircase, Dekker was not there, and this had concerned her. Was he discovered and captured? What could delay him? These were questions with no immediate answers and the longer she waited, the greater her concern grew. Stepping away from the stairs and into the shadows, she had silently told herself Dekker had another five minutes to show up. She had waited longer, of course, and about ten minutes after their scheduled meet time, Dekker appeared. Stepping out of the shadows she expressed her alarm and he had apologized. He also showed her his recovered satellite phone and she nodded her approval.

"Did you find anything out? I have a bit of news from my end," said Hannah.

"Not here," replied Dekker. "We need to get back to the hotel where we can begin to plan."

THE OPEN UPPER deck of the Partner Tut Hotel offered a welcome refuge for Dekker and Hannah. They had not spoken the entire return trip, each digesting what was learned and formulating how best to present facts. Now comfortably seated at a tent-covered corner table overlooking the Nile, drinks ordered and delivered, they were ready to begin.

"I will tell you what I learned from Walid, the man you set me to follow," said Hannah. Dekker gave a sweep of his hand, inviting her to continue. "When I caught up with him, he was already in a meeting of some sort at a cafe on the street at the end of a rear alley. I was able to get an adjacent table and listen, but the street noise and their low tones made hearing difficult. I did understand that Walid was dispatching the two others to Alexandria to meet with a similar group."

"That's good to know," said Dekker.

"There was one more thing: just before the group split up, Walid said something either I didn't hear right or I don't completely understand." Dekker raised an eyebrow in question. "He told the other men that someone named Nebwawi was traveling to England and they should begin coordinating with Germany and America."

This last bit of news caused Dekker to pause and consider. Hannah watched him with curiosity, wondering what it all meant. "That is a bit of news, Hannah. Thank you for following that man..."

"Walid," she said.

"Walid. I think you have put us on a new path. I went into the other room in the building and hid in a coat closet while the man inside finished some business. I found his cloak hanging there and discovered my sat phone, a welcome relief. I followed him to a meeting of twenty or so people. He was giving them instructions, and now I think you have helped me figure it out. It was all in Arabic, of course, so it was difficult for me to follow. The only clear thing I understood was a reference to Kamenwati, to which they all stood and raised their hands. It was a little spooky, like some kind of religious service." Dekker took a long sip of his Scotch. "What you found out, a connection between England, Germany, and America, is significant."

"How so?" Hannah asked.

"These are the three countries with the largest concentrations of Abaddon Brotherhood groups. I don't think there's any question Kamenwati is trying to re-establish that network."

"But for what?" Hannah asked.

"The drone strike was just the first test, and maybe a demonstration that Abaddon has power we cannot match or defeat."

"Why England, Germany, and America?" Hannah asked.

"Lord Geoffrey was in England, Krugerschloss, Abaddon's headquarters, is in Germany, and the United States...Well, there was a group in Washington led by someone named Origen, but there may be a greater reason than just the existence of a group of supporters there." He thought for a moment and struck on the reason. "Of course, that's where UAV operations are located. Kamenwati wants to reestablish the network, but his focus will be on America."

Dekker looked directly at Hannah. "Abaddon plans to start a war, a world war that will have no winners."

"Except Kamenwati," said Hannah.

"Exactly."

"How on earth do we prevent that?"

"We have to find a way to neutralize their command structure and stop Kamenwati before he can expand his reach. We're going to need some help from both our governments. I just hope they will listen."

CHAPTER SIXTEEN

DENNIS WATCHED WITH FASCINATION WHILE Dr. Rimmer assembled an odd looking contraption. It was a tent-like structure built over a shoe box. It looked like an architectural model. Rimmer took deliberate care with every move, stopping regularly to verify some point or other, humming to himself as he worked. Dennis walked around the small model, his own curiosity getting the better of him.

"What in the world is this?" Rimmer looked up from his work and removed a pair of magnifying goggles, the sort worn by jewelers.

"This is a scale model of an EMF deflection tent. Can't you tell?"

"To tell the truth, it looks like a gauze teepee over a shoebox." Rimmer responded with a laugh.

"This is just a first concept, Dennis. The idea is based on a Faraday cage, and the actual device will be on a much larger scale. I'm trying to isolate the specific frequency being used in this drone business, and with a properly constructed EMF tent, neutralize the frequency."

"I've seen Faraday cages in science and technology museums, and from what I remember, the cage shields an occupant from electric currents."

"That is almost right, Dennis, and it points to this particular experiment. We don't need to shield someone from a full spectrum EMF attack, only a very narrow range. I am wrestling with two problems: first, designing a mesh of an appropriate gauge to 'capture' and deflect a 4.9 Hz wave, and then, finding a way to protect an entire building."

"So you are thinking some sort of tent structure like this?" Dennis gestured to the model. "That's impractical."

"You're right, but for the moment, this structure helps narrow down the specific wave interval, which I have determined is 204.081632653 milliseconds. With that we can devise an electromagnetic umbrella."

"I'm getting the vibe there's more," said Dennis.

Rimmer reached out and touched the tip of one end of the tent he had so carefully built. "This line of investigation will give us a defensive tool, one I believe we can implement quickly. What concerns me is our need not only for defense but offense as well."

"What about sonic weapons? I've seen pictures of those mounted on trucks and tanks."

"That is a possibility, but those weapons are essentially huge microwave machines and that is not what we need. My experiment proves the signal has a length of 204.081632653 milliseconds."

"So now you just need to work up a design to cover an entire building in Ft. Bragg." Dennis gave a hopeful grin.

"Give me a little privacy and I will design something that will work."

"In other words, get lost," said Dennis, crestfallen.

Rimmer gave the young man an understanding look and returned to his model as Dennis walked back to the main house.

MORNING WAS BREAKING with a vivid orange glow painted across the high clouds over the mountains of northern New Mexico. The warm morning light was just coming through the rear patio doors as Dennis moved around the kitchen, searching for coffee and wondering if Dr. Rimmer had gone to bed the previous evening.

After leaving the small outbuilding serving as Rimmer's laboratory, Dennis could do nothing but wait for the physicist, finally deciding it was a good opportunity to catch up on some reading. After placing his laptop on the dining room table, he quickly brought up several technical articles he had saved. "I guess this is the time," he said, and immersed himself in articles. Hours later he made a simple dinner, a sandwich and tortilla chips. He wondered how Rimmer was doing , wondered *what* he was doing. Finally giving up, Dennis headed to the guest room for the night.

In the morning, a cup of coffee in hand, he went out the glass doors onto the rear patio to watch the brightening sky and enjoy the quiet beauty of the mountains. The stillness was broken when the door to the outbuilding opened, spilling light outward. A slightly disheveled Horace Rimmer came toward the house. "Dennis! I didn't expect you to be about this early, but this is timely." Rimmer sat in a comfortable patio chair next to Dennis. He looked up to the sky and sighed. "I never tire of the beauty in these mountains. It truly refreshes the soul." Dennis nodded agreement and sipped his coffee. Rimmer redirected his attention to the papers in his hand. Dennis noted they were covered with scientific calculations, lots of $\sum$ symbols and algebraic formulae.

"I believe we have at least the defensive part of our solution. Look." Rimmer offered the papers for Dennis' inspection.

"Impressive," said Dennis, having no idea what he was being shown.

"It's a simple and elegant solution: a tall transmission tower built on the roof of a facility with downward focused EM radiation points connecting to plates on the ground around the building. Can you see the beauty of this design? It may be scaled to any size building, so long as the tower is high enough and the ground discs are in clear view around the building."

"This is an umbrella?" Dennis, shaking his head, looked again at the dense calculations.

"Let me simplify it." Rimmer turned one of the sheets over and began drawing a simple picture. "Here is the building, and this is a tower. We place metallic discs about one foot in diameter around the building." He drew little dots around the building. "The tower emits a very specific signal, 204.081632653 milliseconds, downward to the ground reflectors. The resulting resonance loop creates a covering grid that will shield everyone and everything inside its field."

Dennis was impressed. "This is wonderful! We have to get this to Ft. Bragg right away."

"This only solves one problem, Dennis. You take this to them, but I want to continue to work on the offensive side of this problem after some rest."

"I am such a dummy. You've been working all night. Go to bed and get some sleep, and then I think we should both go to North Carolina." Rimmer was reluctant, but in the end gave in and agreed to travel to Ft. Bragg.

THE FLIGHT TO Atlanta went quickly for Dennis because he spent most of the time on his cell phone. Rimmer spent the flight writing, calculating, and drawing. Dennis began with a call to NCTC headquarters to give Jim Lynch a briefing. He told Lynch about Dr. Rimmer's solution and that he needed some help getting into Ft. Bragg. Lynch was pleased with the progress and promised Dennis special transportation would be waiting when he landed at Hartsfield-Jackson airport. "I'll also call the base commander at Ft. Bragg and have the appropriate people waiting to receive you both." Dennis thanked his boss and ended the call.

The next call was to Dr. Goddard, the Navy physicist who set him on the path to New Mexico. After going through two automated telephone menus and as many administrative assistants, he was finally connected.

"Dr. Goddard, this is Dennis Allende. You remember, the Schumann Resonances?"

"Of course I remember. Did you have any luck finding Dr. Rimmer?"

"More than luck finding him. In fact, I've spent the last couple of days with him working on a solution."

"Wonderful. Did you make any headway?"

"As a matter of fact, we did, and as we speak he and I are heading to Ft. Bragg to meet with their operations people." Dennis went on to outline Rimmer's approach to the problem and how he tested the theories, finishing with a description of the design that Rimmer had indicated could be implemented right away.

"Dr. Rimmer expressed this as two problems. First, we need a device to defend against the brainwave frequency and what he called an infratonic used to control the minds of the drone operators and their machines."

"And the second problem?" Goddard asked.

"He said a defense was not enough, that we need to develop an offensive weapon as well."

"And you thought of me..."

"Yes, sir, I did. May I send you a secure fax when I arrive at Ft. Bragg?" Goddard gave his approval and told Dennis he would await the fax.

When their flight landed in Atlanta, a uniformed enlisted man met Dennis and Rimmer at the gate and escorted them down a stairway to the tarmac and a waiting car. Both Rimmer and Dennis were impressed with the VIP treatment and thanked the young enlisted man as they took a seat in the rear of the car. They never left the airport complex. Instead they drove to a remote area reserved for military flights. The enlisted man parked the government car next to a Gulfstream G150, a small jet but still capable of traveling at .85 Mach. "I guess they want us there in a hurry," Dennis said. Another uniformed attendant met them at the top of the stairs leading into the cabin. The attendant nodded and gestured for them to take a seat wherever they liked in the oval-shaped cabin. "This is much more comfortable than the flight we were just on," Rimmer said.

The jet covered the three hundred twenty mile flight in half an hour, prompting Dennis to remark, "I was just getting settled and we have to land!" The aircraft taxied to a small hangar at Pope Field where another car was waiting. Dennis thanked the attendant, and again he and Rimmer climbed into the rear seat. The driver then drove the car quickly across the airfield, stopping in front of a building with no distinguishing signage. "Is this the place?" Dennis asked.

"They are waiting inside, sir," replied the driver.

As Dennis and Rimmer stepped out of the car, another vehicle came to a stop behind their ride. There was a small flag mounted next to the headlight indicating the car carried a flag officer. Dennis looked on with interest as the officer stepped out of the rear, his uniform immaculate and his left breast covered with ribbons. The officer spotted the civilian pair and stepped over to them, introducing himself. "Mr. Allende? Dr. Rimmer? I am General Nelson Redmond. My team is waiting inside."

Together they stepped through the double glass doors into a modest reception area where an enlisted man immediately stood behind a counter and snapped to attention. He then directed the general to a door on the right. The general swept by the reception attendant almost without noticing him, and Dennis felt he and Rimmer were being dragged along in the general's wake.

The half dozen people in the conference room stood as the general entered and took what Dennis assumed was his customary place in the center seat on the long side of the rectangular table. "Take seats," said General Redmond, which was followed by a simultaneous seating of the group. Dennis and Rimmer were left standing but then they spotted empty chairs and sat at one end of the table.

"This is Mr. Dennis Allende from NCTC in Washington," the general said as he gestured toward Dennis, "and Dr. Horace Rimmer, now retired from Los Alamos Laboratories." Looking to his two guests he continued. "I won't take time for individual introductions around the table. Instead we will hear your presentation and discuss the next steps."

Dennis swallowed and looked around the group. They were mostly men, but there was one woman. Half were in uniform and half in civilian clothes. The uniformed officers were younger, perhaps late thirties or early forties; and the civilians were older, easily in their fifties. All of them were now looking expectantly at Dennis, who felt like a specimen under a microscope, and Rimmer.

"Thank you, General. We have brought you designs with back up formulae and calculations for what we believe will create an electromagnetic shield around your UAV control center." Hopeful looks went around the room. Dennis was seated next to an audio-visual console that included video feeding a large screen mounted on the wall behind him. He began by displaying Rimmer's hand-drawn illustration and looked to the physicist to continue the briefing.

"This is a rough representation of the concept," Rimmer began. "You can see this tower mounted on the roof the height will be determined by both the size and configuration of this building and an emitter on top. This bipolar device operates on a very specific frequency, roughly

4.9 Hz. Its focused energy is coupled with titanium plates on the ground, indicated here by these small circles, and a circuit is created from the emitter to the plates and back to the emitter."

A murmur passed through the room while the general sat still, his fingers tented beneath his chin. "This device will neutralize the effects we have seen?"

Dennis nodded vigorously as Rimmer responded. "Yes, this uses the Faraday principles, somewhat modified but the effect is the same. Let me show you." He replaced the projected drawing with the first page of his calculations, allowing the group to read through it. Dennis didn't understand half of it, but the rest of this group clearly did. After a time Rimmer began changing the displayed pages until he reached the end. There were nods of understanding and a couple of side conversations that continued until the general spoke up. "Dr. Baines, do you have comments?"

"General, this seems well thought out and it operates within established electromagnetic principles." Baines looked to the others who nodded their agreement. "I believe we can build this device in, what, Dr. Eddington, a week?"

Dr. Joanna Eddington, the only female in the group, nodded. "Yes, Dr. Baines, a week. Perhaps less, depending on the availability of materials."

General Redmond nodded his approval. "I want the list of materials on my desk within the hour, and Dr. Rimmer, will you provide the specifications to everyone?"

"Of course, General," replied Rimmer.

The general stood, followed by the rising of the six staff members in unison. Dennis and Rimmer again lagged behind. Once the general left the room, everyone sat down and turned their attention back to the two outsiders. "Well, Mr. Allende, Dr. Rimmer, let's get to it. The general wants a list within the hour," Dr. Baines said.

Dennis discovered the group included physicists, engineers, and a supply officer, each pouring through the information and arguing among themselves as to the best solution to one aspect of the tower or another. Dr. Rimmer chimed in when necessary, and they soon had a list of materials as well as a more detailed tower design, complete with new technical drawings made by one of the officers using a CAD program on his laptop.

Rimmer was confident the new device would work as predicted and he and Dennis excused themselves. Dennis left his contact information with Dr. Baines and headed for Washington and the NCTC.

CHAPTER SEVENTEEN

GALDUR'S DISQUIET ABOUT DEKKER'S SITUATION
only increased over the intervening days. There had been no
communication from his friend, and that was not good. He
decided to contact Salim once again. Making himself
comfortable in the old living room chair, Galdur slipped into
the familiar trance that was the gateway to the Flows. His call
was heard, and Salim greeted his old friend.

Greetings, Galdur.

Greetings, Salim.

*I sense your disquiet, Galdur, and I perceive it emanates
from a concern for Dekker.*

*There has been no contact in many days, Salim. Do you
know where he is?*

Dekker is in Egypt. He escaped an ordeal and has maintained a low profile on the Flows since that time.

Is there reason for concern? A long silence followed and Galdur wondered if the connection with Salim was lost.

Dekker has become involved with forces he is ill-equipped to control. Since our last communication I have looked into the possibility that the Abaddon spirit has take up residence in Kamenwati. It is now confirmed, and the spirit has introduced an entirely new use of the Flows, one which gives it, and Kamenwati, a new ability to control the actions of men and their machines.

It was Galdur's turn to be silent as he pondered the implications of what Salim revealed.

This is terrible! It is a violation of everything the Brotherhood believes and has practiced for thousands of years. How can the Flows be used to control an inanimate machine? It seems anathema to me.

Galdur, as you know, the Flows are a neutral force in this world, neither good nor bad. But the history of our Brotherhood is full of instances of single practitioners, or sometimes an entire group, debasing the power and using the Flows in a misguided effort to change or control societies. How Kamenwati is doing this, I do not yet know, but the implications of his reaching into and controlling modern technology is disquieting.

I should say it is! What can be done?

We must mount an offensive on two fronts: against Kamenwati and against the spirit leading him. I would like you to address the problem of the Egyptian while I attend to the ancient spirit we have battled for so long.

I will do it, Salim.

Craft your strategy well, Galdur. You know Kamenwati is a highly skilled deep practitioner. He will detect your presence, so you must find another way.

Galdur severed the connection and considered Salim's warning, fear for his American friend now greater. How could he get inside Kamenwati's spiritual stronghold without detection? A direct assault would not work. He would be discovered before he ever began, and probably lose his life. As he thought about his dilemma a strategy began to take shape. "What if I could join with an associate, someone close to Kamenwati? Step number one is to find that person, and perhaps Dekker holds the key." He went back into the Flows, this time gently calling for Dekker.

DEKKER REMAINED ON the upper deck of the Partner Tut Hotel when Hannah retired for the evening. He was working on the next move, including considering sending Hannah back to England to follow that lead while he focused his attention at home. The only problem was in Germany, Krugerschloss, and he wasn't sure how to deal with that location.

As he wrestled with the dilemma, he felt a familiar tug in his consciousness that came from the Flows. Looking around for anyone who might witness what he was about to do, he saw only one other patron at that hour, and he was on the other end of the deck. Sitting back in his chair, Dekker slipped into the trancelike state and entered the Flows to connect with Galdur.

My friend, I was concerned when we lost contact.

My apologies, Galdur, but it seemed best to stay off the Flows. Things have been tense these last few days.

I have been in communication with Salim who told me you are still in Egypt.

Yes, that is true.

I need to warn you of danger and offer my assistance. Salim and I have come to realize that the Abaddon spirit is now inhabiting Kamenwati and has somehow given him control over drone operators and their machines. To what end is not yet clear.

I may have some answers. Hannah Ahmed, my SIS partner, and I followed a complicated trail from the original UAV strike site in the Sinai. We were tracked and a second drone was deployed targeting us. We managed to escape but were buried alive in an ancient tomb. We managed to escape and found our way to Asyut, a city on the Nile.

That must be the ordeal Salim referred to.

It was an ordeal. We discovered a resurgent faction here in Asyut, not the Brotherhood exactly but one loyal to Kamenwati. He is the one commandeering the drones and is now trying to establish his authority among scattered Brotherhood groups in Germany, England, and the United States. I believe his end game is to start a war between East and West, leaving both defenseless and at his mercy.

That is a bit of news, Adam, but let me warn you: Kamenwati is dangerous in ways the previous Abaddon host was not. His deep knowledge of Magick gives him a new set of abilities, including controlling machines.

I understand, Galdur, and I agree. Kamenwati is an entirely new type of adversary.

Yes, and I wish to help. You cannot face him alone, if at all. Even I cannot attack him directly. Instead I must use an unexpected method.

What are you thinking?

You mentioned three countries in which he is trying to reach Brotherhood members, and I assume that means he has sent close lieutenants to all three...

Yes, and I was just formulating a plan. I will go to the United States and send Hannah back to England, but I don't know how to cover Germany.

I don't think you need to spread your resources, Adam. If you and your British partner can get close to one of those lieutenants, I can use him to infiltrate Kamenwati's group. Once on the inside, I can alter things just a bit, at least enough to tilt the scales in your favor.

Will I need to be here in Egypt? I don't know Kamenwati's exact location.

That is not important, Adam. Find Kamenwati's man. That is the first challenge.

And after I locate him?

Notify me at once. I will come to you. As a matter of fact, I will leave for America tomorrow. Meanwhile, you will have to find a way to stop his part of the plan. I will work toward the same goal using Magick to stop Kamenwati.

Dekker was satisfied with Galdur's plan and disengaged. He went down to the front desk and asked about the morning train to Cairo. The desk clerk took a well-worn booklet from below the counter and thumbed through it.

"Yes, sir. Train number 991 leaves tomorrow morning at 7:40, and arrives Cairo at 1:30 in the afternoon. Would you like to book that train?"

"That will be perfect," said Dekker. "Make reservations for two people."

A telephone call was followed by an entry on a computer, and the reservation was made. "Will you want to put the charge on your room?"

"Please do. I don't suppose you can make a flight reservation from here, can you?"

"Yes, I can." The helpful clerk made a new entry on the computer and found a flight to New York. "It looks like a Lufthansa flight at 3:55 in the morning still has seats available. It is a fifteen and a half hourflight."

"That's 3:55 the day after tomorrow?"

"Yes, sir. Shall I make your reservations?"

"Yes. Business class."

Satisfied with his planning, Dekker thought about calling Hannah but stopped before dialing. "Let her sleep. I can tell her about these new plans over breakfast."

DESPITE THE LONG day and going to bed late, Dekker was up early. He waited until six o'clock to call Hannah's room and found she was already up and making telephone calls.

"I've been on the line with SIS, inquiring about your Lord Geoffrey."

"Hannah, I know we discussed dividing up last night, but after you left I had a message from my Icelandic friend, Galdur. We've got a new plan now. We are catching the 7:40 train to Cairo." Hannah was silent for a moment.

"I imagine it will be a good idea to pack my things then."

"Let's meet for a quick breakfast in, say, twenty minutes."

They hung up and Dekker collected his suitcase and carry-on bag. Twenty minutes later Hannah joined him in the restaurant.

"Right on time," said Dekker as he checked his watch. Hannah nodded and sat opposite her American partner.

A waiter offered Hannah a menu. She didn't open it but instead ordered toast, jam, and tea. The waiter dutifully made note and disappeared.

"Now, Dekker, what's all this about a train?"

"The more Galdur and I conversed, the greater my belief that Kamenwati's main objective is the drone operations center at Pope Field, part of Ft. Bragg in North Carolina. We know Kamenwati dispatched three lieutenants to consolidate the scattered Brotherhood groups in Germany, England, and America, and Galdur suggested I concentrate on the man sent to the United States because he is closest to the drones. Galdur's plan is twofold: we identify the man so Galdur can mount a 'backdoor' attack on Kamenwati, and meanwhile we focus on protecting the drone center from any more incursions." He reached into his soft messenger bag and pulled out travel documents. "There was no time to waste, so I made arrangements for this morning's train to Cairo. Once there we'll take a Lufthansa flight to New York and then on to Washington to meet with my people at the NCTC."

Hannah's response was one of acceptance, which surprised Dekker. He expected questioning and resistance. He was learning Hannah was not like other women, a quality he appreciated.

After checking out of the Partner Tut Hotel, taking a taxi to the train depot, and finding their train, Dekker sat heavily in his seat. "I'm still bushed after yesterday, and I was up late and early." He looked around the private cabin and put his long legs up on the facing seat. "Hope you don't mind, Hannah, but we've got about five hours on this train and I intend to spend most of it asleep."

"That is fine, but would you mind moving to the seats closest to the window? I don't want to have to climb over your legs when I want to stretch mine." Dekker switched places with her and handed the tickets to Hannah. "I'll let you handle our business with the conductor when he comes around." Hannah took the tickets and laid them beside her. She looked at Dekker. "Sweet dreams."

The time passed quickly for Dekker, if not for Hannah. After sitting next to her sleeping partner for an hour she decided to find the service area on the train. Her query to one of the conductors led her to a self-service snack lounge with small tables and chairs lined against the windows. She purchased a Cairo newspaper and a tea, and she settled in to read, happy to have a distraction.

Forty-five minutes before their arrival in Cairo, Hannah returned to the cabin and found Dekker much as she left him. She looked at him, once again admiring his dark good looks and fit physique. "I can feel you looking at me, Hannah," said Dekker, his eyes still closed and his position unchanged.

"I was trying to decide if I should disturb you," she said, startled and a little embarrassed to have been caught staring. "We're about forty-five minutes outside Cairo station."

Dekker pulled his feet off the opposite seat and sat up straight, stretching his arms behind his head and twisting his torso. "You're right. It is time to wake up. Say, you didn't bring a cup of coffee, did you?"

"Sorry, you'll have to wait until we arrive."

"We're going to have some time to kill. Our flight doesn't leave until three fifty-five in the morning. I guess we should be at the airport around two."

"In that case, I suggest we do some sightseeing," said Hannah. "Do you have any preferences? The pyramids, museums, or the market?"

"I'm hungry. Let's start at a restaurant and decide from there."

THE AFTERNOON PASSED quickly, first at a wonderful local restaurant recommended by Hannah and then on a trip to the Cairo Museum. Now on the Lufthansa flight, Dekker considered what they were getting into. He shrugged and sipped on the flute of champagne given him by the flight attendant. "I guess whatever we're getting into, at least there'll be backup."

Hannah looked at her partner with a questioning look. Dekker gave a small laugh and put the glass of champagne down. "I was just thinking that I've had three encounters with these people and I am wondering how long my luck can hold out."

"Well, you've got about twelve hours before landing to figure out your odds."

"You're a big help."

"I believe luck favors the prepared and the vigilant."

Dekker looked into her blue eyes and saw the conviction there. "You're right, and since we have so much time and a seemingly inexhaustible supply of champagne, let me fill you in from the beginning." Dekker began with his first encounter with the Consortium and their plot to steal technology from Los Alamos Laboratories. He told her about Kelly, who became his wife.

He went on to recount his first direct encounter with Abaddon, derailing a plan to collapse the world's major currencies, and imprisoning him in a stasis. "Galdur called it a Merlin Box." He then told Hannah the stasis was broken by Kamenwati, an Egyptian mystic, and a rebooted plan was put into effect.

He talked again about Kelly, describing her murder at the hands of the brotherhood. Hannah saw how deeply hurt he was over his loss and placed her hand lightly over his, offering unspoken sympathy. He continued, finishing with the death of Abaddon and the disappearance of Kamenwati.

"I thought it was over, that Abaddon was gone from this world, but then this drone stealing episode occurred and I knew it was the same force at work."

The flight attendant delivered breakfast and Dekker realized he talked through the night. "How long until we land?"

"About ninety minutes, sir. Would you like coffee?" Dekker nodded. "And you, ma'm? Would you like coffee as well?" Hannah thanked the flight attendant and gratefully accepted the steaming cup of coffee.

"That is quite a story, and I think I understand now. And through all this you met this Icelander you keep talking about?"

"Yes, and he has proven to be a good friend as has the retired physicist, Dr. Rimmer." Dekker looked out the window. "He is also Kelly's grandfather."

"So that explains your connection. He is more than an acquaintance; he's family." Dekker nodded again and dug into his breakfast.

"The food's been good, hasn't it?" Hannah recognized the change of subject and let it go. There would be plenty of time to figure out this strangely complex man in the days to come.

CHAPTER EIGHTEEN

DEKKER DROPPED HANNAH AT A hotel in Tyson's Corner near NCTC headquarters. He drove to his condo in nearby McLean, where he took a long overdue shower. He wanted to collapse into his bed and sleep, but he first needed to contact Galdur and tell him they had arrived in Washington. He sat on the living room couch, closed his eyes, and entered the light trance giving him access to the Flows. In moments he felt both the rush of the Flows and the calming sense of awareness that came from the experience.

He sent out a call to Galdur, and before long he was connected to the old Icelander.

Adam, how good to hear from you.

And it is good to connect with you, too, Galdur. I have news: Hannah and I have returned to the United States. We just arrived.

We are at the NCTC headquarters in McLean, where I think we need to begin looking for Kamenwati's man.

Very good. How do you want to proceed?

Since the DC area was the center of this group's activity, I am certain the lieutenant will come here for the first step to re-assemble the local cell. My guess is Kamenwati's man will begin at the old Consortium headquarters in Maryland.

Then I must come to you without delay. I am already in Reykjavik waiting for a flight to Washington. I will be there tomorrow.

I will meet you at Dulles.

Dekker broke off the communication, and before lying down he opened his laptop and found that Iceland Air flight #647 was scheduled to arrive at 12:45 PM. "Perfect. I can get some sleep and take Hannah with me to pick him up." He thought for a moment about this first meeting for Hannah and wondered if she would like Galdur. "I can't think about that now. First, sleep."

He slept through the night, waking the next morning at his typical six o'clock hour. He felt refreshed, if a little sore, but none the worse for wear. After a cup of coffee and breakfast, he was ready to take on the world once more. He waited until nine o'clock to call Hannah. Her telephone rang several times before she answered.

"Dekker! I wondered when you would surface. I was just showering." The mental image of Hannah in the shower caused his pulse to quicken.

"Good morning, Hannah. I trust you slept well."

"Yes, thank you. What is our plan for today?"

"I will pick you up at eleven thirty and we'll go out to Dulles."

"Another flight? If we must…"

"We are going to meet Galdur, who is arriving from Iceland."

"So I will finally get to meet the mysterious Icelander. I will be waiting for you at eleven thirty."

Dekker's next call was to the NCTC to get caught up on all the moving parts of this investigation. Jim Lynch picked up his phone almost immediately when Marilyn Stamm informed him Dekker was on the line.

"Dekker, I'm awfully glad to hear from you. Where are you, anyway?"

"Thanks Jim. As a matter of fact, I am here in McLean."

"Are you coming in? There's a lot happening here."

"I will be in, but first I have to pick up Galdur."

"He's coming in from Iceland? I got the impression he doesn't care much for travel."

"He doesn't, but this thing has him wound up and he volunteered to come. His flight gets in at 12:45, and I'm going to pick up Hannah before going."

"Your SIS contact?"

"That's right. She's deeply involved in this and I've read her into most of the background on Abaddon. I'll tell you more about it when we get there this afternoon, but first, can you give me an overview of what's happening?"

"Well, Dennis has been all over the country tracking down a brainwave theory he believes is the source of this problem; and as luck would have it, he ended up with Horace Rimmer."

"Horace? How does he figure into this?"

"A Navy physicist recommended Dr. Rimmer based on his long history of work with resonance theories." Dekker flashed to a memory of the abandoned range station, the battle between Consortium, Russian, and American special forces, and the spectacular implosion of Horace's gravity resonance machine. "Dennis returned just yesterday with Dr. Rimmer in tow."

"They are here? This is great news."

"It seems Dr. Rimmer came up with a shielding device that's being installed at the UAV facility in Ft. Bragg. But he wants to pursue an offensive angle, too."

"I will be eager to catch up with both of them. Send me back to Marilyn and I'll set up a meeting."

Dekker was transferred to Lynch's administrative assistant who was all too happy to arrange a meeting. "Set it for about two o'clock. That should give us time to collect up Galdur and get there."

"Adam, I'm glad you're back safe and sound. I heard about the adventure in the Egyptian wilderness."

"You mean the tomb? It was a little hairy being fired on by our own drone, but we made it out just fine."

"We...?"

"Hannah Ahmed, my SIS partner on this mission."

"Is she pretty?"

"Marilyn, you are a snoop. Yes, she is pretty, and smart and tough too."

"She sounds like a good match." Dekker had a moment of embarrassed silence before replying.

"Why is everyone so interested in my relationships? You, Jim, Dennis, even Horace..."

"We're just concerned, Adam, that's all."

"We'll discuss it when this is all over, okay?"

The call ended and Dekker stood in his condo, looking at his cell phone with bewilderment. He knew Marilyn and the others were looking out for him, and he appreciated the concern. "When this is all over," he said, returning the cell phone to his pocket.

DEKKER AND HANNAH stood in the waiting area outside Customs looking for Galdur. Hannah had no idea what he looked like, of course, but she craned her neck nonetheless, looking for an older man. She was surprised when Dekker walked up to a man who didn't look old at all. The man wore his white hair long and gathered at the back of his neck with a leather strap, his features weathered and tanned. After looking at him for a few moments Hannah saw the years and the wisdom those features represented. The man wrapped his arms around Dekker and kissed him loudly on both cheeks.

"A proper Icelandic greeting between old friends, Adam. It is good to see you again."

"And you, Galdur," replied Dekker.

To Hannah it looked more like a father greeting his son, and she wondered about the extent of the relationship. Her thoughts were interrupted when Galdur reached for her, holding both shoulders and nodding. "You are Hannah," he said, not as a question but as a statement of fact.

"Yes, I am." Hannah was taken by surprise when the Icelander encircled her with his surprisingly strong arms, releasing her after a moment.

"Dekker, I approve of your new partner," said Galdur.

"You don't know how much that means to me," deadpanned Hannah.

"I'm sorry, Hannah. He gets a little enthusiastic," said Dekker.

"Especially with anyone close to Adam," said Galdur.

"Come on, Galdur. Let me take your bag. We're going to a meeting."

Forty-five minutes later they pulled into one of the parking lots surrounding NCTC. "This is most impressive, Adam," said Galdur. Hannah looked with wonder at the sprawling complex that was all but invisible from the highway. "Not at all like our SIS building, a huge monster sitting on the banks of the Thames."

"I suppose the NSA or CIA buildings could compete in that category," said Dekker with a laugh. He parked the car and they entered the building.

A pretty young woman sitting behind a long counter recognized Dekker and greeted him by name. He helped Galdur and Hannah sign in and acquire credentials, and then he led the way to an elevator that took them to the third floor.

Stepping off the elevator Hannah recognized the trappings of a high-ranking bureaucrat: open visitor waiting room with expensive furniture, artwork tastefully displayed on the walls, and a wall of glass providing an impressive view of the forested land surrounding the complex. A luxurious desk in the Louis XIV style, looking like it came from Versailles, sat before the large double doors leading to an inner office. Marilyn Stamm, sitting behind the desk, was about fifty and quite attractive in a tailored jacket worn over a soft white blouse with a matching skirt and jacket. She arose as they stepped off the elevator and beamed at Dekker. "We were all worried about you!" She stepped around the desk and gave Dekker a warm hug and then stood back. "You don't look any worse for the wear."

"Marilyn, this is Hannah Ahmed with British Intelligence." Marilyn shook Hannah's hand. "And this gentleman you know but only by reputation. He is Galdur, from Iceland."

"Galdur!" Marilyn's pleasure meeting the man Dekker, Lynch, and Dennis spoke about so often was obviously genuine and heartfelt. "How wonderful to finally meet you." Another set of doors set into the wall opposite Marilyn's desk opened and two men entered the room.

"Horace. Dennis. I'm glad to see you both," said Dekker. Hannah stood to the side as the pair surrounded Dekker, excitedly asking overlapping questions. Dekker looked at Hannah and stopped the welcoming committee. "Horace Rimmer and Dennis Allende, I would like to introduce Hannah Ahmed of the British Secret Service." The elder Dr. Rimmer and the youthful Dennis took turns shaking Hannah's hand and welcoming her to America. She was touched, not only by the greeting but by the sense of family existing between these people, a feeling she longed for.

Marilyn took charge of the group, heading them to a conference room. "I'll get Mr. Lynch," she said, closing the door behind them.

Sitting at one end of the rectangular conference table, each of them launched into broken accounts of their various activities. Making sense of it all was impossible for Hannah. She sat back quietly, offering an occasional *yes* or *no* to questions about her involvement in Dekker's adventure. They were interrupted by the entry of Jim Lynch, a slight man of medium height and nondescript brown hair, the perfect combination for a former CIA operative, nothing memorable or notable. He greeted Dekker and then introduced himself to Hannah. After a few pleasantries, Lynch began.

"This is a most unusual assembly of talent. Each of you has already helped identify both the source and the means of attack on Ft. Bragg, and I am grateful to you all. Dekker and Hannah, you have established Kamenwati as the source of the attacks, while Dr. Rimmer and Dennis developed a counter-measure for the brainwave frequency used in the attack. And Galdur, since Dekker has brought you here I can only assume the central issue here has, shall we say, a supernatural angle. It seems we are once again facing Abaddon." Everyone nodded except Hannah, who was still new to all this hocus-pocus business. While espionage and subterfuge were integral to her job, what Adam described to her during the long flight from Cairo seemed improbable, even unbelievable. There must be another explanation, she thought, but clearly all those around the table accepted this otherworldly version, even the Deputy Director of the NCTC. Hannah was bright enough to know there were strange things in this world, and so perhaps this business of Magick and Flows really did exist, but she would withhold an opinion until she saw more.

"Now," Lynch continued, "let's get a complete report from each of you, beginning with Dekker."

With all eyes on him, Dekker launched into a report on his movements, beginning in London at SIS headquarters and being introduced to Hannah. His story moved through the Sinai desert and following the suspicious group across the Nile. "I could feel the men ahead, but then lost them. I knew we were being tracked by another drone aircraft and we escaped into a canyon. There we discovered the entrance to an ancient tomb and took shelter just as our car was blown up by the drone."

Hannah interrupted with her episode following Walid and discovering that Kamenwati's other disciples were departing for Germany, England, and America.

Dekker finished, telling the group they changed plans and traveled to the United States as recommended by Galdur.

"Dennis, what about your efforts?" Lynch asked.

Dennis picked up the story, beginning with his meeting when Lynch offered an alternative theory for the mysterious attack on Ft. Bragg. His research revealed well established theories relating to brainwaves and the Schumann Resonances. Finding most literature on brainwave resonances led to the US Navy and their deep water investigations, he visited Dr. Herman Goddard who suggested finding Dr. Rimmer. "Of course, I knew right where to find Dr. Rimmer, and went to Los Alamos."

Rimmer picked up the narrative, telling how he isolated the specific brainwave frequency being employed. "And thanks to Dennis' volunteering to be a test subject, I designed a solution to mask a person or facility from such an attack."

Dennis jumped back in, telling the group they traveled to Ft. Bragg where they passed the research on, leaving it in the hands of General Redmond and his people. "We intended to go back to Connecticut but stopped here first to brief Mr.

Lynch. That's when he told us to stay put, that you, Dekker, were returning."

Lynch took the floor. "Very good, but there is still one aspect of this we need hear more about. Galdur, will you share with us what you know?" With a nod of his head, Galdur began.

"I have been consulting with Salim. You will remember him from our last adventure in Germany. He is the most senior of my order and the one who sits at the Flows point-of-origin in ancient Babylon. We suspected, and later confirmed, that Kamenwati is the new vessel for the Abaddon spirit, an ancient entity with designs to possess and control all men. When we realized Kamenwati had accepted the spirit, we became concerned for Dekker. It was, after all, Adam who was responsible for defeating that spirit." Hannah looked quizzically at Dekker, once again surprised. "I contacted Dekker," Galdur said, nodding in Adam's direction, "and suggested he focus his attention on America for this it is where Kamenwati will make his push toward world war and where he must be stopped."

Lynch leaned forward. "Won't Dr. Rimmer's electronic umbrella stop this man, Galdur?"

"I fear not. I believe that only through the use of Magick and the Flows can he be stopped. We must find Kamenwati's envoy. I will insinuate myself into his mind and strike Kamenwati where he is not expecting."

Dekker spoke up. "Wouldn't Kamenwati be more off balance and less vigilant if he were lured from his hideaway? Can we get him to come here?"

"That is an excellent suggestion, Adam." Galdur tented his hands before him, contemplating the question. "This plan requires subtly and a soft touch, and if we can get him to America, away from his center of power, we stand a better chance of stopping him."

Jim Lynch stood and gathered the papers before him. "Good. We have the beginning of a plan." He looked at each member of the team. "It sounds like the first task is finding this envoy. Dekker, keep me informed of progress." Dekker nodded his understanding and watched Lynch leave the conference room.

WHEN THE CONFERENCE room door closed, everyone's attention turned to Dekker. "It seems we have to accomplish three things in the short term. First, we need to find Kamenwati's emissary. Dennis, would you check with Immigration at every airport with flights from Cairo?" Nodding his head, Dennis began tapping on his laptop. "What Dennis finds out will determine our next steps." Dekker turned to Rimmer with a question. "Horace, can you find out how much progress they've made at Ft. Bragg?"

"Of course, but there's more I need to do."

"What is that?"

"The electronic cover I've designed for the Ft. Bragg building is defensive, and sooner or later it will be penetrated. I want to confer with the Navy scientists in New London to discuss an offensive solution." Dekker hadn't considered this idea, and it was apparent Galdur had not examined the idea either. "Find out about Ft. Bragg, then you can pursue this other thing." He stopped for a moment before speaking. "And when you go to Connecticut, I would like Hannah to go with you."

"Dekker! What do you mean?" Hannah was caught off guard by Dekker's directive.

"There is danger in every aspect of this operation, Hannah, and you are the only other trained agent in this group. I want you there to look out for Horace. I don't know that anything is going to happen, but if it does I want you there." The British agent accepted Dekker's reasoning.

"When Dennis finishes his research, I will take him with me and track down our mystery man. Meanwhile, Galdur you have to convince Kamenwati he needs to come here, and we have to find a way to neutralize him."

"I understand, Adam, but first we need to identify the disciple," said Galdur.

"We may be onto something here," announced Dennis, beaming as he looked up from the laptop. "There are only a few flights from Cairo: the Lufthansa flight you were on, Dekker, and a couple of EgyptAir flights. The manifests for those flights list mostly families and couples, and our guy was flying solo. I checked through the Immigration logs and found there were only six individuals traveling alone, and two of them were women. That leaves us four men to track down."

"Who are they? Where are they?" Dekker asked.

"Whoa. Hold on a moment. I've only just filtered the information. Give me a little more time to trace them and we can get started."

"Is there a telephone I may use?" Rimmer looked around questioningly. "I should give General Redmond a call."

"Of course," said Dekker. "If you go over to the shelf on that wall, you'll find a drawer underneath, and in it is a telephone." Rimmer went to the back of the room, found the telephone, and dialed.

Forty minutes later Rimmer hung up and returned to his seat at the conference table. "They are highly motivated at Ft. Bragg. It seems they have completed installation of the transmission tower on the roof and placement of the refracting discs around the building. The general tells me they tested it two hours ago, and it seems to be working."

"That's a relief," said Dekker. "At least they have some protection. Now, on to Kamenwati's man."

Dennis held up a hand, his index finger extended, signaling everyone to wait. He tapped furiously on the keyboard and then stopped, pushing his chair back several inches. "I believe I've found our man."

"What's his name?" Dekker asked.

"Rahotep," said Dennis.

"Is that it? No first name?"

"That's it, and it's what caught my attention. First, the ancient Egyptian name. I looked it up and it's from the third dynasty and I thought, who would have such a name?"

"One of Kamenwati's 'true Egyptians' I expect," said Hannah.

"That's how I interpreted it. He landed a week ago at Dulles, and the document he filled out for Immigration indicates he is staying at an address in Maryland."

"How convenient," said Dekker. "Let me guess. It's that big old house of Origen's."

"Yep, it is, and I looked into property deeds in Maryland and can't find record of a transfer of that property to the government or anyone else."

"Typical bureaucratic snafu. It's either on the bottom of some clerk's to-do list or they overlooked it entirely. Once Origen was out of the picture they cleared the house out."

"I guess it's worth taking a look, don't you?" Dennis was excited.

"Hold on, Dennis. We can't go in there guns blazing, so to speak. We need to do some reconnoitering and observation."

"Adam is right," said Galdur. "We must take care not to give ourselves away. It is important this Rahotep have no knowledge of us or any sense we are about."

Dekker continued. "Have you considered he may have moved on from that Maryland address? He probably had contacts here among the old Consortium people, and he would waste no time getting to North Carolina."

"All the more reason to get out there," said Dennis.

"You're right. So here is where we part company again. Horace, you and Hannah head to New London. Dennis, you stay here with Galdur and get things ready to go the moment I give the signal, and I'll check out the manor house."

CHAPTER NINETEEN

THE DRIVE FROM MCLEAN TO Patuxent River Road in Maryland is a distance of about forty miles, but traffic on the Beltway and I-595 extended it to more than an hour. It was the first time Dekker had returned to the site of his kidnapping, and some of the memories of that ordeal were dim due to the drugs they used. "Scopolamine," he muttered, shaking his head as he remembered the effects of the so-called zombie drug.

He turned down Patuxent River Road, remembering scattered images from his departure more than a year before. The images played out like a slide show rather than a movie: still images at odd angles, faces and trees and houses. It seemed a long drive out, even at the speed they must have been traveling, yet this trip was not so long at all, perhaps one mile. The road came to a dead end at the manor house. Dekker pulled up in front of the main entrance and looked at the house where he began what was supposed to be a trip to his death at the hands of Abaddon.

Dekker mounted the wide stairway leading to the balcony-covered front door. Before trying the door he went to the window on the left and looked in. "No movement," he said and tried the door. It was locked. He walked back down the stairs and turned right, going around the side of the house where he remembered a portico. He had flashes of memory, now of his escape from the limousine and stumbling into the woods where he met Rusty Strickland. He couldn't remember exactly what happened, but he was recaptured and driven away. Closing his eyes tightly, Dekker returned to the present and inspected the portico entrance to the house. The door was unlocked, and he entered.

It was quiet inside, and he stopped to sense if others were in the house. It seemed empty. No, almost empty. He felt a presence, a single person, in the rear of the house. Dekker moved down the rear hall with a stealth that was second nature to him, stopping just before reaching what he recalled was the security office. Pressing himself against the wall, he looked around the door frame and saw someone seated in a chair, feet up on what had been the control console and reading a book, a graphic novel. It was a young man. Moving swiftly Dekker grabbed the man from behind and lifted him backward, over the chair.

Sammy had been minding his own business when out of nowhere he was grabbed, finding himself in a chokehold and struggling for his life. The man holding him was big and strong. He couldn't fight him and soon stopped struggling. The man loosed his arm around Sammy's throat, simultaneously pulling a gun and holding it to his head.

"You're going to talk," said the man, as yet unseen by Sammy. "If you don't, I will put a bullet in your head." Sammy was terrified and could not speak.

The man shoved Sammy back into the chair and his eyes went wide with recognition. "You! I remember you, the guy who got by our security, the guy we drugged and stuck into the hall closet. Your name is Dekker."

"It is so nice to be remembered," said Dekker, the composite weapon never wavering. "I want to know what you are doing here."

Regaining some of his composure, Sammy looked curiously at the pistol pointed at him. "What kind of gun is that?"

"Never mind that. What are you doing here?"

"I'm just watching the place. Honest."

"Who else is here?"

"No one, I swear, at least not now. I mean, there was an Egyptian guy and he had me find some of the old staff."

"This Egyptian, what is his name?"

"It's like a Pharaoh's name, Ra something."

"You can do better than that." Dekker moved aggressively close to Sammy.

"Rahotep! That's it. Rahotep."

"Good boy. Now how many colleagues did you manage to bring here?"

"There were four, five including me."

"What were they doing? What was their plan?"

"I'm not exactly sure. They talked a lot about flows and someone else that was going to take control. I'm not sure of what. All I heard was this other person was going to control something."

"Where did Rahotep and the others go?"

"North Carolina. I don't know exactly where. They never said."

"When did they leave?"

"Yesterday. They left yesterday."

Dekker let loose the grip he had on Sammy's shirt and stood back, pointing the composite weapon upward. He looked closely at Sammy. "Why did Rahotep leave you here?"

"I dunno. He just said I should stay here and wait for them to return."

"I'll tell you what. You are going to leave here and never come back."

"What about the others coming back?"

"Don't worry about them. I'll be their welcoming committee."

Sammy needed no more encouragement and quickly gathered his graphic novel and cell phone. He almost ran out of the house, muttering under his breath, "Ain't gonna have no more to do with this Consortium stuff." He disappeared down the road and into obscurity.

Dekker paid no more attention to Sammy's retreating figure and sat in one of the front porch rocking chairs. He used his cell phone to call Dennis. "Dennis, I'm at Origen's place and found it occupied."

"Is everything okay?"

"Yes. The guy's gone, but I have some important information for Galdur."

"Let me put you on speaker." There was some rustling and a click. "Okay, you can go ahead."

"Galdur, I just rousted a young guard from the Origen house. He told me an Egyptian named Rahotep was here. He also said he had collected four of Origen's men and they all left yesterday for North Carolina."

"That is good, Adam. We now know who the disciple is and where he is going."

"This is moving faster than I expected," said Dekker. "Whatever you plan to do, you'd better begin. I'm going to return right away."

RAHOTEP WAS NOT considered a deep practitioner of Magick, and his skills were limited, but they did include knowledge of the Flows. His leader and teacher, Kamenwati, instructed him in the basics of communicating through the medium. He sat cross-legged on the floor in the small motel room, his eyes closed, concentrating on the spot within himself he was taught to seek. It took time, but he was finally swept into the Flows. Keeping himself out of the main stream. His teacher warned him he would be swept away if he ever fully entered in. He inexpertly called out. He sat patiently waiting for Kamenwati to respond, and after ten minutes came the reply.

My worthy Rahotep, report on your progress.

Teacher, I used the list you gave me and assembled a small group of men who are ready to do your bidding.

You have done well, Rahotep.

Teacher, when will you strike the Americans again?

This very day, Rahotep. Prepare and observe.

Do we stay where we are?

No. I want you closer to the drone operations. Find a new location. It will be easier to focus my power when you are close.

The communication ended, and Rahotep went to the single window in the motel room and pulled the shades aside. He gazed outside. "Today you will again feel my master's power."

HIS COMMUNICATION CONCLUDED, Kamenwati's thoughts turned to England. He was not happy with Nebwawi. His disciple was having difficulty locating Brotherhood followers. There were many Druids, Fairy and

Forest worshippers, and Satanists, but those who followed Lord Geoffrey and the Brotherhood were nowhere to be found. Kamenwati had to acknowledge the Brotherhood in England was dissolved and members were passing into other beliefs, and it would require a great deal of effort, his personal effort, to resurrect the organization. Contacting Nebwawi, he instructed him to temporarily abandon the search for local followers and concentrate instead on locating British drone centers.

Despite the setback in England, in America Rahotep delivered good news. Kamenwati would use Rahotep's proximity to amplify his newfound power. Settling into the soft floor cushion, he quickly entered the Flows, and as before he sought the Abaddon spirit for assistance.

You do well to contact me, Kamenwati. You recognize this power does not flow from you but from me.

Yes, Master, I do know that. I am ready to strike the Americans again and I wish to know your will on the target.

You will take control of two operators. Send one drone aircraft to Incirlik Air Base in Turkey and another to the Bundestag in Berlin.

Why these places, Master?

The air base in Turkey will widen understanding that neither side of the Islamic conflict is beyond my reach. It is also home to American air forces.

And Berlin, Master?

Berlin is the heart of the European Union and the home of the German Parliament and key to all of Europe.

I understand and will obey.

Kamenwati waited one day for Rahotep to be in place at Ft. Bragg before reaching out to the drone operators. Concentrating, he unleashed a Word of Power and was surprised to find an emptiness. He tried again, and it was as if his command was redirected, or more accurately, slid off the intended target. Confused, he tried several more times, each with the same result. "It must be my distance from both a Flow line and Rahotep." He recontacted his lieutenant.

Rahotep, I want you to prepare to receive me in North Carolina. Our mission is more difficult than before and I need to be there.

As you wish, Teacher.

I am leaving for America tonight.

I will meet you at the airport, Teacher.

Kamenwati stood, called one of his aides and made plans for travel to the United States. While changing from his traditional Egyptian dress to a Western business suit, he found a place of fear deep inside, a fear of failure, a fear of Abaddon.

CHAPTER TWENTY

JIM LYNCH ARRANGED A HELICOPTER to transport Hannah and Dr. Rimmer to the Naval Station in New London. A car was waiting when they arrived and drove them across the tarmac to a large building with a sign reading Joint Operations Command. "This looks like the right place," said Hannah. Rimmer nodded in agreement.

They were greeted inside by Dr. Goddard, who shook Rimmer's hand. "My God, Dr. Rimmer, I am delighted to meet you."

"As am I, Dr. Goddard." Rimmer turned to Hannah. "I would like you to meet Agent Ahmed of the British SIS."

"Welcome to Ft. Bragg, Agent," said Goddard. "Shall we get started?"

They entered the building which was laid out as a large workroom: tables blanketed with papers and laptops, drafting tables lining the walls with mechanical drawings, and a rolling chalkboard filled with exotic symbols Hannah could not interpret. Two men rose to greet them, Dr. Kurt Cheetham and Dr. Joe Linden. *They are polite enough,* thought Hannah, *if a little standoffish in an awkward, engineering way.*

"Doctors Cheetham and Linden have been working on something since the earnest young man from the NCTC left us," Goddard said.

"Dennis Allende," said Rimmer. "He came to me presenting a problem in brainwave entrainment, a question posed by you, Dr. Goddard." The physicist nodded, acknowledging the credit. "Having some experience with resonances and this particular phenomenon, I created a model for a screening device that we delivered to the authorities at Ft. Bragg."

"This is wonderful, Dr. Rimmer," said Goddard. "Then the immediate threat is countered."

"But I fear it is not stopped," replied Rimmer. "I began looking at this entrainment incident not so much a way to control people but as an entirely new class of weaponry. And if it is a new weapon, we need countermeasures, a focused and deployable anti-brainwave defense system."

"It is interesting you should say that, Doctor. Your young NCTC friend sparked much the same thinking here and I asked Muir and Bedlow to help Cheetham and Linden work on viable options." The two scientists nodded to their superior and the others, hearing their names, stood and looked at their boss. "As you know, our expertise is in the area of underwater transmissions, but the notion of using the Schumann Resonances suggested a theory we could develop on dry land. May I take you through our current thinking?"

"I would be honored, Doctor," said Rimmer.

The men launched into an esoteric discussion of physics, mechanics, and resonance theories that made Hannah's head spin. She wisely stepped back and watched, taking her assignment as protector of the kindly old scientist seriously.

Many cups of coffee later the group of six scientists, surrounded by empty Styrofoam cups, sheets of paper, and stacks of books, came to a halt in their discussions. Rimmer stood back with a satisfied look on his face. "By God, Herman, I think we are onto something here." Goddard looked up and nodded in agreement.

Hannah, totally bored by the dense scientific language, had drifted into a daydream state that was suddenly interrupted by Dr. Rimmer's exclamation. She stood and looked expectantly to the elder scientist, expecting to find him holding…Well, she didn't know what but holding something. Instead, his hands were empty and she clinched her brows in confusion. She looked to Goddard and saw a sparkle in his eye as he replied, "Yes, Horace, I believe we are onto something."

The next hours were spent with Rimmer and Goddard hunched over a drafting table while the other engineers worked on the chalkboard scribbling scientific calculations. The scientists completely forgot about meals, but fortunately Hannah did not. After a lengthy telephone inquiry she was connected to the base commissary where she arranged for box lunches.

The work continued and Hannah found a reasonably comfortable couch to nap on. She awoke to the sound of something being dropped and sat up, a little angry at herself for sleeping, and then realized the sun was up. "What time is it?" Hannah asked. Rimmer looked over as if just realizing she was still in the room. He looked at his watch and grimaced. "My goodness, it's eight o'clock. It seems we worked right through the night."

"And your work? How is that progressing?"

"Quite well. As a matter of fact, I believe we are ready to build a prototype." He looked at his fellow laborers, all exhausted to a man. "But I think we'll need some help."

RIMMER AND GODDARD assembled a larger team and began building a prototype. The process developed in fits and starts. Some tasks went smoothly, others encountered problems requiring team members to go back to the beginning and rework their thinking. After two days Rimmer realized Hannah was still hovering, and he felt sorry for her.

"Miss Ahmed, I have a proposal for you."

"Go ahead, Dr. Rimmer. I'm all ears."

"You can see this is going to take some time," he said, waving his arm in a wide arc that encompassed the room. "As a matter of fact, it looks like it will take weeks or even months to develop a viable prototype." Hannah's countenance did not change, but in her heart she was disappointed. "So here is what I propose: you return to Washington and rejoin Dekker."

"I can't do that, Doctor. I was sent to keep an eye on you."

"Of course, Miss Ahmed, but we are in the middle of a highly secure military base. I don't think anything will happen. I believe your time would be better spent with Dekker." Hannah considered his offer, and he was right about security, it really was not a problem on this base. He was also right about returning to the action. An open-ended babysitting gig was not a duty she relished.

"You are right, Dr. Rimmer. I will return today." She started for the main doors but stopped. "But you must promise me, if there is any trouble you will call."

"Of course," he said.

Rimmer gave the situation no more thought and returned to his work.

CHAPTER TWENTY-ONE

THE FLIGHT TO NEW YORK and onward to Raleigh-Durham was long and exhausting, yet Kamenwati stepped off the airplane looking crisp and refreshed as if rising from a full and restful night's sleep. Rahotep and one of his American followers looked at one another in surprise, wondering how their leader managed to arrive in such condition. Kamenwati sensed their amazement and smiled, knowing these two had no idea the Flows conferred rehabilitative powers.

As he followed Rahotep outside the terminal, Kamenwati stopped and looked upward as if hearing a sound.

"Teacher, is something wrong?" Rahotep asked. Kamenwati did not answer but continued staring into the sky. Rahotep waited, not knowing what his teacher was doing.

Kamenwati broke out of the strange trance and looked around. "An adversary is coming. We must set a trap, Rahotep. Do you know a remote location near the base?"

"Yes, I do. When you asked me to move closer to the base, I scouted the area. There is a forested area around Overhills Lake, which is about five miles from the base perimeter."

"We will need all your people for this, Rahotep. Please assemble them for instruction."

"As you wish, Teacher. It is only fifty miles from here to Spring Lake, which will give the others time to return to our base."

Kamenwati nodded and thought deeply on the coming meeting with Adam Dekker.

HANNAH WAITED FOR Dekker at the NCTC complex. She had called him before leaving Rimmer in New London and he agreed with the decision to return. She did not have to wait long. In a huge hurry, Dekker blew into the lobby and spotted Hannah sitting quietly with her single bag at her side. "Let's go, Hannah. We need to get to Pope Field. Our target is Rahotep, and we have to find him."

She stood and grabbed her bag. "I'm ready."

The military transport was waiting for them at Dulles, only a few miles from NCTC headquarters. As they took off Hannah noticed Dekker staring out the window with a distinctly unfocused look. After more than thirty minutes he seemed to return to the here-and-now. "Is everything okay?" Hannah asked. He looked at her and shook his head. "There is danger waiting for us, for me, in North Carolina, but it's non-specific."

"How do you know that?"

"It's a Ranger thing, a feeling, a premonition. Sorry, but it's something I've learned to respect. It has often been the difference between success and failure, life and death." Hannah understood field instincts and often followed them herself, but Dekker's intuition was, well, spooky. "How do you want to proceed when we land?"

"We'll first see Horace's setup. I'm not sure if the threat is at drone operations or somewhere off base."

They were met by a government sedan upon landing and were quickly transported across the airbase to adjacent Ft. Bragg. An officer was waiting at the entrance to the UAV Operations building and greeted Dekker with a salute. After quick introductions Dekker asked to inspect the new EM installation. "We'll have to step back a bit so you can see the tower on the roof," said the youthful officer. He led them into a parking lot where Dekker and Hannah could view the tower, unremarkable except for the oval device on the tip. On the ground they saw silver discs completely encircling the facility.

"Any new attacks, Lieutenant?"

"No sir. Everything is normal," said the officer. "I guess that means this contraption is working."

They entered the building to inspect the small control room for the EM equipment. The captain on duty accompanied Dekker and Hannah, pointing out the primary components and commenting that all were operating within nominal ranges.

"Thank you, Captain," said Dekker. "Is there a meeting room we can use, one with a telephone?"

They were led back through the lobby and the duty captain handed them over to another enlisted man who showed them to a small windowless room. "Nice and homey, wouldn't you say?" Hannah said.

"At least it has a phone," replied Dekker. "I'll call the office." He sat at the circular table and dialed. After briefing Lynch, he was transferred to Dennis.

"Dekker, where are you, man? Last I knew you were out at that estate in Maryland," Dennis said.

"I did come in, but only for a moment to gather up Hannah."

"I thought she was in Connecticut with Dr. Rimmer."

"Change of plans, and now we're at Ft. Bragg."

"You're in North Carolina? When did all this happen?"

"It was kind of sudden, but here we are. Dennis, I would like you to begin searching the hotels around this area and look for someone named Rahotep. He's the person we believe has been sent by Kamenwati to carry out his plan whatever that is."

"No problem. I'll get on it right away."

"Is Galdur still with you?"

"He's sitting across from me."

"Good. Put me on speaker."

A soft click was heard and then Dennis. "You're on. Go ahead."

"Galdur, I know you prefer to use the Flows to communicate, but I had to speak with you directly."

"Of course, Adam. I am overwhelmed by this technology fortress Dennis seems to preside over."

"I had a very strong feeling, you know, my danger alarm, and it was redlining during our flight. I checked out Horace's installation here, and it seems to be working just like it's supposed to."

"What is the problem then, Adam?" Galdur asked.

"The feeling isn't going away. If anything, it's stronger, and I need to zero in on it."

"Dekker, you don't know what you might be getting into," interrupted Dennis.

"I've got Hannah with me, and she is more than capable, as she's already proven." Dekker looked at the SIS agent, and she nodded her acknowledgement of the compliment. "Galdur, I need your help as well."

"Certainly, Adam."

"Can you monitor the Flows, on the down-low like you've done before, to see if you can get an idea who has it in for me?"

"Of course, and I will also alert Salim about this strange aberration in the Flows."

"Just see what you can find out from the Magick side of things. I may need your help."

Dekker ended the call, and Hannah looked perplexed. "What did you mean about magic? How in the world will that help whatever situation we're heading into?"

"I wasn't talking about 'abracadabra' magic but Magick with a K, and it's not at all what you think."

"Perhaps you can enlighten me."

Dekker gathered his thoughts before speaking. "For as long as I can remember, I had an ability to anticipate danger. It's what kept me one step ahead as a Ranger. I relied on this danger radar, as I called it, and it never let me down. And then I met a man in England right after the strangest event of my life: I saw five gray-hooded people appear from the stone walls of a Scottish castle, and one formed what I can only describe as an energy ball, propelling it across the room and killing the man I was there to protect.

"A man I met later knew what I had seen and understood what I experienced. That man, Ulrig, told me about a world I had no idea existed, a world where events and people are influenced by Magick, an ancient belief system predating even the Jewish faith. Magick influenced the world for millennia until mankind turned to technology and all that implies; technology is anathema to Magick, and in the end its practitioners were unable to stop the change in worldview and interaction that technology brought about." He looked up from the telephone sitting before him and into Hannah's disarmingly blue eyes. "I knew at an intuitive level Ulrig spoke the truth, and more importantly, I knew Magick was used to kill my client. I decided to learn as much as I could about this unseen world and agreed to meet Ulrig the next morning in a more private setting.

"The next morning I went to the place we agreed, but Ulrig wasn't there. In fact, he had been murdered. I found his body on the rocks along the quay, and later, investigating his cottage, I was almost burned alive. I was saved by an old root cellar that protected me from a fire set by what I came to know as the Brotherhood, modern practitioners of the ancient belief system.

"I escaped the fire along with a box containing a diary of sorts, as well as an ancient map showing what I discovered were lines of energy circling the Earth, or the Flows. The diary referenced an old friend of Ulrig, an Icelander named Galdur, who helped in my first encounter with Abaddon and instructed me in other aspects of Magick. I don't claim to be a deep practitioner like Galdur, but I do know this other reality exists. I can't explain it. It just is, and I've learned to be comfortable with it. Magick is behind everything since this episode began: the drone theft, burying us in the tomb, and everything we heard and saw in that building in Asyut. That is what I believe we are facing."

Hannah sat back trying to take in what Dekker was saying. "I'm not sure I can believe what you've said about this Magick, but it's clear *you* believe it and so I cannot dismiss the idea. If you don't mind, I will hold my decision until I know more."

"Fair enough. Now we wait for Dennis to do his thing. I wonder if there is somewhere we can get some lunch."

THE MEETING ROOM at the Hampton Inn at Spring Lake was neither spacious nor elegant, but it would do for Kamenwati's purposes. The two additional recruits were already at the hotel when Rahotep and his associate arrived with Kamenwati. They went directly to the hotel conference room, and once everyone was seated, Kamenwati began.

"Gentlemen, first I want to thank you for your loyalty and commitment to our ongoing struggle. I will assume you all have some level of experience with the Flows and principles of Magick." Kamenwati looked to each of Rahotep's recruits, assessing both their commitment and their sensitivity to the extra-normal powers of Magick. Satisfied with the men, Kamenwati continued. "We will face an adversary today, one I know well. He is not an Adept, but he does possess natural skills and he twice defeated Abaddon. Now I represent Abaddon and he has instructed me to deal with the man, and that is what we are going to do."

Kamenwati launched into an intensive instruction, much of which Rahotep already knew but the others did not.

The teacher's intention was to capture Adam Dekker and confine him in something he called a Merlin Box. Rahotep was somewhat unclear what such a box might be, but his leader was confident it would take care of Dekker. After a full afternoon learning to exercise Words of Power, the followers were ready to assist Kamenwati in the ritual.

"Teacher, how will we lure Dekker in?" Rahotep asked.

"We need only go to our site and I will call him."

"Won't he suspect a trap?"

"Of course, but I will issue a call as a friend asking for a cordial meeting."

"He will sense us close by," said Rahotep, "even if we are hidden."

"You will all be covered in the cloud; you need only stay still. He will be focusing on me while your screening will deflect any sense of your presence. When you see I have created the Merlin Box, you will step forward and bind him with the Words I have taught you."

"We are ready, Teacher. When do we begin?"

"Right away. My plans will not work as long as Dekker is in this world."

DEKKER AND HANNAH found the Officer's Club and enjoyed a pleasant meal. It was late in the afternoon and they were discussing where to stay when Dekker suddenly stiffened. "What's the matter, Dekker?" He did not answer Hannah's question but instead closed his eyes and remained stiff. She waited and finally Dekker opened his eyes. "I've been invited to a meeting," he said.

"A meeting? Where? How?"

"The Flows, of course. It is Kamenwati. He is here in North Carolina and he's requested my presence to 'discuss matters of mutual concern'."

"Dekker, this can't be anything but a trap."

"I'm not so sure. I told you we have a history, and I may be able to talk him out of whatever he's doing."

"I have a bad feeling about this," said Hannah.

"But I've got you for backup, Hannah. You can keep an eye out for any others he may have with him."

"I'm not so sure what with all this Magick business. I'd feel better if we had Galdur here."

"Not a bad idea. I'll call Dennis and ask him to come down with Galdur. Meanwhile, we are going to that meeting."

DEKKER HAD NO trouble finding the meeting location because Kamenwati had shown it to him in the Flows. He knew it was near Overhills Lake and just a few miles from Ft. Bragg. As they traveled into the heavily forested area, Hannah's uneasiness grew. Dekker seemed singularly focused and dismissed her misgivings, telling her there was nothing to worry about.

They reached a place intended for picnics that had tables and benches, fire pits, and a lavatory building. It was a pleasant setting, but there was no one around. "I don't like this, Adam. No one is around," Hannah said. Dekker got out of the car he borrowed from the base motor pool and walked into the clearing. Hannah got out as well, but she lagged behind, extracting her weapon and looking left and right for threats.

As soon as Dekker reached the center of the clearing a man stepped out of the forest, someone he recognized. "Hello, Kamenwati."

"Mr. Dekker, it is good to see you again." Kamenwati gestured with open hands. "You have nothing to fear. See? I am alone." Dekker looked around and saw no others, and then he looked over his shoulder and saw Hannah alert, weapon in hand. He probed, seeking any sense of others who might be hidden, but there was nothing.

"Okay, Kamenwati. What do you want to discuss?"

"Your future, Mr. Dekker. You have placed yourself in a dangerous position."

"How is that?"

"I think you know it is your opposition to Abaddon. If you continue to oppose the power, it will cost your life."

"I have been threatened by better men than you, Kamenwati. You can't do anything I am unable to counter. It is you who is in peril here."

Kamenwati's countenance changed. His normally passive face contorted and an evil look came over him. Dekker took a backward step, not understanding what was happening. "You defy me, you inconsequential man!"

Dekker felt a constriction around his body and he was unable to move. He had experienced this before and knew Kamenwati, or was it Abaddon, binding him. He turned his head and saw Hannah similarly immobilized, her hands hanging at her sides, her weapon pointing harmlessly downward.

"Kamenwati!" he shouted.

Four men emerged from the trees, three standing around Dekker and the other walked to Hannah. The three men lifted their right arms, palms facing Dekker, each exercising a different Word, and Dekker saw a translucent cube above him. He struggled against invisible bonds but was unable to break them. He knew it would be only moments before a stasis cube, Kamenwati's Merlin Box, was lowered and he would be trapped. He had to calm himself and concentrate on the one binding him, but it was not one but all three men. Kamenwati had set his trap masterfully and Dekker knew he would not escape.

The translucent cube, the Merlin Box, floated for a moment over Dekker, and with a quick movement of his arms, Kamenwati slammed the box downward onto Dekker. At the moment he was captured in the cube, the binding force was released, but it was much too late to do Dekker any good. Spinning around inside the cube, he peered through the translucent walls and saw Hannah, still immobile, her eyes wide with amazement. She shouted something, but Dekker could not hear.

The world went white as if a huge spotlight was turned on, and Dekker could no longer see through the walls. He realized now what the man Kambrian, the previous host to the Abaddon spirit, experienced when he, Galdur, and Kara confined him in a similar stasis. Dekker pounded the walls, floor, and ceiling. He even tried to use the composite pistol, but oddly, it would not fire. He would have to consider that phenomenon.

He finally exhausted himself and sat down, defeated. He shouted, "Hannah! Bring Galdur!" Dekker had no idea if his SIS partner could hear him, probably not, but his shout reminded him there was some hope out there. "If anyone can help, it's Galdur. And I almost forgot about Salim who can help as well." With those thoughts he settled down. It was to be a long wait.

HANNAH STOOD BESIDE the car, her weapon in hand, ready for…what? She had no idea, but she remained watchful. Dekker stood at the center of the clearing. She watched a man emerge from the trees and she became alert. She heard Dekker call to the man. It was Kamenwati. He began talking with Kamenwati and Hannah relaxed. "Perhaps he is right about this meeting."

After several minutes of interchange, something changed in Kamenwati. Dekker went stiff and she was about to rush to his side when she discovered she was immobilized. It felt like she had been wrapped in ropes, holding her in place. Her arms hung at her sides, the Beretta Nano hanging uselessly in her right hand. Then four men stepped out of the forest. "Where did they come from?" Hannah wondered. She watched helplessly as three men stood at equal points around Dekker and the fourth came to her. All she could do was observe, her anger rising at her inability to move or do anything for Dekker.

Kamenwati raised his arms and spoke into the air and Hannah couldn't believe what she saw: a large translucent cube appeared over Dekker. The cube slammed down, but it did not crush Dekker. Instead he appeared inside. How could this be? The cube seemed to be made of light and pulsed with ever-increasing frequency and intensity, ending with a blinding flash. And then nothing. The cube, with Dekker inside, was gone! In her confusion she did not see Kamenwati and his men leave, and she realized after a time she was no longer being held. She was free.

Hannah stood for a moment trying to process what she had experienced as she made her way to the spot Dekker had been standing. She turned in a complete circle, still unwilling to believe Dekker was gone. She made a half-hearted search in the surrounding woods but knew Kamenwati and his followers were long gone. Whatever they did to her, she was immobilized until they had escaped. Returning to the clearing she noticed a scorched area where the cube stood. "I suppose this means I'm not crazy." Unhappy with the outcome of this adventure, she returned to the car, trying to decide what to do next. "How in the world do I explain this? Who would believe it?" She had to tell somebody about Dekker's disappearance, and then she remembered Dennis and Galdur. "They will understand."

Sitting in the car, Hannah called Dennis and told him what she saw. "Holy crap! I'll tell Mr. Lynch and we'll be there as quickly as possible. Can you get back to the base?"

"I have the car Dekker borrowed. I'll drive back and meet you at the UAV Operations Center."

"Hold on, Miss Ahmed. Help is on the way."

Hannah ended the call and sat back in the seat, now feeling less alone. "We'll find you, Dekker," she said.

CHAPTER TWENTY-TWO

KAMENWATI AND HIS FOUR FOLLOWERS made their way through the dense North Carolina woods to a small road and their parked van. The men were silent as they departed, trying to process their experience in the clearing. Rahotep, who had seen many examples of his master's power, was no less awed by the Merlin Box than the others. Todd Fowler, the driver, seemed intimidated, even afraid, of Kamenwati who sat in the seat next to him. The others, Paul Moor and Bill Sexton, sat on the second bench seat behind Rahotep. Moor and Sexton carried on a muted conversation, both amazed and wanting to ask what happened but both afraid to voice a question. Rahotep sensed their unease and spoke for all.

"Teacher, what we just witnessed was truly amazing. What was it? Did you kill Dekker?" Kamenwati looked over his seat and noted the troubled looks on his followers' faces.

"No, I did not kill Dekker. He is worse than dead. He is confined in a Merlin Box, a trap he cannot escape."

"Where is he, sir?" Fowler asked. Kamenwati looked at the driver with a bewildered look. "Why, he is right where we left him."

"I don't understand," Fowler said.

"The stasis, or Merlin Box, is an energy field drawn from the Flows. When someone enters, he steps out of time and space as the world understands it. And unless one is a deep practitioner of Magick, there is no escaping the box. It has been used only once in my memory, and that was to confine my predecessor."

"How did he escape?" Moore asked.

Kamenwati gave a surprised look. "I released him, of course." The men went silent, considering the power this man must have.

"And Dekker? Does he have the power to escape?" Rahotep asked. Kamenwati shook his head with a slight smile. "No, he does not possess the skills of a deep practitioner. He will be confined in that limbo forever."

The men were further awed and fell silent for the remainder of the ride to the hotel.

"DID YOU KEEP the meeting room for the day?" Kamenwati asked as they entered the hotel lobby. Todd Fowler responded in a manner suggesting he did not want to do anything that would upset his new leader. "Yes, sir, I made sure we have the room until tomorrow morning, and longer, if you want it."

"Today will be sufficient," Kamenwati said.

Rahotep took his master's cue and led the way to the meeting room. Once inside they waited for Kamenwati to sit before taking their chairs. Kamenwati straightened his tailored coat and folded his hands on the table. He looked at each member of his small cadre, and while he did not exactly smile, he did nod briefly to each. "You all did well today but our task is far from over. Now we must renew our assault on the military drones, and we must expand our reach to control several operators and their drones simultaneously. Before coming here I attempted to strike again, but my power had no effect." The men looked to one another with astonishment. "It is true, and I believed it was a screening effort from the man we dealt with earlier. But now I know it was not Dekker shielding the drone operators. Nor was it anyone I could detect, and yet the facility is somehow shielded." The men responded with surprised exclamations. Kamenwati allowed them to vent for a few moments and then calmed them down.

"This is actually a good thing since we can surmise there is no practitioner of Magick involved." Turning to Fowler, Kamenwati asked, "Are you able to get on the base?"

"Yes, sir, but not without some kind of cover like a work order." Rahotep stepped into the conversation to help his man. "The men have been positioned outside the fences in strategic observation positions."

Kamenwati thought for a moment before replying. "We must get on the base and go to the drone facility."

"I think there is a way, sir," said Fowler. "I can get the van masked as a service vehicle and counterfeit a work order. That should get us through the gates. Once inside we can make a direct observation of the drone facility."

Rahotep had a quizzical look. "By 'mask the van' you mean paint it?"

"Not exactly. I can get a wrap job it's like a giant sticker so we look legitimate, and when we're finished it strips off." Rahotep nodded his understanding and tilted his head toward Kamenwati, looking for affirmation of Fowler's plan. Kamenwati thought for what seemed an eternity but in fact was only a few moments. Fowler waited expectantly, as did Rahotep.

"Yes, this is a good plan."

Rahotep was pleased and turned to the three Americans. "What sort of service vehicle would the van become?" One man suggested a package delivery company, like UPS or FedEx; another thought a floral delivery service; and another suggested a plumbing company. Fowler came up with the final solution. "An exterminator that's the answer.

No one questions an exterminator and we wouldn't have to get elaborate decoration, just simple door decals."

All were in agreement and stood to leave while Fowler reassured Kamenwati, "I'll have it done right away. I can be ready tomorrow, the next day at the latest."

THE WRAP JOB took longer than Fowler expected, however. It turned out only one body shop in town produced removable wraps, so the job took two days to complete.

"It is most important you men do not use cell phones, texts, or any other means of electronic communication," Kamenwati reminded the two men assigned to surveil the Ft. Bragg facility. "You will take notes only."

"How about photos? My phone takes pictures and they stay right on the phone." Kamenwati weighed the relative risk of discovery and decided it was extremely low. "Yes, you may take photographs."

With that, Fowler and Moor got into the van, now proudly announcing itself as belonging to F&M Pest Control, and drove off.

A small line of vehicles waited at the base's main gate. Fowler looked calm, but his companion, Paul Moor, was nervous. Fowler noticed Moor's discomfort. "Hey, you gotta stay calm, ya' know?" Moor looked forward, unresponsive. "Look, I've done this a hundred times before at bases and government facilities in DC. We just have to tell them what we're here for and wave a work order around." Moor shifted the legal-pad sized aluminum case around on his lap. He opened the lid and took out the work order Fowler had prepared for this purpose and clipped it to the outside of the case. "That's good, Moor. You don't have to say anything; just let me do the talking."

The van reached the sentry box and Fowler leaned out his window. The enlisted man on duty looked the driver over but did not show much interest. "Your destination, sir?"

"We've got a pest problem to deal with. The work order says someone saw rats around the commissary." He motioned Moor to hold up the faked document.

"Okay," said the enlisted man. "Do you know where you're going?"

"No, we don't. You gotta map?" The young man went back into the sentry shack and returned with a base map.

"It's right here," he said, pointing to a location on the map perhaps a mile from the gate.

"Thanks, Chief," said Fowler.

"It's Corporal."

"Sorry, and thanks again." Fowler rolled up his window and drove onto the base.

"See? I told you, nothing to it." Moor visibly relaxed as they turned a corner out of the view of the sentry point.

"All these bases have maps, and that's what I really wanted," said Fowler.

They parked the van near the commissary and got out. Fowler looked closely at the map and seemed to find what he wanted. "The building we're looking for is part of a complex on the other side of the base. Too bad. It would have been easier if we could walk to the place, but you gotta take what you get." Moor got back into the van and they drove away.

Fowler had shown him where they were heading, and so Moor was able to give him directions as they drove along. "Left up ahead. That should take us where you want."

They discovered the area was all concrete and buildings with none of the park-like settings found in the front of the base. Driving slowly, Fowler read off the building numbers and tried his best to read the small signs in front of each building. "Building A-4. I can't read the sign, but it doesn't look like an operations center," Fowler said. They continued, and on a whim Fowler made a turn down a narrow alley between buildings C-1 and C-2. He stopped short before leaving the alley. "Will you look at that?" Fowler said. "Now that looks like an operations center."

The building ahead had tall glass windows across the front and a large double door entry. "This has got to be the place," said Fowler. "Take a picture," he ordered Moor, who tapped his smart phone photo app and snapped off several pictures.

"Do you see that tower on the roof?" Moor asked.

"Yeah, I do. You got that, right?"

"Yes, I did."

"Okay, we're going to drive out there and go around the building. I want you to snap pictures so we can build a complete 360 degree image."

"Right."

"But look around before you take any photos to make sure no one is watching."

"Right," said Moor with a small gulp, realizing discovery would probably land them in jail.

Fowler and Moor in their disguised F&M Pest Control van circled the building, and when the circuit was complete, left the base by a different gate.

Thirty minutes later they arrived back at the hotel. Fowler called Rahotep's room and told him he needed a few minutes to assemble their photos. "Can we meet in, say, thirty minutes? We can go back to that meeting room since we've got it all day." Rahotep agreed. Moor followed Fowler to the breakfast lounge area, now empty of other guests.

"You know how to stitch the images together to make one big one?" Fowler asked.

"Yeah. Give me a minute and I'll put together a 360 of the building."

After thirty minutes, the pair were ready to meet with Rahotep and Kamenwati.

FOWLER AND MOOR arrived at the meeting room first, giving them an opportunity to prepare their presentation. Fowler had arranged a small video projector that he aimed at a blank wall. Moor connected his smartphone to the projector and, after pressing a few buttons on the projector, got his images to display. Rahotep and Kamenwati entered and sat, saying nothing.

"We got on the base with no problem," said Fowler.

"Did you find the operations center?" Rahotep asked.

"Yes, and we took pictures. Moor was able to stitch them together to show you the full circuit of the building. We weren't sure exactly what you're looking for, but hopefully the pictures will reveal what you want." Moor began with the shots from the alley, those directly at the front of the building.

"Here's the building. We figured this had to be the place; it just looks like an operations center."

"And it's much different from the buildings around it," added Moor.

"And see this?" Fowler stood and stepped to the wall, pointing to the tower on the roof. "That doesn't look like a radar or any sort of tower I've ever seen before."

"Can you zoom in on the image?" Kamenwati asked. Moor responded with a small gesture on the phone's screen, zooming in on the odd shape on the tip of the tower.

"Interesting," said Kamenwati. "Show me the rest."

Moor tapped in a few commands and a new image opened on the wall. Using his finger on the cell phone screen, Moor scrolled across the long image. When he returned to the starting point, Kamenwati ordered him to do it again but this time to zoom in on the ground around the building. In moments they saw the silver discs set at regular intervals.

"Go back to the full image," said Kamenwati. "And scroll it again."

Moor followed Kamenwati's order and made the image flow across the wall. Rahotep observed his master closely, noting how his breathing increased and a look of victory came over his face. "Teacher, what do you see?"

"I know what they have done to deflect my will. Do you see those discs and the tower on the building? It is a system to emit a signal, a very specific signal, to neutralize my commands through the Flows." He looked to Fowler. "You must return to the base. I want you to remove one, no, two, of those discs. That will create an opening for me. But you must do it in a place where it won't be noticed."

Rahotep thought for a moment and then asked his master, "Can we create something that looks like those discs, a decoy?"

"I suppose," said Kamenwati.

"Hey, I think I know how to do that," said Fowler. "You know that shop where I got the wrap job done? Well, they could probably make up a couple of plastic circles and put a silver wrap on them."

Kamenwati thought for a minute, weighing the relative merits of Fowler's plan. "Yes, that would work well. Instead of leaving a blank area, it will look like everything is in place."

"That's right, boss. Should I go back and get a couple of those silver plates made?"

Kamenwati nodded his head and Fowler smiled.

THE NEXT MORNING Fowler was back at the sign shop ordering two silver twelve-inch silver discs. The shop owner raised an eyebrow, wondering what this customer was doing. "You playing Frisbee or something?" Never missing a beat, Fowler replied, "You've found me out. Got a little competition down at the park and I want to stand out. It impresses the chicks, ya' know?" The shop owner seemed satisfied with the explanation.

"They'll be ready in about two hours." Fowler thanked the man and left.

Two hours later Fowler collected his Frisbees and thanked the owner. Moor was waiting at the van. "Everything go okay?"

"Yup. Here, hold these, would ya'?" Moor took one of the silver discs from the paper bag and noticed the curved edge.

"Why did you make them like this? They only need to be flat."

"Had to give the shop owner a reasonable explanation, and so I asked him to make two twelve-inch Frisbees."

"And he bought that?"

"He did and there were no questions. Now, get out that work order from yesterday and get ready to wave it around again."

Thirty minutes later Fowler and Moor were back at the base entrance with a different soldier on duty. "Destination, sir?"

"We're back to check on a job we did yesterday at the commissary. It won't take long." Fowler gave the soldier a wink, and the young man waved the van through.

"Which ones are we going to replace?" Moor asked.

"The boss said it didn't matter, just that we grab two that are side-by-side. I'm thinking in the back, opposite from the entry."

In a few minutes the van approached the rear of the drone operations building. There was a small parking lot on the opposite corner and Fowler pulled in.

"Come on, Moor. Bring the bag and order box with you."

The pair left the van and walked across the road. There was no sidewalk on the rear side of the building, only grass. Fowler made a point of gesturing up and down, looking like someone who should be there. They stopped at the first disc in from the corner and turned away from the building. "Gotta look like we're interested in something else," said Fowler. Moor put the bag and his aluminum order box down as if to tie his boot. He took one of Fowler's new Frisbees out of the bag and replaced the titanium disc in the grass.

"It's light, not nearly as heavy as I expected," said Moor.

"Just put it in the bag and move on," said Fowler.

They finished the swap operation, returned to the van, and drove off the base.

"I'm glad to have that done," said Fowler.

"You and me both," Moor agreed.

CHAPTER TWENTY-THREE

KAMENWATI WAS PLEASED TO SEE THE titanium discs Fowler and Moor delivered. "A breach has been opened. Now I want all of you to take up positions around the base and be ready." The three men grunted their understanding and shuffled out of the conference room. Fowler stopped at the door to ask Kamenwati a question. "Where will you be?"

"Here, in my room, but Rahotep will accompany you three, allowing for a complete encirclement of the base. It is most important you take up positions at the meridian points." Kamenwati turned to Rahotep. "Will you make sure everyone is properly placed?"

"Yes, Teacher, I will," replied Rahotep.

"Be ready in one hour. Remember my instructions. They are critical to what I will be doing." All acknowledged their understanding with a nod and Rahotep said, "It will be done."

Kamenwati waited for the four men to leave then went back to his room. Everything was ready for him: pillows placed on the north wall, shades drawn, and only a single dim light glowing. He took off the Western suit he wore and changed into the comfortable galabia robes of his native Egypt. Thus attired, he was ready to begin.

He sat cross-legged, hands stretched out on his knees, palms facing upward. Kamenwati closed his eyes, fell into the light trance, and entered the Flows. He was able to observe his team driving to their points, dropping off a man, and moving on. He knew it was only a matter of minutes before all were in position and so he began by checking on Dekker in the Merlin Box. Sweeping his consciousness to the wilderness area where Dekker was confined, he saw the brilliant glow of the stasis chamber. It was totally opaque and hung in the air, an immovable, impenetrable prison. He smiled at his solution to the troublesome American, confident there was no escape for him.

Kamenwati turned his attention back to Ft. Bragg and from a high point of view, saw that his people were in place. He also observed the tower on the roof of the operations center. From within the Flows he saw the energy cover surrounding the building. *This is why my previous attempts failed*, he thought. But the cover was now incomplete; a small section was open. *Perfect!*

He moved to exercise his new skills in Magick and control men in the operations center, and through them, direct drones to Incirlik in Turkey and the Bundestag in Germany. Focusing his thoughts on the operations center, his mind slipped through the electronic opening and found two operators with active drones. The man he previously used was not in the facility. *No matter*, he thought. *These will do just as well*. Kamenwati could feel the amplification of his powers coming from his associates around the base and knew he would succeed. With a small nudge of his mind, the two operators quickly went into a daydream state, unnoticed by others around them or by their supervisor. His mental suggestions were carried out without either operator knowing what was happening. They were under Kamenwati's power and could not resist.

At Kamenwati's direction the first drone, intended for a strike in Syria, changed course to the northwest, moving toward Turkey. As that drone made its way to Incirlik Air Base, he turned his attention to the other operator. This man was flying a drone from a base in Italy eastward toward a target in Ukraine, but under Kamenwati's influence and control, his drone was diverted north to Berlin. *Now I must wait and watch.*

HANNAH WAS RECOVERING from her initial shock at seeing Dekker first immobilized and then swallowed by a glowing white cube appearing out of nowhere. Her shock was turning into anger now and she tried to sort out the experience, but it was beyond her. It was all too impossible. As she approached Ft. Bragg her anger grew and she wanted answers, any answers to explain what she witnessed. She only hoped her new NCTC friends could help.

Ninety minutes later a government sedan came to an abrupt halt in front of the UAV Operations Center and two men threw open the rear doors and rushed into the building. Hannah was waiting and stood as she recognized the new arrivals.

"Dennis, thank God you are here." Hannah grabbed his shoulder and began ushering him toward a lobby seating area.

"Hold on, Miss Ahmed. Galdur is way more important to Dekker's disappearance than me."

"I'm sorry. Of course, Galdur, my apologies."

"None necessary, my dear," said Galdur. "Can you tell me exactly what took place, what you saw and what you heard?"

They sat and Hannah recounted her experience, how she was somehow immobilized while Dekker faced a man she identified as Kamenwati. "And then four other men came out of the woods, three of them circling around Dekker and the other one came to me. I couldn't do anything. I'm ashamed to say my weapon was in my hand, but my arms were held tightly at my sides by...I don't know by what, but it was like I was wrapped up in ropes or cellophane. Then I saw a glowing cube hanging in the air, right above Dekker. He looked back to me with an expression I'll never forget: resigned, almost defeated." She recalled the strange actions of Kamenwati and the others around Dekker. "And then the box dropped straight onto Dekker. I thought he was dead, but then I saw him *inside* that cube. He was shouting to me, but I couldn't hear what he was saying and the cube was becoming more opaque. After a moment the cube seemed to explode with light. I was blinded and I think I must have blacked out. When I came to and recovered my sight, I was free from the invisible bonds and the cube was gone, just gone. Kamenwati and his four men were gone, too." A stern, angry look came over her. "I cannot begin to explain what happened, but I need to find out what it was that swallowed him and took him away—and I need to find Dekker."

Galdur was silent for a moment before responding. He looked into Hannah's eyes, recognizing the anger and the fear in them. "Miss Ahmed, you have had your first experience in the world of Magick."

"Dekker told me about that. I couldn't believe it and told him I'd try to keep an open mind. So this is what he was talking about..."

"Yes, there were a couple of things going on, and I'm sure you were confused by them," said Galdur. "You were in the middle of a battle that began years ago, one that drew Dekker in, and by extension, Dennis here, and of course, myself."

"He told me some of the background, about the death of his wife and his confrontation with someone called Abaddon. It all sounded too fantastic, but I could tell he believed it. We went through some tight spots in Egypt, but I never imagined it would end like this."

"It's not over, Miss Ahmed. If it gives you any consolation, Dekker is alive."

"Alive? Then where is he?"

"My guess is right where you last saw him, in that clearing."

"But I looked everywhere and the only thing I saw was a dark impression where the cube last sat."

"Excellent! Can you find that place again?"

"Yes."

They were interrupted by an alarm sounding throughout the building. "What's that?" Dennis asked. Several people rushed out doors on the left and right of the reception area while three uniformed officers came through the front doors. Hannah, Dennis, and Galdur watched the activity with questioning looks. "This can't be good," said Dennis.

"I think I know the cause," said Hannah. "This facility has been breached."

Galdur and Dennis exchanged a look and turned to Hannah. "May we help?"

CAPTAIN TIM DUNN, restored to duty after the investigation into the drones was complete, was pleased to be exonerated and happy the new defensive measures were in place. He felt everything was once again normal and he could return to a non-crisis posture. Captain Dunn could not have anticipated Kamenwati's move to breach the invisible security curtain, and so went about his duties blissfully ignorant of the new attack taking place.

Dunn had one primary responsibility: overseeing UAV operations. He knew the operators and trusted them. They were the troops on the front line, so to speak, and as such were given authority to handle their UAVs as situations warranted. This is why he did not notice when two drones were redirected to new targets, and it was only when the first UAV launched missiles at the airbase in Turkey that Dunn took note. He was astonished. "What the hell?"

As Dunn stood, frozen with indecision, another operator noticed his fellow drone-driver staring oddly at his monitors. Leaning over, he touched the man's shoulder but there was no response. He looked up to Dunn in the office overlooking the operations floor with a stricken look. This got Dunn moving and he rushed down to the operator's position. The other operator was shaking him, calling his name. "Michaels! Hey, Michaels! Come out of it!" Dunn looked at the operations monitor and saw the destruction at the airbase. "Oh, my God, it's happened again."

Dunn noticed the other operators leaning out of their cubicles to see what the excitement was all about. All except one. Dunn realized this other operator must also be affected by the strange force and rushed to the cubicle. He could see the drone was far off course, and checking the target coordinates on the console, realized the UAV was now headed to Germany, specifically, Berlin. Quickly the captain pulled the man back in his chair, away from the control console. He took the operator's place and regained control of the errant drone, sending it back to the base in Italy. Dunn ordered another operator to manage the flight and then went to a newly installed wall alarm and pulled the lever. Klaxons sounded throughout the building and all drone flights were recalled. Men and women rushed around, checking to be sure there were no other UAV compromises. The atmosphere in the control center It wasn't chaos but it was hectic.

After a few minutes, everyone settled down but there was still tension in the air. A senior officer and his aides entered the operations center and went straight to Dunn. "What's happened here, Dunn?"

"Sir, I don't know how, but we've been compromised again. This time two of my operators."

"What about the new defensive system we installed?"

"I don't know, sir. It has been working perfectly."

"Show me."

Dunn led the general and his aides to the room where the infratonic device was housed. "Is anything wrong in here?" the officer asked. Dunn looked around, flipped a switch or two, and shook his head. "No, sir. Nothing obvious. Maybe it's the tower on the roof." That suggestion caused the group to rush into the lobby and out the front doors. They did not notice Hannah, Dennis, and Galdur standing there, watching.

The officers outside looked at the tower on the roof. "Nothing wrong that I can see from here," said Dunn.

"What about those men, the operators. Where are they?"

"Back inside, sir. I haven't had a chance to debrief them yet."

The entourage returned to the building, and the senior officer was not pleased.

HANNAH TURNED WHEN Dunn's group reentered the lobby. She took a step toward Dunn, who recognized her from a previous meeting. "Not now, Miss Ahmed. We've got a bit of a situation here." Hannah moved to intercept Dunn before he and the other officers disappeared into the operations center. "I can see that, Captain, and we may be able to help," she said, gesturing to Dennis and Galdur standing behind her. "Wait right here. I'll be back."

Dunn followed the others into the operations center and to his station where he summoned the UAV operators. "The men will be here in a moment, sir; and if you will excuse me, there is something I must attend to."

"Go ahead, Dunn. We can handle everything from here," said the senior officer.

Reentering the lobby, Dunn found Hannah and the others in a deep conversation. "Miss Ahmed? What is it you think you can do?"

"You've had another incident, am I right?" Hanna asked.

"Yes. We thought the new system would prevent that," said Dunn.

"Some very strange things have been happening today, and I believe the individual behind it all is here, near the base, and he's found a way to penetrate the electromagnetic shield. Will you allow us to investigate?" Dunn looked at Hannah and the two men with her, one young, the other older.

"I can't let you in the operations center right now, but if you can conduct your investigation elsewhere, have at it." Dunn spun around and returned to the operations center.

"Okay, we can't go in, but we can take a look around outside," said Dennis.

"As I was saying a moment ago," said Galdur, "I don't know about all this technology, but I do know about the Flows."

Dennis nodded. "Yes, but I was with Rimmer when he worked up this scheme. He identified the specific brainwave frequency used to put the operators into a trance, a daydream state. He called it an entrainment resonance, something modeled on the Schumann Resonance theory. It's all a bit complicated, but he showed me a model of what they've installed here. I think we should begin by inspecting the components of the infratonic device."

"Excellent idea, Dennis," said Hannah.

WHEN THEY WERE outside, the group stood in much the same place as Dunn just a few minutes before. Looking up at the tower they saw no obvious defects. "I presume Captain Dunn inspected the control room and found nothing amiss," said Hannah.

"It may have nothing to do with the tower," said Dennis. "Dr. Rimmer's model had small discs surrounding the building. If I were going to sabotage these defenses, that's where I'd begin." As a group they made a circuit of the building, noting the placement of the discs. Dennis was unhappy. "I was sure there would be a disc missing," he said.

"Perhaps we should inspect these discs more closely," said Galdur.

With no other ideas to act on, they began looking closely at each disc, tapping each in succession but taking care not to disturb the placement. It was tedious working from disc to disc all the way around the building.

"This isn't looking very promising," said Hannah.

"We're coming to the end of the back side of the building, so there are only a few more," said Dennis.

They came to the corner, preparing to cover the last short side, when Hannah made a soft exclamation, "Oh, what's this?" Dennis and Galdur came to her side and stooped down.

"What is it?" Galdur asked.

"Listen." Hannah tapped the disc with her fingernail. It did not sound metallic, and the color was somewhat different from the other discs they inspected.

"You're right. This one is different," said Dennis. He went to the next disc and noticed it too was similarly discolored. He bent down and tapped it. "I think we've found how they breached the security measures."

"Don't touch anything," said Hannah. "Let's go find Captain Dunn."

CAPTAIN DUNN HELD the Frisbee-like discs in both hands, looked up to the tower, and shook his head. "This is terrible," he said. "And thank you, Miss Ahmed, and your people as well, for finding this. I can tell you there was one strike at an airbase in Turkey and we stopped a second strike in Germany." Dunn nested one disc in the other and turning, looked at the empty spots in the ground. "We'll replace these, of course, and get the system back in operation. Effective immediately, there will be twenty-four hour patrols." Dunn shook hands with all three and left.

"This has been quite a welcome," said Galdur.

"I for one am happy you two came as quickly as you did," Hannah said. "But we still have the situation with Dekker." Looking at Galdur she continued, "You said he is still in that forest clearing, and that is where we should begin."

"Yes," Galdur said.

"Then let's get going. I can't even imagine what he's going through."

CHAPTER TWENTY-FOUR

DEKKER HAD LONG SINCE EXHAUSTED his strength attempting to get out of the stasis box. He tried punching the walls, which simply absorbed his blows. He tried jumping, but again had no success. He tried shouting for Hannah, but the box seemed to suck up the sound and he was sure nothing got out. Frustrated with his impotent efforts, he sat down. He had to think his way out. Throughout his life there was always a way out, no matter how slim. But this box, this stasis, was altogether different, and for the first time he felt fear gripping his heart.

He knew generally what trapped him, it was the same stasis Kara created to hold Abaddon. He and Galdur had assisted Kara, but the box was her work. He remembered how the box formed over the unsuspecting Abaddon and how

Kara brought it down with a crash, the man's form visible through the translucent sides. There was a brilliant flash of light that shot upward and upset the three megalithic stones leaning on one another over the ancient altar below. The stones fell and crushed Kara to death. At the time Dekker had no idea where the stasis box holding Abaddon went, only that the evil was gone. Galdur later told him Abaddon was not dead, only confined, but it was a trap he would be unable to free himself from without outside help.

"Outside help...I need to look at my situation differently."

Dekker worked to calm himself, and in time he managed to reduce his heart rate and respiration to an acceptable level. He began to think about his prison, which is how he thought of the weird, white shape that defined his world. What did he know about it? What could he deduce? He tried desperately to remember every word Galdur said about the stasis. "He called it a Merlin Box." And that set him on another line of mental inquiry. "What do I know about Merlin? Is there an answer in that legend?" Merlin was supposedly a wizard to King Arthur, another legend. He tried to remember everything he ever read about Merlin and found his prison, this Merlin Box, allowed access to memories long buried. "There was Merlin, Arthur, Nimue, and Morgan le Fey. They were the key players in Merlin's life. How did that history go?"

Deeper and deeper he went in his mind, unknowingly connecting with the Flows. It was like an amusement park ride climbing up, shooting down, and whipping around corners of his consciousness. He focused on the one element of the Merlin story that related to his present predicament: Merlin's entrapment. There were several versions of the story, but the key features were Nimue's plot to steal Merlin's secrets and her anger with his refusal to share his power with her. She entrapped Merlin as he slept, placing him in a stone chamber, or a tree, or a glass box..."Merlin's Box," he said, understanding it was meant as a prison, one Merlin would never escape.

"I already know escape is possible," Dekker said. "Abaddon's return proved that. How did that return, that resurrection, happen? It was through Kamenwati."

Dekker found himself adrift in the Flows, far from any familiar point of reference. But there was no fear. "How odd," he said.

He noticed the white haze that obscured the walls begin to clear. He saw people and events, and he realized this might be his way out. He began by returning his consciousness to the location of his entrapment and realized he was still in the clearing in the woods. How long had he been in this prison, this limbo? He had no way to tell. It could have been minutes, hours, or days. There was simply no point of reference. "But that no longer matters because I can at least communicate through the Flows."

Dekker set his mind to summoning Galdur, calling out and waiting.

There was no reply. Galdur did not answer his call. "What is happening?" He withdrew back to himself, returning to the white room.

He thought about his situation for a long time, going over what he knew, resorting the cards, and looking for some clue to escape. He once again went over the circumstance of Abaddon's confinement in Desolation Field below Krugerschloss. "Abaddon was confined, restricted, imprisoned...Kara believed it was a permanent condition, a belief shared by Galdur. I watched him disappear from this plane of existence. Later we discovered Abaddon had been released." That was the key an external force freed him from the Merlin Box. "Even Abaddon could not escape while inside." Dekker slumped down against a surprisingly soft wall.

"The Flows allow me to see beyond these walls but not to communicate." He looked upward. "I am well-and-truly screwed. The only hope is someone outside understands what is going on and can free me. Does Galdur have the power? I don't know."

GALDUR WAS DISTRACTED by the discovery of Dr. Rimmer's infratonic device. It was becoming clear to him the divide between Magick and the modern world was rapidly closing; this demonstration of active interference with the

Flows was proof. His initial shock that a mechanical device could interfere set him back. After a lifetime of following the Old Truths and the use of Magick, it was inconceivable a mechanical contrivance could actually block the Flows, and yet here it was, successfully screening those inside the building from Kamenwati's attack.

As he considered the situation, his initial disbelief gave way to acceptance. "Perhaps this is best. We have been at odds with the world for so long, and now this man, Horace Rimmer, has shown a way to bridge the divide, shown us a path to reconcile the old ways with the modern. I think, in the end, this is good."

Hannah was eager to find Dekker, as was Dennis. They stood a short distance from Galdur, and aware of his state, Dennis held the British agent back. "Just a moment. There's something going on with Galdur," he said. After a few moments Galdur seemed to snap out of it and looked over to Hannah and Dennis. *His face is different*, thought Dennis. *I wonder what just happened.*

Hannah, who did not know Galdur, did not see what Dennis saw but did notice a change in the older man's posture: a slight slump or bowing of the sturdy Icelander's back. She attributed it to the tension of Dekker's loss and the discovery of a new attack on the UAV Operations Center. She didn't know there had just been a tidal shift in Galdur's world.

"Are we ready to go?" Dennis asked. They walked back to the car with him, Hannah with resolute purpose and Galdur in quiet contemplation.

They drove to the clearing in silence, each caught up in their own thoughts.

Once again in the picnic area, they left the car and walked to the clearing. Hannah pointed to the spot where she last saw Dekker. "It was right here. You can still see the outline of that box on the ground." Galdur was careful not to step into the area Hannah indicated. Instead he circled it, looking up and down as he made the circuit. He then did something strange. He stopped and faced the area in the grass, lifted his arms and let out a loud shout. His outcry startled Hannah and Dennis, who looked to one another in confusion.

Galdur remained with arms raised and eyes closed as Hannah and Dennis remained rooted where they stood. One minute passed, and then another, and another. He seemed to be holding the statue-like posture for a very long time. And then it was over. As unexpectedly as he began, Galdur dropped his arms and turned to his companions. "I am unable to release Dekker." His simple declaration swept away any hope held by Hannah and deflated Dennis' unwavering faith in Galdur.

"Is there no way to recover him?" Hannah asked. Galdur hung his head, and then he looked up at Hannah.

"There may be another way." He turned to Dennis. "We need to reach Dr. Rimmer. Is that possible?"

"Yes, of course. What do you have in mind?"

"Combining Magick and technology, my boy."

DENNIS ARRANGED A flight directly from Pope Field at Ft. Bragg to the Naval Base in New London. En route he called Horace Rimmer, who in his absent-minded way, greeted Dennis as if he had just left. "Ah, my boy. There you are!"

"Dr. Rimmer, I want you to know I will be there within the hour."

"Are you on the base? Wasn't Miss Ahmed just here?"

"No sir. Hannah is now in North Carolina, but I'm coming to you. We need to talk about your activities there."

"Yes, yes, we've been making good progress. We've managed to…"

"Hold on, Dr. Rimmer. Don't discuss anything on an open line. We'll talk when I get there."

"You are right, of course, Dennis. No discussions on anything using electromagnetic frequencies." Dennis signed off and the flight continued on to New London.

The military flight was met by a gray sedan that took him to a nondescript building on the far side of the naval base. A young lieutenant, junior grade, met Dennis at the door and escorted the guest to a large workroom, a place Dennis had not seen before and he was impressed. It was large and open, and there were desks, workstations, whiteboards, chalkboards, and large video monitors scattered throughout the space. He looked around for Dr. Rimmer and spotted him hunched over a table working on something.

"Dr. Rimmer," Dennis called out. The elderly scientist looked around, spotted Dennis, and broke into a wide smile. He hurried over and grabbed Dennis' hand. "It is good to see you, Dennis. I hadn't kept track of time. So much to do here. Come, come. Let's go over to the meeting area and you can tell me why you're here."

Dennis followed Dr. Rimmer to a corner of the room that was set up for meetings: a large, rectangular table surrounded by swivel chairs, flip charts on easels, and a fold-up projection screen with a compact video projector on the table. Taking his seat, Dennis began. "Dr. Rimmer, I'm afraid I have disturbing news. Dekker has been taken." Rimmer's face showed confusion combined with a hundred questions. "I really hope you're working on something that can help free him."

"Oh, my. Free him from what?"

"He was placed in a stasis cube, a so-called Merlin Box, much like the one created for Abaddon some years ago. It was a prison he managed to escape. Since you created the device that is shielding the drone center, I hoped you might have another trick up your sleeve."

Rimmer gave him a quizzical look. "We have been working on combining the Navy's research in ultra-low frequency transmission and my infratonic field theories, but we are still some time away from any workable model."

"You said the system for the base was only a passive defense, that we needed to develop a tactical field weapon," said Dennis. "That's why I thought you may have answers."

"Tell me more about Dekker's confinement," said Rimmer.

Dennis recounted Hannah's story, her invisible binding, and Dekker's disappearance in a white cube, the Merlin Box. Rimmer was silent, deep in thought. "Tell me, do you know how this Merlin Box was made? Is it an electromagnetic construct?"

"I believe you would call the forces entrapping Dekker electromagnetic." Rimmer nodded his head, stood, and went across the room to an area covered with papers and arcane drawings on a chalkboard. He shuffled through a few pages, found what he was looking for, stuffed them into his coat pocket, and wheeled the chalkboard into view.

"Let me show you what we've been doing."

Laying out the pages from his coat pocket, he launched into a monologue about Schumann Resonances, Infratonic Qui Gong machines, Faraday cages, and brainwave entrainment. The entire lecture was dizzyingly complex but Dennis was able to follow what Rimmer was talking about.

"So we are back to where we began, using the brainwave frequency of 204.081632653 milliseconds, but this time I am happy to report we have developed a means to issue an EM projectile at a specific target."

"You mean an electromagnetic bullet?" Dennis exclaimed.

"A little more than a bullet, I should say," Rimmer replied. "More like a cannon ball or a torpedo."

"Awesome!"

"However, I am not sure this new object, this Merlin Box, operates on the same frequency," said Rimmer. Looking at a now discouraged Dennis Allende, Dr. Rimmer said, "Take heart. There is always a way."

After some discussion Rimmer was at an impasse. "If only we had one of these boxes to study," he said.

Dennis looked up and slapped his forehead. "Why couldn't Galdur create a box for you?"

"I'm not certain he can, Dennis."

"But he did it before, at Krugerschloss," Dennis said.

"True, but as I understand it, he had help."

"Dr. Rimmer, you need to test your electromagnetic torpedo on a facsimile of your target. Galdur is your only hope."

Rimmer made a call to Dr. Bedlow, who in turn called Dr. Goddard. In short order they moved from the open lab to Goddard's office. Rimmer laid out the problem they faced and how the newly developed weapon might help.

"But, Rimmer, we haven't even built a prototype," said Goddard.

"I know, but before we even begin, we must know what frequency to target and only Galdur can help us."

"I see," said Goddard. "What do you need?"

"We need to set up shop at Ft. Bragg. Is it possible to move our lab there?"

Goddard thought for a moment and then nodded. "Yes, it's all theories and paperwork at the moment and so you should be able to pick up and move." He lifted the telephone and dialed. "Bedlow? Your team is going on a little field trip."

THE RESEARCH TEAM was soon loaded onto an aircraft and transported to Pope Field, where they were met and escorted to a building set aside for their use. Dennis introduced the scientists to Galdur and turned to Hannah. "You already know Miss Ahmed." Horace Rimmer immediately explained to Galdur what they needed from him. Galdur nodded but understood almost nothing of what Dr. Rimmer said about this electromagnetic thingamajig.

"Are you able to make a stasis chamber, a Merlin Box?" Rimmer asked.

"Yes, although I may not be able to sustain it like the stasis holding Dekker. That requires a level of power and control I do not possess."

"That is fine," said Rimmer. "We only need to know if it is possible."

Galdur looked around the room that would serve as the development laboratory. "Is there somewhere less, um, sterile? Someplace quiet with trees?"

Rimmer looked to Hannah who gave him a bright smile. "I think I know a place."

Hannah led the group to an unexpected oasis in the center of otherwise plain buildings: a courtyard, small but pleasant, with grass, trees, and benches. Galdur looked around approvingly. "This will do nicely." Rimmer and Bedlow went to collect instruments they would use to analyze the phenomenon Galdur was about to create.

Dennis and Hannah stood to one side while Galdur moved to the center of the courtyard. It didn't look to them like much was happening. "Was it like this before, Dennis?" Hannah asked.

He shook his head. "I wasn't actually there when Kara and Galdur created the stasis, and so I don't really know." Hannah folded her arms and waited. Rimmer and Bedlow reappeared, now loaded down with equipment.

"Anything yet?" Bedlow asked. Hannah looked at the array of esoteric measurement devices for testing and analyzing. Shaking her head she said, "Not yet." They all stood in silence, waiting for Galdur.

But then Galdur lifted his hands above his head and they saw a small, swirling cloud appear about ten feet above him. There was no specific form to the cloud but colors were shooting through it, soft pastels swirling within the white mists of the cloud. Rimmer exchanged a surprised glance with Bedlow while Hannah seemed dumfounded. Only Dennis was unaffected by the situation.

The apparition transformed into a cube with translucent sides and a continuing swirl of colors. Galdur slowly lowered his arms and the cube came to rest on the ground before him. Rimmer and Bedlow stepped up to the cube holding devices before them. They circled the remarkable construct. Galdur remained in place, his eyes closed while focusing on maintaining the Merlin Box. After ten minutes of probing, measuring, and assessing, Rimmer and Bedlow stepped away.

"Thank you. We have what we need," said Rimmer. Galdur's posture slumped and the cube disintegrated into nothingness.

Dennis and Hannah went to Galdur, holding him up and leading him to a nearby bench. The two scientists were already gone off to the laboratory to analyze their findings. Sitting with Galdur between them, Dennis and Hannah processed the experience.

"I wouldn't have believed it had I not seen it for myself," said Hannah.

"This was my first time seeing it, but I was already a believer," Dennis replied. "I hope they get what they need." Looking to Galdur he saw the man was spent. "Is there anything we can do, Galdur?" The old Icelander shook his head. "Thank you, Dennis, but no. I just need to catch my breath." Looking around the courtyard, he smiled. "And this is a perfect place to do that."

They remained seated on the bench, each occupied with his own thoughts.

THREE DAYS PASSED, and still Horace Rimmer was in the laboratory. Dennis checked on him several times each day, mostly to make sure he was eating and getting some sleep. On this, the dawn of the fourth day, Rimmer wasn't at his usual place at the drafting table. It wasn't that he was resistant to computers, he told Dennis when they were in his workshop back home. The tactile interface with paper and pen, the table, the T-squares, the rulers, and other implements of drafting made him feel closer to the subject. So when Dennis found him absent from the drafting table, he had a moment's hesitation, a small fear for the kindly old scientist. But that fear quickly disappeared when he heard Rimmer's familiar voice calling to him.

"Dennis! You must bring the others. We have a solution. At least I think so."

"I'll have them here in ten minutes, Doctor." Dennis left the laboratory and returned to the Bachelor Officers Quarters where Hannah, Galdur, and he were billeted. He delivered Rimmer's news and they quickly reassembled in the laboratory where Rimmer waited.

Dr. Rimmer was clearly excited and fell into his lecture mode.

"We began from the solution to the drone hijacking situation. Dennis, as you will remember, we calculated a frequency of 204.081632653 milliseconds, and using that figure designed an EMF shield. We spent a good deal of time analyzing Galdur's cube and got seriously sidetracked debating how he manifested this phenomenon. We could not answer that question, but it is clear that there is another science at work, and Galdur, along with our friend Kamenwati, are able to manipulate forces in ways unknown to us. In the end we decided to table that discussion, learning how Galdur does what he does and how that interacts with modern science, albeit an important one. What we witnessed has opened my mind to new possibilities…But I digress.

"Our readings from the cube indicated it was indeed an electromagnetic force, a field of energy if you will, that is very much like the Faraday cage we discussed in New Mexico. This force field is somehow constructed on the same principles of charged particles, and so when it is fully formed it exhibits a charge only on the surface. There is no effect on the interior. To put it into practical terms, think of it like an airplane flying through a thunderstorm. Lightning strikes the airplane…"

Dennis raised his hand, bringing it down quickly and feeling a little foolish. "Doctor, do you mean airplanes can be struck by lightning?"

"Oh, yes, and in fact they are struck with regularity but the airplane and passengers are unaffected because the body of the aircraft creates an EMF shield, a Faraday cage, and the charge from the lightening passes harmlessly over the surface.

But back to my point: the cube Galdur created is an electrostatic induction object with the positive and negative particles winding up on opposite sides of the conductor field. The result is an opposing electric field that cancels out the field of the external object's charge inside the cube, making the cube's net electric charge zero." Rimmer stopped for a breath. "The opposing field, the surface of the cube, shields the interior from static charges and electromagnetic radiation."

"Like the airplane," said Dennis.

"Exactly. So the notion of developing something that emits a certain wavelength has no significance."

Hannah leaned forward. "So how do we get Dekker out of that thing he's locked in?"

Rimmer continued. "Our Faraday cage example can only point us in the right direction. As you may know, the Faraday, or EMF cage, is just a wire mesh. The effectiveness of the shielding is directly proportional to the cage's construction, by which I mean how tightly a mesh is made changes the overall effectiveness. But in this case there is no mesh, no metal construction. Galdur's cube is totally smooth. There are no holes."

"So there is no way in?" Dennis asked.

"I didn't say that, but coming to that understanding caused our inquiry to take a turn. Instead of designing a device to emit a signal in a very narrow and specific range, we moved to an EMP solution."

"EMP? What's that?" Galdur was finally grasping some of what Rimmer was saying.

"An electromagnetic pulse. They were discovered early in the atomic bomb experiments, massive bursts of electromagnetic energy that spread out from the blast point, knocking out power grids, telephones, radios, basically anything functioning within the electromagnetic sphere."

"Are you saying that you are planning to explode an atomic bomb on Dekker's head?" Hannah asked with alarm.

"Goodness, no. I was simply explaining that we've known about, and experimented with, EMPs for decades. In fact, the military has been testing variations on EMP technology." Rimmer paused again before continuing. "Here is our solution: the creation of a device, a weapon, to fire a focused pulse of electromagnetic energy at the EMF object. We believe such a weapon will open a hole in that Merlin Box and release Dekker."

"This will work?" Hannah asked.

"In theory, yes," replied Rimmer. "But first we must do some testing." He looked to Galdur. "Can you make another cube?"

Galdur nodded. "Yes, but I'm not certain your theory will work."

"We must try. It is Dekker's only hope."

"Very well. When do you want to conduct this experiment?"

"We must first build the device and then come up with a solution to power it. The Navy can easily deal with that on their nuclear ships and submarines, but we need something much smaller and portable."

"How long will this take? A day, a month, a year?" Hannah asked with some frustration.

"Piggybacking on the Navy's research and testing, I'd say we'll be ready to test within weeks."

Rimmer's response seemed to satisfy Hannah and Dennis. Galdur only shook his head.

CHAPTER TWENTY-FIVE

KAMENWATI WAS UPSET THAT ONLY one of the hijacked drones struck its target. How did they discover his intrusion into the command center? This was a question requiring an answer because he would be held accountable, and for that he needed a very good excuse. Still in the Flows, he probed once again and found the opening to the control room remained open; but he sensed a different energy within. It was someone with power, a practitioner of Magick who was somehow brought to the base. Who could it be? It certainly wasn't Dekker, now safely out of the way. "It can only be my old friend, Galdur." Kamenwati withdrew from the Flows, taking care to leave no trace of his presence. Looking up, he noticed Rahotep.

Rahotep, seeing concern on his master's face, greeted him with his usual deference. "May I be of service, Teacher?" Kamenwati pushed past his trusted lieutenant without responding. Sensing something was amiss, Rahotep followed his master awaiting the reply he was confident would come.

After dropping himself on a couch, Kamenwati looked up. "Rahotep, there is a problem at the base."

"A problem, sir?"

"I have sensed a new presence in the operations building."

"Surely it must be traces left by the man we confined."

"Dekker? No, it is not him. It is someone else, another deep practitioner." Rahotep gave no reply. "I believe it is a man I knew long ago and was friendly with, the Icelander, Galdur."

"Does this interfere with our operation?"

"Interfere? I should say so. He is one of the few able to challenge me, although I now have more power than he."

"Why not simply put him into a Merlin Box, like Dekker?"

"He'll not be as easy to fool as Dekker. No, Galdur has great subtlety and can see many things, and so I do not think getting him to stand still while I conjure another Merlin Box will be possible." Rahotep stood mute, unsure what to say. "I need to eliminate Galdur. I need you to find him and kill him."

Rahotep was unsure how to fulfill the order. "As you wish," he said and left Kamenwati brooding.

Kamenwati's next order of business was checking on Nebwawi in England and Sabu in Germany. Their parts were not as immediately important as this operation in the United States, but they did play a role in the world's response to the drone attacks.

RAHOTEP, UNSURE HOW to carry out his orders, realized the Icelander could be the undoing of a plan only in its first stages. He would first have to gain entry to the military base, locate the Icelander, and then kill him. Deciding to address these questions one at a time, he looked for Fowler, Moor, and Sexton. He found them lounging by the hotel pool, which was not surprising since their task to infiltrate the base and create an opening in the electromagnetic shield was complete.

"Gentlemen," said Rahotep. "I see you are relaxing, but I have a new assignment." Sexton tipped up the brim of a wide hat woven from artificial palm fronds. He looked the part of a self-indulgent tourist. "Won't you join me at the table over there?" The three men extracted themselves from lounge chairs, grabbed their towels, and went to the table.

"There is someone involved in this affair who opposes our master. We have been ordered to kill him."

"Whoa, I'm no killer," said Fowler. He looked to his two companions. "None of us are, and that's not the work we signed up for."

"You will do as Master Kamenwati orders," said Rahotep, irritated at the mutiny. "If you do not he will snuff out your life where you stand." The men grumbled and Fowler, the leader of the group, spoke up. "We don't want to upset the master, but the plain fact is we have no experience in that sort of thing."

Rahotep sat back, thinking. He would not be served well by these men with no skill for the task. "Does the van still have the markings of an exterminator's vehicle?"

"Yeah. We haven't gotten around to removing the wrap," said Fowler.

"Very well. I will do the job myself, but I need your assistance, Mr. Fowler, to capture the man." The three men looked relieved. "Can we get back on the base?"

"That shouldn't be any trouble," said Fowler.

"We will wait until next week when the high state of alert is lifted," said Rahotep.

TEN DAYS PASSED before Fowler drove the van to the base, dropping Moor and Sexton outside the gate. Rahotep's plan was to enter the base, find the Icelander, disable him, and transport him back out before anyone knew what was happening. There was a Walmart near the base, and the two men would not be noticed waiting around. The store's large parking lot would also be a perfect place to strip off the wrap and move the hostage to a place where Rahotep could complete the job.

The fake work order was once again presented to the duty guard. The young man remembered them, or at least their van, and waved them through with little scrutiny. Rahotep let out the breath he was holding through the exchange with the gate guard. Fowler looked at his passenger and smirked. "Hey, I told you there wouldn't be a problem. Where to?" This was the part Rahotep was unclear about, having no idea where on the massive base he might find Galdur.

"Do you have a map of this base?" Rahotep asked.

"Hold on. I think it's here somewhere," said Fowler. He pulled over and rummaged around in the van, finally finding the map under the seat. "Got it!" He returned to his own seat behind the steering wheel. "What are we looking for?"

"He must be staying on the base, so look for housing," said Rahotep.

Many minutes went by while Fowler studied the map, turning it this way and that, mumbling to himself. "I think I've found it," he said finally. "Here." He placed his index finger on a cluster of buildings surrounding an open space. "Looks like base housing."

Rahotep looked at the map and agreed. "Take me there," he ordered.

Fowler looked at the map once again and, reorienting himself, drove off. In fifteen minutes they were cruising around the complex. "Definitely housing. Do you think your man's here?"

"Yes. Now drive slowly around so I can get a feel for the place."

An exterminator's van was not remarkable cruising around the apartment buildings, so there were no questioning looks from the few people they did see. They came to a road leading into a central courtyard that was part park and part playground. "Pull up here," said Rahotep.

They saw children playing on equipment at the far side of the courtyard and a group of mothers sitting at a table keeping an eye on their children. Closer to the van Rahotep noticed three people sitting on a bench under a large tree, an old man, a woman, and a younger man. Rahotep leaned toward the windshield as if trying to hear what the three were saying. "They're too far away, you know," said Fowler.

"Quiet! I need to concentrate," ordered Rahotep. Fowler, stung by the rebuke, sat back with his arms folded across his chest.

They watched as the three people on the bench conversed and then, as if agreeing on some point, stood and walked away. The older man, Galdur, stopped halfway across the courtyard and looked around. His companions did not notice, but Rahotep did, and he ducked down in his seat. "Get down! He may see you," Fowler complied but after a few minutes he'd had enough of the uncomfortable position and sat back up. He noticed the children and their mothers had gone home for the afternoon.

"All clear. There's no one out there."

"Ah, I see the old man entering the building to our right," said Rahotep. "That must be where he is staying. Can we remain parked here?"

Fowler looked around. "It should be fine. But let me fix it so people won't think we're up to something." He reached into the door pocket, extracted a folding windshield cover, and placed it against the glass. "Now we should be able to sit here without attracting attention."

The sun was setting and soon lights began to appear in windows surrounding the courtyard. "What time is it?" Rahotep asked.

Fowler looked at his wristwatch. "Just after seven. How long are we going to wait here?"

"We wait until the lights begin to go out."

Around ten o'clock, they noticed lights being extinguished. "Thank God they go to bed early around here," said Fowler.

"Give it a little more time, and then we can move in." Fowler squirmed uncomfortably in his seat but said nothing.

Forty minutes later, Rahotep seemed ready to move. Fowler carried the few supplies they had prepared for the abduction: rope, zip ties, duct tape, and a pillowcase. They moved to the building's rear door and found it open. Rahotep, while not a deep practitioner or even an Adept, nonetheless had skills in the practice of Magick. Concentrating, Rahotep remained unmoving in the hallway. After a few moments, he moved to a stairway, looked up and then ascended with Fowler following. When they reached the landing, Rahotep looked down the hall and once again held still while seeming to listen. Then he moved quietly down the hall, stopping briefly before each door before moving to the next.

The last door seemed to catch Rahotep's interest. He stood for a long time with eyes tightly shut and then whispered to Fowler, "This is the one. He is inside and I sense he is asleep. You mentioned you have skills with locks?" Fowler nodded and reached into a pocket, presenting a soft bundle for Rahotep's inspection. After unwrapping the cloth, Fowler looked through the several slender metal picks, selecting two that seemed to please him. He knelt so the door handle was at eye level and inserted a flat-bladed pick that he pressed down while inserting another slender one. Keeping the flat pick steady, he moved the narrow pick in and out, searching for tumblers.

Rahotep stood back, giving Fowler room to work. He also looked anxiously back down the hall, fearful someone would leave their apartment and discover them hunched suspiciously before the door. But no one entered the hall and Fowler finished picking the lock. He turned the handle and slowly opened the door. He noticed a sconce fixture on the wall across from the door and pointed to it. Rahotep understood and unscrewed the bulb, throwing the hall into darkness.

Fowler opened the door and entered with Rahotep following. The apartment was small and the furniture sparse, only a couch, a chair, and a small dining set with two chairs. There was a single door leading to a bedroom. Rahotep stood before the bedroom door, concentrating once again. Motioning Fowler to his side, Rahotep slowly turned the doorknob and pushed the door in slowly. The room was nearly dark, but they could see a form on a bed set in the corner of the tiny room. Rahotep had previously laid out their plan: he would hold Galdur down while Fowler taped his mouth. Once silenced, Fowler was to restrain Galdur's hands and feet while Rahotep rendered him unconscious by depressing his carotid artery. The final step was to cover the Icelander's head with the pillowcase.

The pair moved quickly, subduing the Icelander before he knew what was happening. With all steps of the plan followed, Fowler lifted the unconscious man over one shoulder and nodded his readiness to leave. Rahotep led the way, looking carefully down the hall. "All clear," he said. They moved as quietly as possible back to the stairs and out the rear door. The courtyard was empty, and except for one small lighted window across the way, their path was clear.

Rahotep opened the side door of the van and Fowler laid Galdur across the bench seat. They drove off with lights extinguished, and then as they turned onto the main road,

Fowler turned the headlights on. As they passed through the gates Fowler began to breathe easier. "It's a good thing they only care about who's coming and not going out," Fowler said.

They pulled into the Walmart parking lot and drove slowly past one set of entry doors. "Where the heck are they?" Fowler wondered. At the second set of doors they found Moor and Sexton leaning against the wall, obviously bored. When they spotted the van they stepped forward and let themselves in the rear sliding door. Looking at the figure lying across the seat Sexton commented, "Looks like it went well." Moor and Sexton lifted Galdur and placed him on the last bench seat, and then they took their seats, ready for a small trip.

CHAPTER TWENTY-SIX

IT TOOK ONLY TEN DAYS for Rimmer and his team of scientists to debate, haggle, and come to a consensus on the energy source for the weapon. The team had gone through the relative merits and shortcomings of a Marx generator, pulse forming networks, and even a railgun. Dennis liked the idea of a railgun because it sounded deadly, but Rimmer's team quickly dismissed that option because it is based on the principles of the homopolar motor: parallel conducting rails accelerating a sliding armature with an electromagnetic current flowing down one rail, into the armature, and back along the other rail, generating enormous energy and speed. But the armature carries a physical projectile and so they moved on.

A Marx generator is essentially a huge capacitor operating at a single frequency and its output, while great, is not scalable. It is also heavy and would require a retrofitted chassis on a very large truck ,or even a railcar, to support such a unit.

They decided on a pulse forming network. The PFN can be scaled for the application, can be "tuned" to a specific EM frequency, and can be carried on a truck. The biggest question was power. After more discussion the group agreed on a series of capacitors built from fifty-five gallon drums to provide sufficient direct current to handle what they hoped was a reasonable load.

"The stasis is not created by a field generator; it comes from the mind," Rimmer told Dennis. "We don't know how much power it takes to keep it in place, but with Galdur's help, I believe we can discover the answer." The others agreed and began a debate on the nature of the delivery system.

Tasks were divided between Drs. Rimmer, Goddard, Muir, and Bedlow. Rimmer and Goddard worked on the delivery mechanism while Muir and Bedlow focused on the problem of portable capacitors. The drum capacitors were complete before Rimmer's focusing device, but he was well on the way.

Dennis and Hannah were sidelined, and since there was nothing for them to do, they hung around the laboratory. They watched with interest as Muir and Bedlow built several plastic fifty-five gallon drums into capacitors. "These are basically jar capacitors, like the ones first developed by Daniel Gralath in the eighteenth century," said Muir. Dennis nodded and watched. They began by lining the inside of the drums with thin sheets of titanium followed by a number of thicker sheets that slid vertically into place. When finished, the drum was a tightly packed unit.

"How many of these do you have to make?" Hannah asked.

"We don't exactly know," said Muir. "I think we will start with six containers and see if it is sufficient."

When the six drums were fabricated, they were placed against one wall of the laboratory.

Dennis kept tabs on Dr. Rimmer as he worked, but it had been a day since he last checked on him. In fact, Galdur, Hannah, and Dennis made regular visits to the courtyard to talk and enjoy the relaxing environment. When Dennis did visit Rimmer, his eyes went wide with amazement. "What in the world..." The device Rimmer fashioned looked like something from Buck Rogers, a central tube surrounded by glass rings, each diminishing in size. It was much larger than a handheld pistol or even a rifle. In fact, it was six feet in length and mounted on several wooden stands.

Rimmer noticed Dennis and beamed like a proud new father. "Do you like it, Dennis?"

"We'll, yes, but..." Dennis struggled for a polite way to put his question. "But what is it?"

"This is a PFN channeling unit. See here? These wires will connect to the capacitors, and over here…" He walked around to a small box on a pole. "This is the activator."

"You mean a trigger?" Dennis asked.

"I suppose you might call it that. In any event, the keypad is used to enter a frequency and when the toggle is switched, the full energy stored in the capacitors is discharged through the channeling unit."

"At Dekker's prison?"

"Yes, of course, but before we tackle the logistics of charging up the capacitors and transporting them to a remote location, we are going to run some tests."

"And that's where Galdur comes in…"

"He does, indeed. Now, let me finish."

Dennis left the laboratory talking excitedly to Hannah about Rimmer's ray-gun. They searched for Galdur when they reached their quarters but could not find him. "Wherever has he gotten to?" Hannah asked.

"Dunno," said Dennis. "Now, if I were Galdur, what would interest me? Our little park, I'll bet."

They found him in the small park of grass, trees, and playground equipment. Galdur was sitting on a bench beneath a tree enjoying the sounds of children shrieking alternately with joy and distress, a background sound that seemed to calm him.

"Galdur? We couldn't find you," said Dennis.

"And now you have located me," Galdur replied. "What is it you wish?"

Dennis and Hannah sat on the bench. "We have news: Dr. Rimmer and the others have almost finished, and they are going to need your help."

"Oh?"

"Their device is in pieces, but Dr. Rimmer says they need to test it on a Merlin Box," said Dennis.

Galdur looked around at the children playing. "I imagine this would not be the place to do that, although it is peaceful."

"I suspect they'll want to conduct experiments in the lab. Is that possible?" Hannah asked.

"Let's visit tomorrow and see." Galdur stood and looked up into the blue sky. "It's been days since I last stepped foot in the lab, and perhaps the environment may be altered to suit my needs."

The three companions walked back to their quarters.

HANNAH AWOKE THE next morning with an uneasy feeling. She couldn't put her finger on it, but the disquiet was a sensitivity she learned to respect over her career in SIS. Her apartment in the transient officers quarters was on the first floor. Dennis and Galdur were on the floor above. She showered and dressed, thinking that might shake off the feeling, but it didn't. She stepped into the hallway, and instead of going out to the small cafe in the building next door, she decided to check on Galdur. Reaching the second floor, she passed Dennis' room on the right and headed for Galdur's room at the end of the hall. She knocked gently on the door and waited. She knocked again with more urgency, and there was still no answer. She tried the knob and discovered it was not locked. Her heart tightened.

Her senses were on high alert, and instinct from a hundred missions took over. Extracting her Beretta Nano, she crouched to create a lower profile. Pushing the door open, she scanned the room. Nothing. She slipped silently to the left, keeping her back to the wall and scanning the room with her weapon. Satisfied there was no threat, she stood and walked to the bedroom door; she noticed it was slightly ajar. She held the Beretta with both hands and pushed the door open with her foot, ready for any surprise. The room was dark, shades pulled tight over closed venetian blinds. Hannah moved to the single window and pushed back the drapes while keeping one hand on her weapon. A quick look revealed rumpled bedclothes, but it wasn't until she opened the blinds that she discovered the bed was empty. At that moment she knew Galdur had been kidnapped. There was no evidence for her conclusion beyond the covers in disarray, but she knew deep inside that Galdur was not simply up early.

Hannah left Galdur's room and ran to Dennis' door. Her furious knocking woke Dennis from a deep sleep and he was rubbing his eyes as he opened the door. "Hey, what's all the racket?" He saw the frantic look on Hannah's face and knew in an instant there was trouble. "Hannah, what's happened?"

"Galdur is gone," she said. "It must have happened in the night." Dennis looked at her, not fully understanding what she said.

"Maybe he's just up and out. You know, Icelanders like to rise early." He was still not fully awake and reaching for an excuse.

Hannah shook her head. "No, Dennis. He's been taken."

Dennis had a slightly confused expression and leaned out the door to look down the hall to Galdur's room. "What do we do?"

THIRTY MINUTES LATER Hannah and Dennis were standing in General Redmond's office explaining Galdur's disappearance. The general looked worried, pacing with hands clasped behind his back. "First Dekker and now the Icelander? I can understand Dekker's disappearance. He was, after all, off base and out of our control. But this incident, disappearing like that..." Redmond stopped behind his desk, grabbed the telephone, and gave crisp orders for a sweep of the base for any sign of Galdur.

"Thank you, General," said Hannah. "I don't need to remind you how important Galdur is to solving this infratonic assault."

"We can only do so much, Miss Ahmed. Beyond base security, you will have to engage the local authorities. Should that be necessary, I will be happy to make a call for you."

"General, I don't believe we will find Galdur on the base. He has been taken, and I think I know who would do this. My fear is for his life. You see, he is the one person who can help us release Dekker." Hannah turned to Dennis. "Will you go to Dr. Rimmer and his team and tell them what has happened?" Dennis nodded his acknowledgement and left the office.

Turning back to General Redmond, she said, "If you wouldn't mind, General, will you make that call? I don't see why we shouldn't be trying to find Galdur both here on the base and in the community."

"Of course," he said and picked up the telephone once again.

"And if you wouldn't mind, may I have the use of an automobile?"

"I'll do better than that. I'll get you a car and driver. You don't know your way around so a driver will be helpful."

General Redmond made the call to the local sheriff's office and to the motor pool. Now Hannah had to decide where to start looking.

THE SHERIFF OF Cumberland County was not especially helpful. He only took Hannah's statement and told her his department would keep a lookout for Galdur. She knew his efforts were pro forma, but she thanked the sheriff all the same and left the office. Returning to the car she got in on the passenger side and sat without saying a word.

"Is everything okay, ma'am?" asked her military driver.

"No, not really. I shouldn't have expected anything, but still, I hoped the sheriff could be of some use."

"Where would you like to go next?"

Where, indeed? She had to get into the mind of the abductors, into the mind of the man giving them orders. Her search would have to begin at the base, Ft. Bragg, a huge facility covering some 250 square miles but somehow the abductors gained access. "Back to the base security office. I want to check something out."

They drove back in silence, the driver obviously respecting his passenger's mood. The car pulled up to a surprisingly large building and the driver looked over to Hannah. "Here is the security building, ma'am. Should I wait for you?"

"May I call you if I need you again?"

"Of course. Here's my card and number. Call any time."

She glanced at the card. "Thank you, Matthew."

Hannah got out and watched the car drive away before entering the security building. She walked up to a window in the lobby and announced herself, and she dropped the general's name as leverage. She was soon in the office of the duty officer explaining what she sought.

"I would like to view last night's logs from all gates. Is that possible?"

The officer scratched his chin and gave her a doubtful look. "I spoke with General Redmond myself about an hour ago and I've sent out security details looking for your man. I'm not sure what good the gate logs will do."

"I'm hoping to find a vehicle leaving the base at a late hour."

"We only log entries onto the base, not departures, and I've got to tell you, there are a lot of entries."

The officer's comment gave Hannah pause, and she looked around as if the answer might be on the ceiling or walls. She was about to give up when she had an idea. "Do you keep track of who was on duty at the various gates?"

"Certainly."

"May I have a list of the guards and the hours they were on duty?"

The officer made a call to an assistant to provide Hannah the duty roster for the previous evening. "Good luck with this," said the duty officer as she left the office.

In the outer office Hannah was met by another MP officer who promised to schedule an interview with each person on the duty roster. He then took her to a small room. Hannah thanked the military policeman and began poring over the roster.

THE INTERVIEWS BEGAN within the hour, and Hannah found the reports of the various guards beginning to blur: they all said the same thing and remembered mostly personal vehicles passed on and off the base. But then Corporal Scott Hostler did recall something a little unusual. "I was close to the end of my duty at the Gruber Gate, so, ya' know, I was keepin' an eye out for my replacement. Then I see lights approaching, and I think it's the duty jeep bringing him up; but no, it's not a jeep it's a bug van." Hannah thought perhaps she did not understanding American slang.

"Bug van? What's that?" The young corporal sat up a little straighter, hoping to impress the attractive woman questioning him.

"A van with markings of an exterminator. I thought it was a little weird because of the hour, but then I forgot about it. It was only you questioning me that brought it back. Do you think there's something important about the van?"

Hannah was way ahead of Corporal Scott Hostler. "Do you have any idea where the bug van went, Corporal Hostler? There is an intersection not too far from the gate."

"Yeah, now that you mention it. The bug van went left at the intersection. I don't know after that."

"That's fine, Corporal. You have been a great help," said Hannah. "You can go now." Hostler was sorry to leave the company of the pretty lady but stood and left. Hannah closed up the file folder in front of her and retrieved the card given to her by Matthew Strand, the driver. He answered almost immediately, a cell phone Hannah surmised, and told her he would pick her up in ten minutes.

Hannah felt she finally had something to go on, even if it was the barest thread.

IT WAS WELL into the afternoon when Hannah climbed into the waiting car. "Thank you for coming so quickly." Matt Strand, her driver, smiled and gave her a small salute. "Where to, ma'am?"

"To the Gruber Gate, please. I'll direct you from there."

It took only a few minutes to reach the gate, and Hannah asked Matt to stop for a moment. She got out and went to the guard shack and spoke with the duty guard. Matt couldn't hear what she asked but when she got back into the car she seemed pleased.

"We may be onto something," Hannah said. "The guard told me he has the duty three times each week and he remembered a new exterminator coming and going about a week ago. He wasn't familiar with the vendor, but he said they had a work order and so he didn't think anything of it."

"An exterminator?" Strand asked.

"Yes, and the guard had the van logged in yesterday afternoon: F&M Pest Control, one driver and one passenger, and they said it was a follow-up visit."

"So we're looking for this pest control van?" Strand asked.

"Head out the gate and turn left," ordered Hannah. "We'll see where that takes us."

The road passed along the perimeter of the base fence, intersected Honeycutt Road, and turned into a wooded area. They continued to follow the road, looking for the F&M Pest Control van, but there was no sign of the vehicle and Hannah was becoming anxious. When they reached Haw River she looked over her shoulder. "We passed a small road a few minutes ago. Let's go back and check it out."

Matt swung the car around and headed back down the road. After traveling about one mile, they came to a narrow chip-sealed road leading deeper into woods.

"Let's slow down," said Hannah. "I need to look around. They may have pulled off."

"Fine by me," said Matt. "This road won't let me go very fast anyway."

After driving for a while, they came to a turn and Hannah saw something. "Stop! I think I see something up ahead." Matt pulled over as far as the road allowed, which wasn't much, and came to a stop.

"Wait here," said Hanna. As she left Matt noticed her pulling a piece. *I wonder where she was hiding that,* Matt thought.

Hannah followed the curve in the road but then stopped and dropped to the ground. Matt watched with some alarm, trying to figure out what was happening. He watched her move off the road into the cover of the trees and then disappear from sight. His tension grew as the minutes crawled by. He wondered what the SIS agent was doing.

The quiet of the forest was shattered by the sound of two shots. "What the hell!" Matt was truly concerned and wondered if he should stay or go. He decided to stay.

Minutes passed, and then Hannah came around the curve in the road and she wasn't alone.

HANNAH APPROACHED THE curve in the road looking for the glint she had seen through the trees. The glint did not reappear, but her curiosity was raised. After moving around the curve, she froze. There, just ahead, she could see the rear of a van. She dropped to the ground and waited. A minute went by without an alarm being raised. She breathed easier and moved into the underbrush that grew up to the edge of the chip-sealed road.

She moved through the bushes and trees to a better observation position. "That's a van, all right," she said to herself. The van seemed empty, but the open passenger side door suggested otherwise. Hannah listened carefully and was about to approach the van when she heard a voice.

"How long are we going to wait, Fowler?"

"Not much longer. I think the old man is coming out of it."

That was as much as Hannah needed to hear, and she moved silently out of the woods to the rear of the van. She peeked through the tinted windows but had a hard time making out what was going on inside. Then she made out three figures hunched over another spread on the rear bench seat. She needed to lure them out of the van and away from Galdur, and she had to come up with a plan and quickly.

The opposite side of the road was as heavily wooded as the other, but it didn't face the open side door of the van. In a crouching run she dashed across the road and picked up a handful of loose pebbles. "These will do nicely," she said. From behind a tree she sent one pebble sailing upward. It landed on the roof of the van. The discussion from inside stopped for a moment and then resumed. Hannah repeated the interruption, and again she heard the talking stop. She couldn't see well through the tinted side windows, but this time one of the figures separated from the others and went to the open door. Hannah let him poke his head out, look around, and return to the others. Hannah tossed another pebble and this time the entire group stepped out to investigate.

"What the hell's going on out here?" Hannah heard the exclamation from the opposite side of the van.

"I don't know Fowler. I came out and looked and there was nothing."

"All right, you and Moor go that way and look around, and I'll go this way." Hannah watched the group separate and waited for things to develop.

Crouching in the underbrush, she watched as two men came around the rear of the van while another rounded the front. She noticed they were unarmed, and that made her gambit all the more viable. The two men joined the one Hannah guessed was the leader, Fowler, and another discussion ensued, one that stopped short when Hannah fired a shot into the air. The three men instinctively crouched and looked for the source of the shot. Hannah stepped out onto the road behind them.

"You need to leave," she ordered. "Now."

The three men stood, gaping at her, obviously wondering where she came from. Fowler gave a sneering, superior look to his companions, but Hannah was ready for them. "Don't even think about it."

Fowler made a move toward Hannah, but she was much too fast. She fired another shot, showering Fowler with bits of rock. Her steady hold on the weapon kept the other two in place. "I said, leave."

The abductors were obviously convinced the woman was not kidding, and as a unit, turned and ran up the road. Hannah watched with satisfaction but knew it was only a matter of time before they regrouped and returned to ambush her. She holstered her weapon and went to the van where a groggy but ambulatory Galdur sat, looking around in confusion.

"Where am I?" Galdur asked, and recognizing the SIS agent, gave a weak smile. "Miss Ahmed, I am very pleased to see you."

"We have to get going. Can you stand? Are you able to walk?"

"I believe so," said Galdur, who stood and stepped uncertainly to the open van door.

"Let me help you," said Hannah, and she draped his arm around her neck.

She moved Galdur as quickly as possible back around the curve to the waiting car and Matt Strand. She waved to him with her free hand, indicating they needed to leave in a hurry. Matt understood and started the car. When Hannah and Galdur reached the car, she helped the elderly Icelander into the rear seat and got into the front seat. "Let's get out of here."

"Roger that, ma'am," said Matt, who executed a quick U-turn and flew back down the road, not even trying to avoid the ruts, grooves, and potholes. When they reached the main road Matt really let the car open up, racing back to the base.

Hannah leaned over the front seat to see how her charge was doing. "Are you better?"

Galdur nodded. "Yes, much better. Thank you, Miss Ahmed, for rescuing me."

"Why did they want you?"

"I'm not certain, but I suspect it has something to do with Kamenwati. He may perceive me as a threat and was trying to eliminate me."

"That makes sense, and we are going to place you in a more secure location just in case those thugs have a mind to try again."

CHAPTER TWENTY-SEVEN

FOWLER, MOOR, AND SEXTON STOPPED running when they rounded another curve in the road. The adrenaline was dissipating and Fowler's mind was clearing. "Hold on, boys. We need to think this thing through." The other two came to a stop and waited to hear what Todd Fowler had to say. Fowler's bruised ego needed some sort of satisfaction, and he squinted, looking furtively back down the road. "We've got to go back. Rahotep's coming and we need to have that guy trussed up and waiting for him."

"But what about the woman? She looked like she knew how to handle that gun," said Moor.

"Yeah, and we don't have any of our own," added Sexton.

"True, but there are three of us and we can surround her, then take her," said Fowler.

They all agreed and split up, using the cover of the woods to hide their movements. When they reached the van, Fowler realized they were too late. Their hostage was gone. Sexton looked over Fowler's shoulder and saw the empty van. "Ooh, this is not good."

The men went back down the curve in the road and moved cautiously until they realized the road was empty.

"She must have had a car waiting," said Fowler.

"What are we gonna do?" Sexton asked.

"We tell the Egyptian the truth: we were ambushed and fired on. For now we go back to the van and wait."

An hour later Rahotep stood looking at the open van door, his anger rising and his worry growing. The trio launched into overlapping excuses as soon as he arrived, but he was able to unravel the story that the men had been ambushed by an armed team who ran them off.

"We were fired on. We had to escape," offered Fowler. "Then we came back for an ambush, but our man was gone."

Rahotep looked around. "Lord Kamenwati will not be pleased. We need another plan, and we need to eliminate Galdur as quickly as possible."

Fowler looked to his fellows with doubt in his expression but said nothing.

It was a very quiet ride back to the hotel.

RAHOTEP FOUND KAMENWATI meditating and was reluctant to interrupt. His master sensed his presence and opened his eyes. "Rahotep, you have returned sooner than expected."

"I do not bring good news, Master. I went to the prearranged place in the forest and found the prisoner missing." Rahotep could almost feel his master's hot rage burning through him. "Our men carried out the abduction as planned and drove into the forest to wait for me to carry out your orders. But somehow they were discovered. They were fired upon, and since they were unarmed, flight was their only option. When they doubled back, the van was empty and there was no sign of the prisoner."

Kamenwati stood and issued a single order: "Leave me."

After Rahotep left, Kamenwati struggled with both the failure and trying to devise an alternate plan. He did not want to report the loss of Galdur to the Abaddon spirit; he must resolve this situation on his own. "How do I get the Icelander now? Surely his people will increase his security." After grappling with his dilemma for a long while, Kamenwati could find only one option leading to Galdur's capture. "The Icelander must be lured off that military base."

The days following saw Kamenwati generating one scheme after another, each discarded, each dead end leading to more frustration. He simply could not think of an enticement for Galdur to leave the base.

Rahotep entered his master's rooms quietly. He was concerned for the mystic's health since he had not eaten much over the last few days and was beginning to show signs of physical weakness. "How are you this morning, sir? May I order you some breakfast?"

Kamenwati looked up at Rahotep, his eyes now looking bruised, the dark, puffy flesh below the lids contrasting with the pale, somewhat sickly whiteness of his complexion. Kamenwati heard the question but didn't seem to possess the strength to answer. He simply shook his head.

"Master, you cannot continue like this. You need to eat and sleep." Kamenwati responded by dropping his chin to his chest as Rahotep continued. "Perhaps I may help. Can you tell me what troubles you?"

Kamenwati lifted his chin, looking at his follower with a grateful smile. "I wish you could help, Rahotep. Since the Icelander's escape I have been trying to devise some plan to lure him out where he can once again be captured. But think as I might, I cannot find a compelling reason, the bait, that will entice him to come to us."

"Sir, perhaps you have been approaching the problem from the wrong angle." Kamenwati was desperate for an appeal that would both reach and attract Galdur. He sat up straighter and listened to his oldest ally.

"This man is an adherent to the Old Ways, is he not?"

"Yes."

"Then we assume he is not familiar with modern technologies, relying instead on Magick and the Flows."

"I'll give you that."

"Then that is what we use to lure him out."

"I've gone through those options, Rahotep. I considered reaching out to him in the Flows, but there is nothing to offer him, nothing to entice him."

"But sir, there is one thing, the man we entrapped in the Merlin Box. Perhaps there is a way to offer him to the Icelander."

Kamenwati's face lit up. "Rahotep, you are a genius! It was right here before me and I failed to see the obvious." He stood and paced, his mind now working on Rahotep's suggestion. He could find no immediate problems with the strategy, but a way to implement it would require more planning. He felt suddenly hungry. "In answer to your previous question, yes, you may order me some breakfast." Looking at his rumpled shirt and bare feet, and was slightly embarrassed. "I believe I will shower first."

Rahotep, quietly excited for his victory, picked up the telephone and called room service, deciding a full English breakfast was in order.

GALDUR'S RETURN WAS hailed as a victory by Rimmer and the others on their project. Galdur was by now quite clear-headed and he first sought out Dr. Rimmer.

"I am ready to begin on your experiments, Dr. Rimmer," said Galdur.

"Are you certain? We could wait a day so you can regain your strength."

"Not necessary. Icelanders are a robust people, and I am ready to do what I can to release Adam from his prison."

"Then we begin," said Rimmer. "First, however, we must complete the PFN device. Allow Miss Ahmed to show you to new quarters right here in this building. It will be much safer than before." Hannah led the Icelander out of the main laboratory to a converted office on the second floor that overlooked the lab.

Rimmer turned to his support staff and said with some urgency, "It is now our turn to get to work, gentlemen. We must have a workable solution as soon as possible." With that order, all disbursed to different sections of the large room, each focused on a different aspect of completing the PFN cannon: the pulse-forming network itself, the focusing system, a modulating mechanism, and finally a reliable transportable power supply.

The PFN device was not remotely ready the next morning and that meant Galdur was on hold. Dennis was fully occupied shadowing, and pestering, the scientists. Hannah remained on guard, accompanying Galdur on walks within the base confines while he explained the principles of Magick and the Flows. Although the inaction grated on her nerves, she did not mind the duty. She enjoyed listening to

Galdur and learning about a world she knew nothing about. "Do you suppose I might learn a little of this Magick you talk about?" Hannah asked. Galdur thought about the question.

"The answer is both yes and no. Given time almost anybody with the desire can become an acolyte and perhaps develop to the level of an Adept; but that requires years of study and there is no time to begin training you, Miss Ahmed." Hannah was a little disappointed. "Unless you exhibited natural abilities, sensitivities, like Dekker," Galdur added.

Hannah was encouraged. "I am a full Egyptian, and we are taught from a very early age about what my mother called spiritual things. You know, the unseen things around us." Galdur nodded his head in understanding. "And please, call me Hannah. I feel we have become friends."

"Very well, Hannah. And to your point about heritage, perhaps you have a latent gift that may be unlocked. If so, that may prove quite valuable in coming events, the opposition we can count on from an unexpected quarter." Galdur looked at the SIS agent and thought once again what a nice couple she and Dekker made. He turned his mind back to the subject at hand and let out a long breath.

"It seems we are to have time on our hands, and so I suggest we begin your training."

THE PLAN WAS simple. Kamenwati would reach out to Galdur through the Flows and offer a deal: Dekker's release in return for a private meeting. That offer held little personal risk for Galdur, and in fact, it was an opportunity for two old, if estranged, friends to clear the air between them. Satisfied with his logic, Kamenwati entered the Flows and set his plan into motion.

Galdur...Galdur, I wish to speak with you. Kamenwati waited patiently for Galdur's reply, which came quickly.

I perceive it is my adversary, Kamenwati.

It is I, Kamenwati, and I hoped you might see me less an adversary and more the old friend of years ago.

In light of your actions in Germany, and of late in Egypt and here in America, I see you only as a foe.

I think you misunderstand my motivations, Galdur. If you perceived my intentions your opinion might change.

You are a fool, Kamenwati. Your use of a stasis, a Merlin Box, only proves your malicious intent.

Kamenwati saw his opening and took it. *Perhaps I can make a peace offering. I will release Dekker if you will agree to meet.*

Galdur was cautiously interested. Any opportunity to release his friend from that vile prison was worth a face-to-face meeting. *Very well, I will meet you, but you must first release Dekker.*

The response was not unexpected and Kamenwati was ready with a rejoinder. *And I must be assured you come alone, old friend. I will make this concession: the Merlin Box will be visible but its occupant will stay inside. If you are truly alone, I will release my hold and your friend will walk free.*

Galdur found no fault with the plan. *Where shall we meet?*

We meet in the picnic clearing in the forest. Do you know where that is?

Yes, I do.

Good. We will meet tomorrow at dusk. The connection was severed. Kamenwati summoned Rahotep and his men to ready them for a new abduction.

Galdur knew he could tell no one about the meeting, or almost no one. He would confide in Hannah and ask her to take him to the picnic clearing.

CHAPTER TWENTY-EIGHT

AFTER DISENGAGING FROM THE FLOWS and his interaction with Kamenwati, Galdur was uncertain how to proceed. He would speak with Hannah, of course, but how to manage Dekker's release was the dilemma. Surely Kamenwati wanted something, but what? He would have to rely on Hannah for advice. After all, he had spent the last two days in her instruction and she seemed to understand the principle of the Flows. In addition, he was pleased to find that beneath her government service exterior was an openness to Magick, and he told her she had promise.

He left the tiny converted office that was now a bedroom and walked to a small lounge area above the laboratory floor where he found Hannah fully engrossed with her smart phone. "Hannah, may I interrupt you?" She looked up quickly, a little embarrassed to be caught wasting time with a game app on her phone.

"Sure. This is nothing important," she said laying the phone on the low table before her.

"I have just been in contact with Kamenwati."

"How? Where?"

"In the Flows, of course. He wants to meet with me, and he says he will free Dekker from the the Merlin Box."

"That is wonderful! But why would he do that? What does he want?"

"That is the question. He says he wishes to make amends, to explain what he is doing." Galdur took a seat next to Hannah. "I do not trust him, and more importantly, I do not trust the spirit he has taken on."

"Spirit? What do you mean?"

"The Abaddon spirit, an ancient evil that, it seems, cannot be eradicated. It now controls Kamenwati, moving him toward…what? I do not know, only that it is ultimately deadly for the host and promises destruction for civilization."

"I don't scare easily," said Hannah. "We will meet this head-on."

"Very well, but I need your advice, your military skills, to plan for this meeting."

"Fine. Where is the meeting to be? What sort of terrain?"

"He asked me to come to the picnic area in the forest."

"That's the same place I saw Dekker trapped in that box. I know it well."

"Kamenwati is expecting me to come alone, so that is our first obstacle."

Hannah became energized by the prospect of this mission, an undertaking for which she was well suited. They talked for hours, exploring different scenarios and theories about Kamenwati's objective. In the end, Hannah had only two possible outcomes, neither of which were good. "He will either try to kill you outright, or he will entrap you as he did Dekker. The question remains: why?"

"I am a threat. It is as simple as that. He obviously has a plan and we have to anticipate it, neutralize it, and retrieve Dekker."

"We should tell General Redmond, who can give us a Special Operations unit for support."

"No. Kamenwati would know about such a plan before we ever got there. This trip to retrieve Dekker is up to us alone."

"We may go in alone but we're not unarmed." She drew her weapon and drew strength from its feel.

Galdur nodded but knew such a weapon would not decide the outcome of the meeting.

HANNAH PARKED THE car in a turnout before reaching the picnic area. She and Galdur had discussed their roles in this upcoming meeting. His was to face Kamenwati while she concealed herself in a convenient observation position. "Be sure to remain absolutely still. He will be able to detect you if you move." They parted company, Galdur continuing down the narrow road and Hannah slipping into the forest.

Galdur walked across the stone-paved parking lot serving the picnic area. The sky was bright blue above the trees and the mulch surface around the four picnic tables created a peaceful setting. *That it were so*, he thought. As he approached the edge of the parking area he noticed a shimmering against the trees and then a discernible form: a large cube. It was almost transparent, but as the moments went by, the cube seemed to gain more form until it was translucent. It was floating about two feet from the ground, and inside the cube he saw the form of a man. Dekker.

Kamenwati appeared seemingly from nowhere and was standing several feet in front of the cube. Galdur approached, reaching out himself to learn if Kamenwati brought others with him. He sensed no others, but that did not mean Kamenwati did not have treachery planned. He took some consolation in Hannah's presence but knew she could not defeat Kamenwati.

Turning his attention to the Egyptian, he sensed a power much greater than the man himself.

"My old friend," said Kamenwati. "How good it is to see you again."

"Yes, the last time was in Krugerschloss. I'm sure you remember that."

"As it turns out, that day was not one of defeat but of victory."

"How do the circumstances of Abaddon's demise not equate to defeat?"

"The human host for the true power was found lacking and the spirit of Abaddon allowed the man to die. But surely, Galdur, you know a spirit cannot be destroyed. It simply moves on."

"And you became its new host," said Galdur. The Egyptian nodded. "You must know the spirit of Abaddon cannot be controlled. It works through subtle seduction."

"The spirit has given me vastly more power and clarity."

"So you say, but let me warn you, as a friend, of the doom you bring on yourself. You promised if we met you would release Dekker." Galdur gestured to the Merlin Box behind Kamenwati.

"I confess, he was the bait in my trap, a means to lure you here by yourself."

"You cannot do to me what you have done to Dekker, and you know it," said Galdur. "You are a fool if you try."

"Silence!" The command was harsh and carried with it a power Galdur had never encountered. With the word Galdur felt himself restricted and knew at once Kamenwati was exercising a restraining word. Under normal circumstances it would be easy to break the restraint, but this was much more and he knew the spirit would supply as much power as necessary to keep him immobilized.

Kamenwati smirked. "I did not bring you here simply to confine you." He gestured toward the trees and four men stepped forward. "Today you die, Galdur, and I will continue unhindered in the creation of a conflict that will consume the world."

The men approached Galdur, clearly ready to bind him with physical restraints. But at that moment Hannah stepped from her place of concealment, weapon held outward covering the men.

"Stop right there or I'll shoot."

DEKKER WAS LANGUISHING in the murky limbo, all his efforts to break out of the stasis to no avail. Neither physical attacks nor mental assaults using his knowledge of Magick proved potent enough to crack the hold on him. Time did not seem to pass within the stasis; and Dekker, despite his normally reliable sense of time, had no idea if he had been inside the stasis for a day, a week, or more. He only knew there was no way to communicate with the outside, not even with Galdur.

And then something changed. He began to see trees around him, and then ground below. "Something is happening!" Dekker's spirits lifted.

The cube continued to materialize in the physical world and Dekker hoped that meant rescue was imminent. He splayed himself against the translucent wall facing the open space before him. He saw a figure, Kamenwati, standing before him, and then out of the mist came another figure. "Galdur!" Dekker could hear the conversation between Kamenwati and Galdur, although it was muffled, as if he were listening through a door.

Dekker followed the conversation as best he could, but he definitely heard the tone on both sides harden and turn loud.

"Today you die, Galdur, and I will continue unhindered in the creation of a conflict that will consume the world," he heard Kamenwati say.

He watched helplessly as four men stepped from the surrounding forest, clearly intent on carrying out the Egyptian's promise. But there was someone else, a woman, also emerging from the trees. It was Hannah!

"Stop right there or I'll shoot."

Dekker watched the tableaux before him: Hannah with her weapon trained on the four men, all who stopped quickly when she appeared. The moment was broken when Kamenwati shouted. No, Dekker decided, it was more guttural, more like a raging lion or an enraged spirit. With that screech the transparency of the cube returned to the flat, opaque white, but he could still hear what was taking place outside. Shots rang out and there was a scuffling of feet, and then nothing.

"What happened?" Dekker wondered. "Hannah shot at someone, but whatever the plan was, I'm still trapped."

He slid down the wall, sitting with his with knees up as a new determination to find some means to get out rose within him.

"If only I could reach Galdur."

HANNAH WATCHED THE picnic area through the thick brush. She crouched perfectly still as Galdur instructed, watching and waiting. Galdur walked across the small parking lot to the edge of the picnic area, and she saw the Merlin Box materialize. Even though she experienced this phenomenon before, she was no less startled by the cube appearing from thin air than she was when it appeared previously and then vanished.

She listened as Kamenwati greeted Galdur and the conversation that ensued.

She heard the shout from Kamenwati and saw Galdur suddenly immobilized, much as she had been during that first encounter. Then she saw four men emerge from the forest, including one she recognized, he one called Rahotep. He was accompanied by three others, local recruits she supposed. It was time for action. Hannah stepped into the clearing and, leveling her weapon on the men, issued an order.

"Stop or I'll shoot."

Hannah meant business and the attackers seemed to understand it. They held still for a moment, time enough for her to decide how to handle the situation.

There was a shout from Kamenwati and the Merlin Box seemed to pop out of existence, and Rahotep and his men were propelled into action. Hannah remained cool and took aim at Rahotep, their leader. She fired, and he spun around with the impact of the round. She turned her attention to the others who, recognizing her as a new threat, rushed her as a group. Hannah coolly lined up on the nearest attacker, fired twice, moved to the next, and fired again, then to the last. All three were down, their conditions unknown, but they were at least no longer a danger. She saw Rahotep lying on the ground writhing in pain, and she was satisfied that he, too, was out of the game.

Hannah wondered for a moment if Galdur was injured, but then she realized he was unharmed as he looked around in despair. Hannah approached him, touching his shoulder lightly.

"What is it, Galdur?"

"He's gone," he said. Hannah looked to the place Kamenwati had been standing and beyond to where the Merlin Box had been.

"Do you mean Kamenwati?"

"No. Dekker. He's gone and I am afraid the only chance to release him has been lost."

"No. There is Dr. Rimmer's pulse forming network cannon. Let's get back to the base and take the wounded man with us."

Galdur looked at the other three men on the ground. "Don't you think we should notify someone about these men?"

"You're right." Hannah pulled a cell phone from her pocket. "I'll call Matthew Strand, my MP driver. He'll know what to do."

KAMENWATI WAS SURPRISED by Hannah's appearance. He recognized her as the woman working with Dekker in Egypt, but how did she come to be here? Kamenwati did not have time to consider the question. The spirit was now fully engaged within him and he lost awareness of his participation in the situation. He watched Rahotep spin around. *Was he shot?* There was a shout. *Did that sound come from my throat?* He watched Rahotep collapse, but he callously ignored him, quickly dematerializing the Merlin Box and then placing a masking cloud around himself. To those around he seemed to vanish, but it was only an illusion and Kamenwati took advantage of the confusion to slip away.

An hour later, the Egyptian mystic, now dressed in a suit, presented himself at the Delta Airlines ticket counter at the Raleigh-Durham airport. A cheery attendant greeted him. "May I help you, sir?"

"Yes, I wish to purchase a ticket to London. Do you fly direct from here?"

"I'm afraid not, but I do have a flight through Atlanta leaving at four o'clock." She looked at the time on her computer. "That's only about two hours from now."

"That will be fine," said Kamenwati. He reflected on the events of the last few days, becoming angry, not at himself but at those following him. He would never admit his culpability in the way events unfolded. He would deflect and blame others. That is how he planned to present this outcome to the Abaddon spirit, as the fault of others.

The flight through Atlanta and on to Heathrow took him through the night. He arrived just before nine the next morning, and as he pushed through the crowded concourse and emerged at a taxi stand, he realized he was relaxed for the first time in days. He was away from the complications of his American project and was now on British soil, determined not to make the same mistakes.

"There is still time to make this work, despite the Americans."

CHAPTER TWENTY-NINE

THERE WAS A RENEWED SENSE of purpose among Dr. Rimmer's team. Hannah's report of the encounter with Kamenwati and of seeing Dekker, if only as a shape inside the Merlin Box, sent the team of scientists into overdrive. Hannah was protective of Galdur, given what he experienced, but Rimmer pressed for the creation of a test Merlin Box. "We need to free Adam, and Galdur is the only means to test our PFN device," Rimmer insisted.

"Can you give him just a little space? You don't know what he's just been through," said Hannah.

Galdur, sitting apart in a plastic chair, stood. "Hannah, I have endured much worse over the years, and the reason for my introspection is not fatigue. I have been attempting to understand the scope of Kamenwati's new power and how that may impact our world."

"Are you able to construct a new stasis for us?" asked Rimmer.

"Yes. Where do you want it? They don't move around, you know."

Rimmer guided Galdur to an open space in the lab. He completely ignored Galdur's last statement, but Dennis did not. As the lights dimmed in the laboratory, Galdur began the creation process.

Dennis whispered to Hannah, "Did I hear Galdur correctly? A stasis chamber stays in a single spot?"

"I'm sorry, Dennis. I didn't hear that. Tell me more."

"He said, 'they don't move around' when asked to create the stasis."

Hannah remembered the Merlin Box that appeared in the same place she had last seen it. "This could be very important."

"Darn right," said Dennis. "One of our questions has been where exactly to take this PFN cannon and where to aim it."

"And it follows, if Galdur's his Merlin Box cannot move, then neither can Kamenwati's," said Hannah.

Dennis looked at the small group of scientists surrounding Galdur. "Let's let them finish their tests before we approach Galdur on this." Hannah nodded her assent.

IT TOOK ONLY a few minutes for Galdur to produce a stasis cube. Once formed, the Icelander relaxed into an easy posture with his eyes closed, feet firmly planted, and arms outstretched. The Merlin Box hovered about one foot above the floor, its indistinct sides washing every-so-often with a different pastel color. The effect was mesmerizing, but Rimmer's team did not pay attention. They rolled up the PFN cannon, positioning it one hundred feet from the glowing form in the middle of the lab.

An engineer dragged over a heavy electrical cable and hooked into the PFN cannon. "Be sure we are running direct current, and monitor the levels used with each step," ordered Dr. Rimmer. The engineer gave him a *do-you-think-I'm-a-fool* look and completed the coupling procedure.

"Good to go, sir," said the engineer, who retreated to a panel with many meters and knobs.

"Right," said Rimmer. "Then let's begin."

Dr. Rimmer was a rigorous researcher and insisted on moving in small intervals of power. He knew the frequency, which was thankfully identical to that used to defeat the mind control attack, the "Infratonic Assault" as he called it.

They stepped through increasing levels of power, making notes at each, until finally something happened. The PFN cannon emitted an energy bolt, although it was not visible. But at this particular power level the side of Galdur's cube suddenly changed color. Instead of soft pastels, an angry red spot appeared. It was small at first but grew quickly. "It's working!" shouted Rimmer.

Hannah, who had been observing from a distance, stiffened. "Something's wrong," she said to Dennis. She went to Galdur's side. His posture was no longer easy. He stood stiff with clenched fists.

"This is hurting him!" she shouted. Rimmer looked over and recognized the change in Galdur, and it seemed he got worse as more EM bolts were fired and the red spot increased in size.

"Shut it down!" Rimmer ordered. The scientist manning the voltage flow on the PFN cannon immediately spun a dial counter-clockwise. The red spot glowed angrily for a moment and then began shrinking, finally fading away, and the pastel colors returned.

Hannah grabbed Galdur's arm and spoke softly to him. "Galdur, can you hear me? You must come out of your trance." Galdur responded slowly to her plea, unclenching his fists and his posture returning to an easy state. As his eyes opened, the cube began to dissipate, vanishing when he became fully awake. Hannah looked at him with concern. "Are you all right? What happened?" she asked as she led him to a chair. He was quickly surrounded by Rimmer's team, each inquiring about his well-being.

"Thank you all. I believe I will recover, but not without the consequence of a blazing headache." Rimmer motioned to Dennis, who disappeared into a restroom and returned with a bottle of aspirin and a cup of water. Galdur swallowed the pills, thanking Dennis, and then looking to Rimmer, began describing his experience.

"I don't know how to express this, but let me try. I formed the stasis as before, and then from a point of view above, I watched as you fired your cannon. My stasis held with no ill effects to it or myself at first, but then you must have reached a certain level that changed things. I felt a growing pressure in my brain and as the red spot increased in size, so did the pressure in my head. It was becoming unbearable when I heard Hannah calling and I returned." He looked directly at Rimmer. "Had you not stopped, I believe you would not only have broken the stasis but my skull as well."

"Now, that is an interesting side effect," said Rimmer. "Do you believe we would have penetrated your cube?"

"Not just penetrated. Obliterated," replied Galdur.

Hannah stepped into the conversation. "Would this hold true for Kamenwati?" Galdur stopped at her suggestion, realizing where she was going with the thought.

"The principles governing the creation of the cube, the Merlin Box, are fixed. The stasis has been used through time to prolong life, to avoid conflicts, and the like. What Kamenwati has constructed is no different, and therefore I believe the answer to your question is yes. I think your device will not only free Dekker but will in all probability kill Kamenwati."

Dennis jumped up with his typical enthusiasm. "What are we waiting for? Let's get Dekker and take care of that crazy Egyptian once and for all!"

"But let me caution you: breaching the Merlin Box will unbalance the very stasis that created it. I cannot tell you what will happen to Dekker inside." Rimmer and the other scientists now shared concerned looks.

Hannah, with considerable more calm than the young NCTC geek, asked Galdur for more information. "Dennis mentioned that earlier you said the stasis is fixed to particular place."

"Yes, wherever it is formed is where it stays until its creator removes it," said Galdur.

"Then we know exactly where to find Dekker," said Hannah.

"What are we waiting for?" Dennis asked again. "Let's get going."

Rimmer smiled at the young computer expert. "We will go, and soon, Dennis, but we must first make these components transportable, and we have to calculate how many electrochemical battery drums are necessary."

Within a few hours everything was complete and a convoy of trucks and cars headed for the picnic area in the forest.

AN ASSEMBLY OF cars and trucks parked along the narrow forest road, leaving an opening for a stake bed truck carrying a full load of fifty-five gallon drums. The truck was followed by a transport truck carrying the PFN cannon. Scientists and engineers huddled around the spot Galdur was standing. "This is where I stood when confronting Kamenwati." He shivered slightly at the memory and was glad Dennis, Hannah, Dr. Rimmer, and the rest were there with him.

The stake bed pulled up close, allowing the engineer to connect the power barrels to the PFN cannon. Rimmer and two others inspected the setup, and each announced their satisfaction.

"Be sure to elevate your cannon. Dekker's box is hovering about three feet above the ground," Hannah said to Dr. Rimmer. Slight adjustments were made, and when everything was ready, Rimmer ran down the list of scientists and engineers, each announcing "go" for their particular area of responsibility.

"This is like a moon launch," said Dennis.

With all departments ready to go, Rimmer nodded to the engineer on the stake bed truck. The engineer punched a button on his console and a hum rose from the truck as the series of fifty-five gallon electrochemical cells came online. He watched a meter on his console and when it reached the target charge point he lifted his hand. At the PFN cannon console the scientist operating the device punched a button releasing the charge. The previously empty space now glowed with the outline of the Merlin Box. The PFN cannon was fired again, and the cube became fully visible.

"My God, there he is!" Hannah grabbed Dennis' shoulder with her exclamation.

"Dekker! Can you see us?" Dennis was just as excited as Hannah.

Rimmer stepped closer to the Merlin Box. He could almost see Dekker through the opaque wall, and he hoped his friend saw him. Rimmer gestured for Dekker to move away from the front wall. After a moment, the shadowy figure inside moved as directed, disappearing into the mists. "I hope this is enough to protect you, son." Rimmer stepped out of the line of fire and gestured to fire another bolt.

With each burst the effect on the stasis chamber became more pronounced. The results followed closely their experiment on Galdur's construct in the lab, the wall of the cube first turning from swirling pastels to an angry mix of reds, grays, and blacks. The center point, where the PFN cannon was aimed, began showing a deep angry red spot that grew with each successive charge.

"I pray Dekker survives this," said Dr. Rimmer.

DEKKER WAS SURPRISED to find his tight prison suddenly reappearing in the real world. He wondered if Kamenwati or Galdur had a hand in this. He looked as best he could through the translucent wall and saw a number of people and vehicles. They were all murky as if he were looking through smoke, but he could see them. "It's a rescue!" He placed his palms on the surface of what he considered a wall of his prison and immediately took them away. The box did not really have solid walls but was an energy barrier, and now, for some reason, that barrier stung him when he touched it.

"That's odd," he said. "It hasn't done this before."

Dekker watched as two of the figures waved at him, one of whom could only be Dennis and the other standing next to him was a woman. "Hannah," he said. He waved back but he assumed they were having as much difficulty seeing him as he was seeing them. He watched the cube's color change from the normal swirling pastels to a dark mixture of red and black. Another figure stepped forward, much closer than the others. "Horace, it's you! How in the world did you get here?" Rimmer was gesturing to him.

"He wants me to move back. Okay, Horace, I'll move." He stepped to the back wall. He couldn't lean against it because of the growing charge across the surface, and knew that all that was keeping his feet from burning must be the thick rubber soles of his hiking boots. "Thank the Lord for these," he said softly.

Dekker watched as an angry red spot appeared on the opposite wall. "I hope you know what you're doing, Horace." He crouched to present as small a profile as possible.

The red spot grew to a smudge the size of his fist and quickly doubled, tripled, and then quadrupled in size. The effect on his chamber was increasingly dramatic. The walls, now fully black except for the front wall glowing red, emitted a hum. It wasn't something he heard so much as felt. It was a throbbing, pulsing of energy sweeping across all the exterior surfaces of the cube. He could only imagine what might happen next.

KAMENWATI CHECKED INTO a small hotel outside London and was preparing to find Nebwawi, his follower sent to England. But before he could compose himself for entry into the Flows, he felt a stabbing in the head. Holding his head in both hands, he looked around for a source for his pain; but there was nothing, just his room and its contents. Then as swiftly as it began his pain subsided and he relaxed. "It is probably a delayed reaction to my long flight in a pressurized cabin."

He had just about convinced himself when he was struck again with the pain, except this time it more intense. "What is happening?" Kamenwati shouted to the ceiling. The shots of pain increased and were spaced closer together, no longer allowing him a break between assaults. He tried focusing his mind on the source of the onslaught of pain, something he knew he could not endure much longer.

"Where is this coming from? Who is doing this?" His questions went unanswered until he realized this was originating in the Flows. The more he concentrated, the clearer the solution became. "This is an attack on my Merlin Box! But what is the nature of this attack?" He could not imagine. Never in all the ages of Magick had there been a report of a similar reaction. Regardless, this new assault from an unknown source was having a significant impact on his Merlin Box and on him.

Kamenwati focused on his Merlin Box, and even through the pain he discerned the field was dangerously close to collapse. He was tied directly to the construct through the Flows and knew that, once whatever power was being applied broke through, his brain would literally explode. With a mighty effort of will he tried fighting back but his efforts were futile. In defeat and close to unconsciousness and death, Kamenwati released his hold on the Merlin Box.

"Damn you, Dekker!"

THE TENSION AMONG those observing in the forest clearing was tangible. Everyone watched with growing concern. Would Dekker remain unharmed when the PFN cannon penetrated the Merlin Box? Rimmer and Dennis both added another concern: would Kamenwati be affected like Galdur? All they could do was wait and watch as the PFN cannon was fired over and over again.

They had released perhaps a dozen bolts of energy when Dr. Rimmer held up a fist, signaling the firing to stop. Everyone held their breath. Something was happening to the Merlin Box.

The structure of the stasis seemed to give way, breaking into a million points of light that dropped in a cascade until the Merlin Box was no more.

A cheer rose from the observers when they saw Dekker. He stood with eyes closed and crouched down, arms around his knees. When he heard the cheers and whistles, he opened his eyes. He was out of that terrible cell, freed by whatever Horace had done.

Horace Rimmer, being closest, rushed up to Dekker and held him by the shoulders, looking him over. "Are you hurt?" Dekker shook his head. Hannah was not far behind, and she hugged him tightly. "I was very afraid for you, Adam." He accepted her tenderness, and enfolding her in his arms, he whispered, "I was thinking of you, Hannah." Dekker held her tightly for a long moment before Dennis rushed up, almost tackling his mentor and friend. The others surrounded him as well, bombarding him with questions.

"Hold on, guys. I need to get my bearings and then you can ask your questions," said Dekker. They quieted down and Rimmer began explaining all the exotic machinery arrayed before them.

"A pulse-forming network?" Dekker said to Horace. "I'm afraid I have no idea what that is."

"Never mind, my boy. Let it suffice to say this device fires bolts of electromagnetic energy like cannon balls. The focused energy is tuned to a specific frequency."

"So you just began shooting a hole? What if you hit me?"

"It doesn't work like that, Adam. Inside the EMF cage you were quite safe. The damage was to the surface only."

Dennis spoke up. "Tell him about the other effect, like on Galdur." Dekker raised an eyebrow in question.

"I overlooked that," said Rimmer. "We had Galdur create a similar Merlin Box to test our PFN cannon. It seems the construct is tied directly to its originator and the force of the electromagnetic pulses caused Galdur great pain."

"Yes," said Galdur. "I thought my head would explode."

Rimmer continued. "We stopped before fully penetrating the test Merlin Box to protect Galdur, but we inferred the effect on Kamenwati would be the same."

"And was it? What happened to Kamenwati?" questioned Dekker.

Rimmer shook his head. "We don't know. He escaped after Galdur's encounter with him yesterday, and we have no idea where he is."

Hannah's face lit up, remembering an important point. "I wounded Rahotep and he's alive."

"In the base hospital," added Dennis. "Under guard."

"I think we should question him," said Hannah. "He may be able to tell us where his boss has gone."

CHAPTER THIRTY

DEKKER, HANNAH, AND DENNIS STOOD around Rahotep's hospital bed. He was their only link to finding Kamenwati. He lay in the bed surrounded by various medical monitoring machines, but he was awake and Hannah began the questioning. "My name is Hannah Ahmed, and we wish to discuss your leader, Kamenwati." Rahotep initially turned his head away, unwilling to talk.

"I remember you. You shot me."

"Rahotep, like you, I am an Egyptian, a true native. I can understand your point of view, and you may find I am sympathetic to many things that may be at the heart of what you are doing." Rahotep turned back to face the woman. "But you must know there is a flaw in your rationale."

"I follow Kamenwati," said Rahotep. "He is a mystic of great learning and power."

"That may be so, but something has happened to him, something deeply evil."

"No! My teacher is unchanged except for an increase in his power."

"When did you first recognize that change?" Dekker asked, receiving a sharp look from Hannah.

"When he returned."

"Returned from where?" Hannah asked.

"Germany."

"Do you know what happened in Germany?"

"Not specifically, but he did mention a great struggle, and after that a powerful spirit joining with him."

"And that is when he changed?"

"Yes. Before that time we lived in peace, enjoying the benefits of my master's blessings."

"Let's go back to the morning you were shot," said Hannah.

"The morning you shot me, you mean."

"That morning your master was meeting Galdur, a fellow mystic. He made a promise to release Adam Dekker from the Merlin Box in exchange for the meeting." Rahotep simply nodded in agreement. "But you and three other men were hiding in the forest, and when Kamenwati issued a Word of Power to bind Galdur, you four came into the clearing. What were your orders?"

Rahotep squirmed uncomfortably, struggling with the memory. Hannah waited for his reply, holding up her hand to keep Dekker or Dennis from speaking.

"Death," said Rahotep.

"Your orders were to kill Galdur?"

"Yes."

"Rahotep, there was a period of confusion when the shooting began. Both the Merlin Box and your master disappeared. Can you explain that?"

"No."

"Your master abandoned you, left you to be taken by the authorities." Hannah waved her hand broadly to include Dekker and Dennis, and by extension, the entire military base. "How did that make you feel?"

Rahotep squeezed his eyes closed and shook his head.

"Do you feel betrayed?"

Rahotep snapped his eyes open and, staring at Hannah, whispered, "Yes."

"Then allow us to be the instrument of your revenge."

Dennis moved forward slightly, concerned at the tone Hannah was taking. He began to say something but Dekker silenced him by placing his hand on Dennis' forearm. Rahotep's eyes narrowed and he nodded, accepting Hanna's logic.

"Can you tell us where he is?"

"No."

Dekker moved forward and sat in the chair next to Hannah. She looked at Dekker and nodded her consent for him to join the questioning.

"Rahotep, I have seen that sort of disappearing act before. In fact, I experienced it firsthand, thanks to Galdur. What I know is the phenomenon is not really vanishing but more of a fog or a cloud, a trick of the mind."

"I have seen my master use it once, and I did not understand how he did it, only that he disappeared."

"He didn't disappear," said Dekker. "He fooled you into seeing nothing."

"As he did in the forest clearing," Rahotep observed.

Dekker launched into a new line of questioning. "Can you tell me how you came to be here, to be in America?"

"Three of us were summoned into the teacher's presence. He told us again of his dream of a purified Egyptian nation, a nation free of the invaders from the desert. He said we must go to England, Germany, and America to seek out adherents to the Brotherhood and rally them to his cause."

"What is that cause?" Hannah asked.

"A war between East and West, leaving both decimated and vulnerable."

"And his instrument would be drone aircraft striking both ways, sowing anger and distrust that results in war," said Hannah.

Hannah, Dekker, and Dennis looked at one another in dismay.

Dekker continued the questioning. "You were sent here then?"

"Yes. I made contact with the remnants of an organization belonging to someone named Origen. There was a young man, Sammy, who recruited the other three for me, and then we came here. I had trouble using the master's control technique, and he came here to assist. That was when we found you were using some technology to interfere with our efforts. The master realized another deep practitioner like himself must be involved, and he lured that practitioner to a place we could capture and kill him. Our first attempt failed and so the master persuaded him to meet in the forest clearing. The rest you know."

"You said the other Egyptians were sent to England and Germany?" Dekker asked.

"Yes."

Dekker looked at Dennis. "I'll bet the German destination was Krugerschloss…"

Rahotep brightened slightly. "Yes, that is the name he used."

"And if I had to bet," said Dennis, "the location in England is on the Salisbury Plain, Lord Geoffrey's stomping grounds."

Dekker looked back to Rahotep. "Is that right? Is that the location?"

"It is," said Rahotep.

The three stepped out of the room to confer.

"England or Germany, which would he choose?" Dekker asked.

"Maybe neither. He could have returned to Egypt." Hannah said.

Dekker was quiet, thinking about Kamenwati and his understanding of the Egyptian's motivations. "From the beginning Kamenwati wanted Abaddon's power, and in some unexpected way he got just that. Abaddon's power by joining with the spirit. But from what Galdur told us, the longer he is coupled with the spirit, the more influenced he becomes." He looked at Dennis. "Now, Dennis, what do we know about the Abaddon spirit?"

Dennis constricted his eyebrows in thought. "I'm not sure about this spirit thing, but the Abaddon we encountered and defeated at Krugerschloss was totally consumed with two things: collapsing the world's major economies to bring on a new dark age and seeking revenge on you." Hannah lifted an eyebrow in surprise.

Dekker nodded. "So this drone scheme fits right into that spirit's agenda. It wants to create a war that will devastate the world."

"Yeah, it does," said Dennis.

"Where does that lead us?" Hannah asked.

Dekker crossed his arms and continued. "Running back to Egypt wouldn't further the plan, and so I believe that is out. Krugerschloss in Germany was the place of the spirit's defeat, and there aren't many of the Brotherhood followers left there. The Germans are not much into drone technology either, so it seems unlikely Kamenwati would go there to continue the program." He looked at Hannah. "England is where he would go, to attack the British UAV operations, and I imagine Lord Geoffrey's organization is largely intact."

Hannah nodded her agreement with Dekker's reasoning. "I will contact SIS and get an inquiry going."

"Great," said Dekker. "Let's collect Galdur and hunt down this megalomaniac."

HANNAH INSISTED SIS headquarters be their first stop upon arriving in England. She left Dekker, Galdur, and Dennis in the lobby while she met with Alex Younger, Chief of SIS. After almost an hour Hannah returned.

"How was the debriefing?" Dekker asked.

"It went well, and I have some information on our man. It seems he did arrive in London, congratulations Dekker, but neither SIS nor MI6 knows where he is."

"I'd start with Dugannon Manor," said Dennis. Hannah gave him a quizzical look. "That was Lord Geoffrey's place."

"In the absence of a better plan," said Hannah, "I suggest we follow Dennis' lead."

"Then it's off to the Salisbury Plain," said Dekker.

Hannah drove, taking the M3 out of London. After passing the M25 circling London, Galdur remarked on the countryside. "It is lovely, Hannah. It is quite flat, more so than Iceland."

"We are traveling to the Salisbury Plain, some of the best farm land in Great Britain."

"Will we pass Stonehenge? I've always wanted to see that ancient structure,"said Galdur.

"Yes. Right after we pass through Andover."

Soon Hannah exited at Stockbridge Road and drove through Andover and into the pastoral countryside. Stonehenge came up quickly, and were it not for the parking lots around it, they might have missed the ruins. "There it is, Galdur. Stonehenge." Galdur gazed, saying nothing. He concentrated on the ancient site and nodded his head.

"There is so much history here, so much suffering, so much death," said Galdur. "The history of Stonehenge goes far back in time. One of the last remaining megalithic structures on Earth, it is far older than people realize. It predates the Egyptians and even the ancient Sumerians. It was built when Magick was young in the world, a time when men understood that unseen forces interacted with their world and their lives." He had a faraway look in his eyes. "There are few of us now who know the true history of this place and the few remaining sites of its kind, like the ruins of the temple in Desolation Field below Krugerschloss, where we confined Abaddon."

"And where Kara died," said Dekker.

"Yes, where Kara died and our contest with the evil spirit came into the open."

"Will this ever be truly over?" Dekker asked.

"The battle with the spirit of Abaddon? No. It will not. We must identify and defeat those he possesses and empowers. The longer they are under that spirit's influence, the more they are able to operate in this world with his power."

Hannah looked again at Stonehenge as they drove by, listening to the exchange between Dekker and Galdur, her appreciation for the structure greatly increased.

Dennis, reading a map, chimed in. "It is only a short way to Wilton, and that's where we'll find Dugannon Manor."

"Tell me where to turn," said Hannah. "We don't want to get lost."

A short time later, they were on a narrow road leading through the countryside when, like Nimue rising from the lake, a great structure appeared. "A most impressive building," said Hannah.

They drove slowly up to the great house whose origins went back to Roman times. Years of expansion created the present sprawling structure of spires, gables, turrets and parapets. Pulling around the wide, circling drive, they stopped in front of the main doorway. "I'm not sure what to expect," said Hannah. "With Lord Geoffrey's passing and having left no heir, there has been some confusion as to the disposition of the estate." Hannah used the large knocker, rapping the door twice. "If we're lucky, a caretaker or someone will be here."

No sooner had she spoken than the door opened. Standing in the doorway was a butler in full formal dress. "May I help you?"

"I am Hannah Ahmed with SIS." She showed him her identification. "Were you employed by Lord Geoffrey Stapleton?"

"Yes, madam, I was. What is this about?"

"May I ask your name?"

"I am Benton, the head butler." He looked at each in the group. "What is it you wish?"

IT WAS EASY to view Benton as simply a servant, but he was much more. He had been with the manor his entire life, his father serving as head butler to Lord Geoffrey's father. Benton's relationship with his employer went far beyond personal loyalty; he was tied to Dugannon Manor in a way only the Lord of the manor could understand. His loyalty was first to Dugannon and the history it represented, followed by loyalty to whoever the current Lord may be.

This is not to say he was not loyal to the now deceased Lord Geoffrey, but this new man, Kamenwati, had shown up two days previously and, with *bona fides* presented and accepted, Benton's loyalty was transferred without question.

"We hoped to speak with a man who may have come here in the last few days," said Dekker. "Older, well-dressed..."

Benton did not hesitate. "Yes, the gentleman you ask about presented himself and his *bona fides* establishing his right to take possession of Dugannon Manor."

"His name?" asked Hannah.

"Mr. Kamenwati," said Benton. "He was somewhat odd, but as I said, his *bona fides* were in order."

"Is Kamenwati here?" Dekker leaned forward, a hard look in his eyes.

Benton hesitated, his loyalty to the new lord of Dugannon being put to the test. "No, I'm afraid not sir."

"When do you expect him?" Dekker pressed.

"I'm not certain, sir. He left early this morning."

Dekker's patience was wearing thin and there was something about the butler that struck him as scheming and deceitful. "Do you have any idea where he went?"

Benton clasped his hands and looked away, but he did answer. "I believe he was meeting some people."

"And I suppose you have no idea who those people might be?" Dekker's frustration was showing through.

"No, sir, I do not. Now, if there is nothing more, I wish you a good day." The butler turned and closed the front door.

"Do you find anything strange about the butler?" Galdur asked Dekker as they descended the steps.

"I had the distinct feeling he was not honest with us, and I feel like we've walked into another trap."

CHAPTER THIRTY-ONE

KAMENWATI PREPARED TO LEAVE DUGANNON Manor early in the morning. Benton accepted the departure with his usual decorum. "May I have the driver come around, sir?" After receiving a nod of acceptance of his offer, Benton left the new master of the manor to call Michaels, the groundskeeper and driver. "Bring the Bentley around front, please."

In minutes Kamenwati was in the luxury car heading to meet with Nebwawi near the RAF base in Waddington, a short distance south of Lincoln in Lincolnshire. The base is home to the Intelligence Surveillance Target Acquisition and Reconnaissance group, or ISTAR, and the center of operations for the MQ-9 Reaper. As they drove to the meeting place

Kamenwati was suddenly taken by a disturbing feeling. "Someone is hunting for me."

He did not have to ponder long who his pursuer was. "Dekker." Kamenwati smirked. "What a fool. Has he not yet learned his lesson?" He went into the Flows and quickly connected with Dekker.

You seem to have escaped my Merlin Box.

And I'll bet you are wondering how I did it. There was no response from Kamenwati.

You and your Merlin Box are done, Kamenwati.

No, Mr. Dekker, it is you who are done. You have no idea the power I wield.

Oh yeah? Then let's meet and see who has the upper hand. Dekker's threat was real and Kamenwati paused.

No, Mr. Dekker, I will not accept your invitation.

Where do you think you can go? I will find you wherever you go, and I will kill you.

Bold words, but I think you can search for a hundred years and still not find me. You may have thwarted this effort, but be assured I will have more plans for the future. Good bye, Mr. Dekker.

Communication was abruptly ended.

Kamenwati leaned to the front seat. "Michaels, disregard the previous destination. I wish to go to Heathrow."

"As you wish," said Michaels, heading to the city. Kamenwati sat back, knowing Dekker would never be able to penetrate the cloud covering his island home on the Nile.

DEKKER STOOD OFF from the car, stiff and with his eyes closed. Galdur understood he was in the Flows and gently observed the conversation, and Hannah and Dennis knew better than to interrupt. After a few minutes Dekker relaxed and turned to them. "It was Kamenwati."

"We have to stop him," Dennis insisted.

Galdur shook his head. "He's much too clever and far too slippery. If he knows we are on to him here, he will be gone before we can pick up his trail."

Dekker looked down the narrow road for a long while, finally accepting the reality of the situation. "You're right. He can employ all sorts of tricks to get out of England, but I will not stop chasing him."

Hannah looked at Dekker with a mixture of shared resolve and admiration. "I know, Adam, and I will help you."

www.ingramcontent.com/pod-product-compliance
Lightning Source LLC
Chambersburg PA
CBHW050908250626
47155CB00001B/154